Sparks

LAURA
BICKLE

WITHDRAWN

POCKET BOOKS

New York   London   Toronto   Sydney

Pocket Books
A Division of Simon & Schuster, Inc.
1230 Avenue of the Americas
New York, NY 10020

First Juno Books/Pocket Books paperback edition September 2010

JUNO BOOKS and colophon are trademarks of Wildside Press LLC used under license by Simon & Schuster, Inc., the publisher of this work.

POCKET and colophon are registered trademarks of Simon & Schuster, Inc.

For information about special discounts for bulk purchases, please contact Simon & Schuster Special Sales at 1-866-506-1949 or business@simonandschuster.com.

The Simon & Schuster Speakers Bureau can bring authors to your live event. For more information or to book an event contact the Simon & Schuster Speakers Bureau at 1-866-248-3049 or visit our website at www.simonspeakers.com.

Cover design by John Vairo Jr. Cover illustration by Chris McGrath.

Manufactured in the United States of America

10   9   8   7   6   5   4   3   2   1

ISBN 978-1-4391-6768-7
ISBN 978-1-4391-6771-7 (ebook)

On the astral plane, Michigan Central Station looked much as it did in real life: a shattered black husk.

But here, throngs of people moved past the windows and along the warped steel tracks. Anya could make out hats shading faces, the swish of skirts, hear the chatter of voices and the creak of luggage—images of people from many eras, though no one seemed to notice the disparities.

"They're ghosts." Anya's brow wrinkled.

"This place is what it's always been: a way station for spirits among planes. Spirits come here before they move to the Afterworld, whatever that destination may be for them. From here, you can travel to any plane of reality. And the spirits don't have much choice where they go." Charon paused at the edge of the train platform, peered into the darkness with his hands stuffed into his pockets. "It's coming soon."

"What's coming?" Anya's mouth was dry. She could see light beginning to prickle the edge of the tunnel, hear a terrible sound moving toward them.

"The train. It'll take you where you need to go."

The roar trembled the platform, whipping up wind and a scorching heat that shimmered in the air. A blackness thick as the dark at the bottom of any basement stairs rushed down the tunnel.

"It's going to hell!" Anya shouted, feeling a visceral fear rise in her stomach. That sound could come from nowhere else.

"Not hell." Charon's voice was shredded by the black. "But a road to it."

Sparks is also available as an eBook

Acknowledgments

Thanks to the ladies of the Ohio Writers Network for the chocolate and support: Michelle, Linda, Melissa, Lisa, Rachel, Faith, Tracy, and Emily.

Thank you to my husband for suffering through muse duty without quibbling.

Thanks to my editor, Paula Guran, for the opportunity, advice, and encyclopedic esoteric knowledge.

Sparks

CHAPTER ONE

DEATH, WITH A CHASER OF magick.

Anya wrinkled her nose as the odors burned into her sinuses. Unmistakable, they awakened a primal fight-or-flight response in the most primitive part of her brain. She forced one foot in front of the other, her fingers tightening in a sweaty grip on the handle of her tool kit. Any ordinary person would have license to flee from those smells, but Anya had no choice. She was not ordinary. And this was her job.

The hoarder's house smelled like burned bacon, fetid and greasy. The stench clung to the stacks of newspapers littering the kitchen table, the bundles of *National Geographic* magazines and cardboard boxes stacked along the walls on the scarred black-and-white linoleum. Dishes in the sink were coated with dried lemon dish soap; the garbage reeked of coffee grounds . . . but all the other odors were overwhelmed by the stink seeping through the peeling wallpaper.

A knot of cops milled at the back kitchen door. As if

some invisible ward prevented them from crossing the threshold, the uniforms remained steadfastly outside, their voices kept low, thick with tension. There was none of the wisecracking and bravado gawkers usually brought. Transfixed, they didn't want to walk away from the scene, but were unwilling to enter the house.

Someone had cracked open the window over the kitchen sink, allowing a breeze to creep through. Anya reached over the dishes to pry it open further, hoping to dispel the odor. A hazy film covering the pane obscured her reflection. Her latex-covered fingers smeared the glass, thick with grease. In spite of her gloves, the slickness of it made her skin crawl.

Anya tipped her head. A fringe of chin-length sable hair curtained her amber-colored eyes. Her hair had burned off six months ago and was now at that annoying stage where it still wasn't long enough to pull back into a ponytail. She shoved it behind her ear with the back of her clean hand. The motion revealed a copper torque peeking out over the edge of her hazmat suit. The metal salamander curled around her neck, grasping its tail in a deep V above her collarbone. The collar always felt warmer than her skin, pulsing with its own presence. The salamander torque was always most active around death; she was certain it smelled the death as acutely as she did. For the moment, she ignored it.

"Thought you'd enjoy this one, Kalinczyk."

Captain Marsh dumped a tackle box of tools on the kitchen table. Even in these stiflingly close quarters, her supervisor wore his firefighter's coat open over an immaculately pressed white shirt and tie.

Anya's brow arched. "Something stunk, and you automatically thought of me?"

Marsh's mahogany face creased in a grin. "I thought it might have spooked some of the other fire investigators." He crossed his arms over his crisp shirt. "But seriously . . . we need for this to be kept low-key. Quiet."

She glanced at the cluttered, humble surroundings, brow creasing. There was nothing in the scene that suggested to her a need for secrecy. Sadness, perhaps . . . but not secrecy. And she was certain none of the others could taste the sharp tang of magick in the air, distinct as ozone. "What's the backstory?"

"This house belongs to a seventy-two-year-old man, Jasper Bernard. A neighbor called nine-one-one because she saw strange lights and thought burglars might have broken in."

Anya gestured to the kitchen table with her chin, looking askance. "Does he have anything worth stealing? Anything that could be found in this mess?"

"Yeah, well." Marsh spread his hands. "I guess she could tell that something was different. Police tried the front door, and no one answered. All the doors and windows were locked. When they peered into the windows with their flashlights, they saw evidence of fire in the living room, and broke in."

"They saw fire?"

Marsh shook his head. "No. Just char and ash. The fire was long cold. So was Bernard."

"What did Bernard die of? Smoke inhalation?" Anya

envisioned an old man dead on his couch of a fire started by a forgotten lit cigarette. As far as ways to die went, suffocating in one's sleep was not the worst way to go. Anya had seen much worse. Though she knew the official coroner's report wouldn't be available for a few days, a preliminary opinion would help her move forward with the investigation.

Marsh nervously scrubbed his palm over the scar crossing his bald head. Marsh was rarely nervous, but Anya recognized the unconscious gesture. "No."

"Burns?" Anya winced. There were only two ways to die in a fire: burning or asphyxiation. Burns were the worst.

"You gotta see this for yourself." He jabbed a thumb at the six-panel door off the kitchen. It stood ajar, and only cool shade stretched beyond. "That way."

Heat had lifted the paint into bubbles that burst like blisters under her fingertips. She pushed the door open, sucked in a breath as her eyes adjusted to the half-darkness.

The living room was a pack rat's nest. Above, a bare lightbulb had melted in its ceiling socket. Painted-shut windows had been forced open, allowing gray light to ribbon through bent blinds, over pressboard shelves warping under the weight of books. Anya scanned the titles, but most of them were in incomprehensible Latin. Sculpted shag carpeting was mottled under the weight of years of dirt and too few vacuumings. Unopened mail rattled on a dusty credenza, envelopes curling in a breeze that failed to chase out the bitter reek of death.

As disorganized as the room appeared, the scene was

surprisingly intact from a forensic viewpoint. No scorch marks blackened the walls. It was unlikely that someone could have actually died of burns or smoke inhalation in a room showing so little damage. Only a swirl of carbon smoke stained the ceiling, surrounding the melted light-bulb over the couch.

Anya frowned. Maybe the old man had had a heart attack. Maybe he'd died of cancer. Or a drug overdose. Surely the autopsy would reveal something other than burns or smoke inhalation. There simply hadn't been a fire here big enough to traumatize a mobile adult.

The threadbare couch faced away from Anya, toward a fireplace. The fireplace mantel sagged under an odd assortment of objects: a clutch of brass keys dripping over the edge like the limbs of a spider; a Tiki god beaming over his domain of clutter; a tarnished sword with an elaborate gilt hilt. Smoke had stained a collection of bottles in various sizes and shapes. They were now all the color of gray quartz, nearly concealing their contents: gleaming bones suspended in liquid.

Anya's skin crawled. These things smelled like magick, like rust and salt. Old magick. Not the new, ozone tang of fresh-brewed magick that she had smelled in the kitchen. Anya picked her way around the couch for a better look and nearly stepped into the remains of Jasper Bernard.

Not that there was much of him. A greasy black burn mark spread from the middle couch cushion to the floor, scorching the carpet. A pair of feet in black socks and blue slippers extended from the bottom of the stain. Squinting, she could make out a few finger bones from a right hand at the perimeter of the scorch, but nothing else of Jasper Bernard remained. The burn had chewed through the carpet, leaving white ash on the unmarked hardwood floor. In front of the slippers sat an unharmed TV tray, a microwaved dinner preserved in its compartmentalized plate. Meat loaf and green beans, from the looks of it.

She rocked back on her heels, breathing: "Holy shit." This wasn't a natural fire. It wasn't even a *possible* fire. Human bodies didn't burn like that, not even when they were doused with gasoline and set ablaze in cars. There was always something left behind. Nothing burned like that, even in crematories. Crematoriums had to physically pulverize the remains to get them into a box. . . . Where the hell had Bernard's remains disappeared to?

She knelt to stare incredulously at Bernard's feet. Through a hole in his sock, she could see pink flesh. The intense heat that had reduced his body to ash hadn't touched the lint underneath his perfectly intact toenail.

Marsh's steps scuffed up dust from the carpet behind her. "Is this what I think it is?"

If it was, it was the holy grail of fire investigation. She hedged. She hadn't seen enough of the scene to be positive. "I don't know for sure. We need to collect more evidence, but it has all the hallmarks of it."

"Of what?" He pressed harder, leaning forward on his now-dusty spit-shined shoes. He didn't want to be the first one to say it, the first one to step off the cliff into an irrational explanation.

She swallowed, kept her voice so low that the uniforms eavesdropping past the open door couldn't hear: "Spontaneous human combustion."

Silence stretched. She couldn't believe she'd said it.

Marsh gestured to the open windows. "That's what the uniforms are saying. That's what the press would say if they knew." He looked down at the hole in the carpet where a human had once sat, preparing to eat his TV dinner. "Disprove it. Find the truth."

She rocked back on her heels, voice dry. It was too soon to even begin conjecture, and she resented being pushed. "Sir. I haven't even begun to seriously consider any theory. . . ."

"Find a reasonable explanation for this. Take the time and resources you need, but make this go away." His gaze drifted out the window to the darkening skyline. Somewhere out there a siren whined. "Detroit doesn't need any more things that go bump in the night."

Marsh was right. Anya stared down at the cinders, thinking that Marsh didn't know half the things that wandered unseen in the city. If anyone else really knew what she knew . . . She smothered a shudder. Ordinary people had no idea of what lay underneath the skin of Detroit's sad normalcy.

Anya wasn't ordinary, much as she wished she were.

Her attention wandered over Bernard's collection of bottles. By the look of things, Bernard hadn't been ordinary, either.

Voices rattled from the kitchen door in argument.

Marsh peered through the bent blinds, muttered, "The press is here."

"Already?"

"News van just pulled up outside beside the squad cars. Someone must have tipped them off," Marsh growled, heading for the door. "Work the scene. I'll handle the press."

The wooden door clicked shut behind him, leaving Anya alone with Jasper's ashes.

She pulled her camera from her kit, aimed it toward the door. In the snap of the shutter and the bleed of light through the blinds, she gathered her thoughts as she circled the scene. She blotted out the voices filtering into the room, listening to the creak of heat-warped floorboards underfoot as she minced through Jasper's clutter. Making sure each frame of the last shot overlapped with the next, she let her camera lens devour the images of a sad, ordinary life: bills stacked in piles; a wall clock with glow-in-the-dark numerals tapping out the time; a roll of yellowed stamps; a cardboard box full of record albums, the vinyl curled from the heat.

To say nothing of the extraordinary things augmented through the camera lens. Anya's eyes swept over an elaborately enameled terra-cotta figure of a Foo dog with a broken paw; a plastic zipper bag full of antique coins that seethed like scales when she shook it. A wand of selenite crystal, long as her forearm and slender as her finger, rested on a battered desk, shimmering in the sunlight. A filigreed silver bottle the size of her hand was attached to a stopper on a tarnished chain. To Anya's sensitive eye, these things swirled under a layer of dust, pulsing of mysteries of the ages and magick.

Anya peered through the gap in the blinds. On the street, she could see Marsh looming over a man with a minicam, while cops were stringing yellow tape. The man with the minicam looked persistent, beads of sweat from his well-gelled hair dripping down his neck and onto his expensive jacket. Anya thought she recognized him as one of the evening newscasters.

The reporter looked at the blinds, like a bloodhound sensing movement. Anya retreated into the shade of the room, but not before the blinds scraped the bottom of the windowsill.

In an old house of this era, marble windowsills were common, white stone skin crossed by black veins. But something about the pattern caught her eye, and she gently tugged up the blind cord.

A fine line of salt had been sprinkled on the window ledge, where it had barely been disturbed by breeze.

Anya frowned. She was no witch or magick-worker, but she knew a ward when she saw it. Bernard had been afraid of something magickal, of something magickal getting into his house . . . though there were plenty of magickal things already *in* his house.

It would take forever to process this scene, and to guess at which of those things might have gotten out of his control . . . enough to kill him.

Aiming the lens at the ceiling, Anya shot a picture of

the lightbulb over the couch. The bulb troubled her. In any normal fire, the heat would cause the glass to break or warp. If it warped, it would twist toward the source of the greatest heat, the ignition point of the fire.

But this bulb dripped straight down over the couch. Like a bead of sweat on a runner's nose, a piece of glass had frozen in mid-dribble, pointing to Bernard's remains.

The fire could not have started there. Could not.

Anya's finger cramped on the shutter switch as she snapped the greasy black stain from every angle. The ceiling had a sheen, as if it had been freshly painted, and she squinted at it. Nothing in this house had been painted in years. Could it be the residue of an accelerant, an exotic chemical trace that hadn't burned cleanly away, as gasoline or propane might?

The same gleam glistened on the underside of the TV tray table, snagging her attention. Anya squinted at the sheen, touched it. It was still warm, smelling like candle wax and raw meat. Startled, she realized that it was the source of the unusual smell she'd discovered when she'd entered the house. This residue was what covered the kitchen windows, filmed over the plaster walls. It wasn't an accelerant, at least, not in the conventional sense.

Fat. It was Bernard's burned body fat, evaporated and settled onto his surroundings.

Anya's stomach churned. She'd only read about this kind of thing in textbooks. It was called the "wick effect," the idea that a human body theoretically could smolder for hours, feeding on its own fat. Theoretically.

But where was the original spark? What could have ignited the man in the first place?

Her gaze passed over the untouched dinner in its tray, moved to the fireplace. That would be the obvious place to look. On her hands and knees, she shone a flashlight up into the firebox. Through her gloved hands, the hearth felt cool as stone, colder than the TV table closer to the body.

This wasn't the source. But she smelled the bitter tang of magick here, more strongly. After carefully recording the condition of the firebox and hearth with her camera, Anya pulled a pair of stainless-steel barbecue tongs from her kit and dug into the blackened ashes of the hearth.

A lot of paper had been burned here. Fragments flaked away, irretrievable. Anya was amazed that Bernard had ever disposed of anything. Whatever this was, it must have been important for him to destroy. From the grate, she plucked a corner of an envelope, frowned. Bernard seemed to have stockpiled all of his junk mail. With tweezers, she pulled a scrap of green paper from the envelope's remains.

A check. The watermark was unmistakable. In the upper left-hand corner, a name was legible: *Miracles for the Masses*. The address was for a location in Detroit's warehouse district.

She placed the scraps into an empty paint can to go to the lab for analysis and continued her poking around in the ash. Her tongs rang against something with a note like a bell: glass.

From the grate, Anya pulled the neck of a shattered

bottle, charred black. It was smaller than a wine bottle, stoppered with an ornamental silver seal. Whatever it contained was obscured by the carbon black skin coating it. She turned the broken edge toward the light.

She'd expected it to be an empty vessel, for water or wine. Or perhaps a glass prison like the ones on the mantel, holding preserved fragments of bones. But looking into the darkness of the bottle was like looking into a geode: Shining, rock-crystal teeth glinted back at her, seared obsidian-black from the fire.

Around her throat, something fluttered. Anya's hand slipped up to the metal collar around her neck. A warm shape inside the metal shifted, peeled away from her skin. Delicate salamander toes unfurled and marched down her shoulder as the metal sizzled and released a living creature. Taking the shape of a hellbender, a fire elemental salamander leapt to the hearth, growling at the magick-soaked bottle in the grate. His tongue flickered into the black of the firebox, and he incandesced with an amber glow.

"Sparky," she hissed. She had no fear that Marsh or any other living creature could see him; Sparky was invisible to ordinary humans. But Sparky only bothered to wake himself up under three conditions: when it suited his preternatural whims, when ghosts were around, or when danger was near.

Anya swallowed. As if handling a piece of radioactive debris, she placed the fragment of the bottle on the hearth. Sparky stalked toward it, his feathery gill-fronds flaring. His tongue flickered over the carbon on its surface.

Anya held her breath, watching for Sparky's reaction. She knew he smelled the magick on it, too. But she had no way of knowing how dangerous that broken bottle really was. For all she knew, it could be a magickal time bomb . . . a bomb that blew up Jasper Bernard. A bomb that could still be active.

Sparky turned around, presented his speckled rump to the artifact. He scraped his back feet at the ash disdainfully, as if he were a cat burying a turd in a litter box.

Anya rolled her eyes. The salamander couldn't speak, but he managed to be expressive, just the same. Perhaps the bottle wasn't a source of danger; perhaps the elemental was busy expressing himself and being a pain in the ass.

Or . . . Anya looked around the room, back at the grease stain that had once been Jasper Bernard.

Anya whispered at the stain, "You still here, Bernard?"

Perhaps Sparky was picking up on something else that had disturbed his nap. Perhaps Jasper Bernard hadn't gone peacefully to the Afterworld, and was still hanging around. If so, she could talk to him, get the real story of how he'd managed to dissolve himself from this plane of existence and leave just his foot and slipper behind.

A translucent orb welled up in the grease stain: a balding head and bespectacled eyes. Anya noted that a piece of electrical tape held one side of the glasses together.

"Jasper Bernard?" Anya asked quietly. She didn't want to startle him. The freshly dead were always skittish as feral cats, and she expected Bernard to be no different. She could feel Sparky slithering behind her legs, and she stood on his tail to keep him from crawling forward and scaring the ghost off.

"Everyone calls me Bernie. You . . . you can see me?"

"Yes, I can see you."

The phosphorescent eyes shifted right and left, and panic twitched through his voice. *"The cops didn't see me. The firemen didn't see me. How can you see me?"*

Anya crouched beside the stain in the floor, conscious of Sparky straining beside her. "I'm a medium . . . of sorts. I can see spirits and talk with them."

Bernie's eyes narrowed in assessment. *"I've met mediums. You're more than that."*

Anya chewed on her lower lip. She didn't want to panic Bernie, but she didn't have time to construct a plausible lie. "I'm a Lantern. Ghosts are drawn to me." Anya deliberately left the other part out, the part about how she could destroy what remained of his spirit with little more than a breath. Spirits came to her, moths to the flame, and—if needed—she incinerated them.

The frightened eyes peered over a bifocal glass line at the salamander. *"Is that what I think it is?"*

"Um . . . This is Sparky. He's my friend." *My friend who would also like to have you for lunch.*

Sparky growled at him.

"A salamander? How did you ever tame one of those?" Curiosity and a note of avarice resonated in the ghost's voice.

"I, uh, have had him since I was a child." Again, not the whole truth, but Bernard didn't need to know the whole truth. Nor could Sparky be really considered "tame." Anya eyed him suspiciously. "What do you know about salamanders?"

Bernie's fingertips steepled above the oily black pool. *"I'm a collector, of sorts."*

Anya glanced at the bottles over the fireplace. "A collector?"

"A purveyor of magickal artifacts."

Anya protectively angled her hip before Sparky. "That's why this place stinks of magick."

Haughty eyebrows wrinkled over the glasses. *"My house does not stink."*

"Bernie." Anya crouched before the spirit, mindful not to disturb the grease stain with her knees. Bernie might not have fully digested the knowledge that he was dead, and she didn't want to send what was left of his personality into a tailspin before she could extract some useful information. "Is that what happened to you? Bad magick?"

"I remember . . . the fire." Bernie's lower lip turned down and began to dribble off the side of his face. The force of the recollection was beginning to disincorporate him.

She'd have to work quickly. "Do you remember what started it?" Anya pressed him. "Were you burning something in the grate? Smoking?"

Despite Bernie's magickal surroundings, experience had taught Anya to seek the most mundane explanations first.

The ghost shook his head. *"It wasn't me. It was her."*

The eyes behind the glasses rolled upward. *"Wait. If you can see me, can she see me?"*

"Can *who* see you?"

Ghostly fingers gnawed at the edge of the stain. Bernard's eyes flicked to the ceiling. *"Oh, shit . . . "*

The ceiling opened, a vortex of wind reaching toward the floor, cold as the breath of winter. The vortex didn't disturb any of the physical surroundings, but it reached for Bernie as surely as a child rooting through a toy box for a favorite plaything. Like a marionette jerked on its strings, Bernie's ghostly body was yanked out of the floor. His body, clad in pajamas and a chenille robe, flailed in resistance to the invisible force.

Anya lunged forward, instinctively reaching for the ghost. Sparky grasped Bernie's pant leg with his teeth, growling. The salamander pulled back with all his might, struggling to ground Bernie to the ruined floor. But the old man was rising like a helium balloon, and Anya didn't know how much longer they could hold him. The reek of sour magick, like expired milk, made her gag.

Bernie pedaled in the air, his fingers beginning to char. Ghostly flames licked under the collar of his robe, and the chenille burst into flame.

"Don't let her find the vessel!" Bernie shouted.

The artifacts dealer was yanked from Sparky's grip and fizzled away into the ether. The hole in the ceiling closed up, leaving the room ringing in silence.

Anya landed on her butt on the stained carpet, slack-jawed. Frigid air steamed from her mouth. She'd seen ghosts disincorporate as the result of exorcisms, or willingly, when they chose to walk into the afterlife. But she'd never seen anything like this, nothing so violent. The ghost had been sucked up like an ant in a vacuum cleaner, but . . . to where?

"Bernie?" she called, into the half-light of the room.

No one answered her.

Sparky waddled to the stain covering Bernie's ruined carpet. He circled it twice and began scratching it with his back feet, as if he were burying another dead thing.

CHAPTER TWO

"IT WAS LIKE A BASS on a fishing line . . . he just struggled and got pulled out of the water. To where, I don't know."

Anya stared into her drink. In the milky depths of the White Russian, she kept seeing Bernie being hauled back into the ether.

Her voice carried. At this hour, the Devil's Bathtub bar was nearly empty. The former speakeasy retained most of its 1920s charm, from the polished, railed bar and the original woodwork, to the claw-foot tub containing wish-pennies in the center of the scarred wood floor. The bathtub wasn't original; the original had been destroyed in a botched exorcism several months ago, when Anya had contracted a nasty case of demon possession.

The Devil's Bathtub always retained some degree of secret comings and goings. Though bootleggers no longer brewed bathtub gin there, it was now the headquarters for the Detroit Area Ghost Researchers, a group of paranormal investigators of which Anya was reluctantly a part.

They were the only patrons in the Devil's Bathtub

tonight. Jules, behind the bar, led the group with stern authority. He was still wearing the meter-reader's uniform from his day job, capped off with a Detroit Tigers ball cap. The tattoo of a cross peeped out from under his sleeve. His ebony brow wrinkled as he supervised Max, a Latino kid with sagging jeans, filling water balloons with holy water from a large two-liter bottle shaped like the Virgin Mary.

"Keep your fingers off the Madonna's holy bosoms."

Max rolled his eyes and kept his fingers splayed over her plastic breasts. "You don't want me to drop her, do you?"

"Have some respect for the Holy Mother, willya?"

Max stuck his tongue out and licked the bottle. Jules slapped him on the backside of the head, and the kid yelped.

"Apologize to the Madonna."

"I'm sorry, Madonna, for licking your holy tits. . . . "

Katie snorted, her pale hand covering a chuckle from her perch at a table. Her witch's Book of Shadows lay open before her, scrawled with notes of spells and potions. Being a modern witch, she'd used tiny colored sticky notes to earmark some of the pages. One had even insinuated its way into the curtain of long blond hair over her shoulder.

"You're not helping, Katie," Jules growled.

"Hey," retorted the witch, "she's not my Goddess. Mine has a sense of humor."

"See?" Max ducked another swat from Jules. "Hecate likes having her tits licked. Or Isis. Or whoever Katie's worshipping this week . . . Hopefully Isis. Hecate is a real dog."

Jules snorted. He wasn't a big fan of witchcraft. He tolerated Katie's presence on the team because she was effective . . . lately, more effective than his own methods.

Katie threw a cardboard beer coaster at Max, striking him on the back.

"Ow!"

"Quit insulting the heavenly ladies who protect your scrawny ass from evil, or I'll hex you. I'll make you unappealing to girls until you're old enough to collect Social Security," Katie told him. A witch was not to be fucked with.

"The witch is less forgiving than the Holy Mother. Now, get over here." Jules snagged Max by the ear and marched him off behind the bar to wash glasses.

The water balloons lay on the end of the bar like forlorn breast implants awaiting a home. "You guys getting ready for a run?" Anya asked.

"Yeah." Brian, DAGR's tech manager, looked up from his keyboard. Tucked away in a dim booth, he was surrounded by wires and illuminated by green light from his monitor, looking more machine than man as the glow reflected off his glasses.

But Anya knew better. She admired the muscles moving in his chest as he stretched. She and Brian had been taking things slow. But every once in a while, an unintentional gesture like that made her heart skip.

He caught her watching, and the corner of his mouth quirked up.

Anya blushed, looked down into her drink.

"Typical generic haunting, we think," Brian said. "Interesting because it's a full-body apparition of a woman, but in modern dress. We can't find any record of any suspicious deaths at the location . . . very boring history. The apparition won't speak or tell the owners who she is. She paces through the halls at night, but doesn't interact with anyone."

"Residual haunting?" Anya asked. Some hauntings were like supernatural tapes that played over and over in the spiritual memory of a structure. There was no consciousness behind them whatsoever.

"Maybe. We'll find out when we get there in a few days. Since this one isn't a violent haunting, it's been pushed down on the priority list."

Anya frowned. DAGR had been under too much pressure lately. Jules had even contemplated recruiting more staff. Detroit was suffering from more than the well-publicized economic malaise and spikes in crime. Something deeper was affecting the city, feeding on its despondent psyche. The number of reported hauntings and supernatural happenings had skyrocketed. Bars were full of people trying to deny that the city was slowly slipping away around them. Jails were full of those who'd snapped, and whom evil had taken hold of. Churches were full of penitents trying to wash away the despair. And DAGR's schedule was full of people who were convinced that they'd seen something more, underneath all of it. And what they saw terrified them.

Sitting before the bar's cash register, Sparky slapped the

register keys and was rewarded with a series of electronic beeps. He chortled to himself, tail kinking in delight. He pressed another random series of keys, and the register emitted a foot of tape that curled over the edge of the bar. The only things Sparky could affect, other than Anya, were energy fields. The salamander loved playing with electronic equipment. Anya dreaded his unpredictable effects on it.

Jules stared at her. "Is it . . . is *it* on the register?"

"Yeah." Anya knew that no one else could see him. Just her and the spirits. And animals. Sparky liked to chase cats. Jules had an intense disgust for all nonhuman entities. He'd been trying to be polite around Sparky lately. Anya considered that a sign of progress in human-salamander relations.

"It's okay to touch him. He won't mind."

Jules gingerly glided his hand over Sparky's body. To most humans, the only palpable signs of Sparky's presence were changes in air pressure or temperature fluctuations.

Jules shook his head. "I don't feel him."

"Here." Anya guided Jules's square hand over Sparky's chest. "Feel anything?"

Jules frowned. "Just . . . just a tingle."

Sparky snorted, annoyed at being distracted from the bells and whistles of the cash register. His tail slapped the front of Jules's shirt.

Suddenly, Jules's cell phone blared to life. He jumped back, snatched it out of his uniform pocket and flung it on the bar, as if it were a live snake. The phone smoked and hissed with static, and went dead. His hands shook . . . whether in anger or fear, Anya couldn't tell.

Anya winced. "Sorry about that. I'll pay for it."

Sparky waddled across the bar to the cell phone, licked it. A blue arc of electricity curled from the darkened screen.

"Don't bother. The wife's been nagging me to get a new one, anyway. One with GPS, so that she can track where I am." Jules growled, wiping his hands on a dish towel, as if he'd touched something filthy. "Just keep that thing away from the television. At least while the Lions are playing."

Anya made a face at him. She scooped Sparky up in her arms and placed him, wriggling, on her lap, then reached forward to rub his round belly. The little chunker had been putting on weight lately. Perhaps he'd been nibbling at too many ghosts. She cooed as she rubbed the pale speckles on his amber tummy, and he squirmed in pleasure. Jules looked sidelong at her with barely disguised disgust.

Brian wandered warily over and plucked the cell phone from the bar. In seconds, he had the faceplate off and was tinkering in its tiny copper guts. "Interesting. The battery's totally drained. I mean . . . the motherboard's fried, but that's kind of cool. . . . "

"I thought ghosts drained batteries sometimes," Anya said.

"They can. Video recorder batteries. Camera batteries. It's not uncommon during an investigation to have a fully charged laptop die."

"Why does that happen?" Max stood on his tiptoes to peer over Brian's shoulder. The teen had taken a shine to the electronics, and Brian had begun to take him under his technological wing.

"Well, the theory is that ghosts need to draw power from somewhere to manifest. That's why the temperature drops in a room where ghosts are present . . . they draw energy from air. A battery of an electronic device is pretty much the same thing. Some people who are psychics or psychic vampires can even power down watch batteries."

"What's a psychic vampire?" Max asked.

"They're humans who suck other people's energy fields," Jules said. "Like leeches."

Anya wrapped her arms around Sparky, who burped against her ear. She wrinkled her nose. His breath smelled like sulphur. "Sparky is not a psychic vampire."

"Not saying he is. Just that he might have some survival mechanisms that we don't know about yet. I mean, you don't even really know where he came from," Brian pointed out.

"My mother gave him to me," she challenged Brian, daring him to continue. This was rocky ground for her, and he knew it.

"But where did she get him?" Brian pulled up a bar stool.

Anya let a curtain of hair fall over her face. Her chin-length hair was handy for hiding behind. "I don't know. He just always was around. My mom said he used to curl up in my bassinet with me when I was a baby."

Jules snorted from a safe distance across the bar. "And to think I was nervous when my wife let the cat sleep with our daughter. . . . "

"Can you ask your mom sometime?"

Anya's jaw tightened. This was not terrain she'd covered in her relationship with Brian. Not yet. "She's, um, not around anymore."

"Oh. I'm sorry." Brian stared down at the steam his fingerprints made on the glossy bar, outlining his hands.

"Don't be. It was a long time ago." Anya wound her fingers under Sparky's armpits. Brian said that she used Sparky like a security blanket in a lot of ways. Maybe he was right. But she needed the little guy. She didn't really need anyone else—not the members of DAGR, not even Brian. But she would admit to herself that she needed Sparky.

A wheelchair squeaked along the polished bar floor. Ciro, the owner of the Devil's Bathtub, pushed up to the bar. His ebony face was creased with sadness. He held a photo album in his deeply lined hands. Anya noticed how much they shook when he handed it to her, the album pages opened like heavy birds' wings that smelled of mothballs.

"That's Bernie," Ciro said, pointing to a faded snapshot of a group of men wearing plaid pants and collared shirts. Anya judged by the cut of the collars and the fading orange hue of the photograph dyes that the picture had been taken in the 1970s. The interior of a bowling alley sprawled in the background. Ciro's shaking finger pointed to a man with muttonchop sideburns and a meticulously trimmed, elaborate mustache. Even back then, Bernie sported glasses and a paunch.

Anya's gaze trickled to the other faces in the photo,

grinned as she saw a younger Ciro lounging beside the ball-cleaner. Anya could see the swagger in his posture—he was a young man with the world at his bowling-shoed feet. Young Ciro had hair. Lots of it. His Afro spread out of the view of the camera, as meticulously groomed as a topiary. She bit back a laugh.

"Hey, it was the style back then." A gleam of humor and pride flickered in the old man's eyes.

"It's the style again, Ciro."

Ciro self-consciously rubbed at his bald pate, smiling at the handsome image of his younger self. He'd kept the beard and mustache, but the Afro was long gone. "Time and follicles wait for no man."

"Is this how you know Bernie? From a bowling league?"

"Not just a bowling league. The League of Smooth Operators. We were league champions for three years, till half the team got sent to 'Nam."

"Did you guys bowl after you got back?" Anya wasn't sure how to ask how many of Ciro's friends came back.

The old man shrugged. "Some of us. Off and on. But it wasn't the same." He tapped Bernie's picture. "Bernie was always an odd duck, even then. Though that was a time of . . . well, I guess you could say it was an era of spiritual exploration. . . . "

Max snorted and pantomimed smoking a joint.

Ciro gave him a dirty look. "That's not what I meant. I meant that Bernie was into weirder stuff than the rest of us. And I don't just mean drugs."

"Like what?" Anya leaned forward. Ciro was DAGR's demonologist. He'd forgotten more names of demons than Anya had ever known. For someone to be into weirder shit than Ciro was saying a lot.

"Bernie was obsessed with the idea of astral travel. Out-of-body experiences. He insisted that he'd been all over the world."

"I didn't think that humans could go to the astral plane," Anya said. "Isn't that the same as the Afterworld?"

Ciro shook his head. "You're confusing the road with the destination. The astral planes do include the Afterworld, but much, much more. Not all of those places are happily, heavenly ever after. Astral travel reveals intersection points that connect our world and allow travel to those planes . . . shortcuts." The old man sighed. "But, in general, yes. Humans don't go there. Not without paying a terrible price."

Anya recalled the anguished expression on Bernie's face as his ghost was pulled out of the room. "I can visualize that."

Ciro continued. "When Bernie said he was plane-hopping back then, we thought he was just tripping. But once or twice he managed to bring physical objects from his travels."

Anya's eyebrow crawled up into her hairline. "Really?"

"Small stuff. Chinese coins, crucifixes . . . One time he came back with a piece of stone he said was from an archaeological dig in Egypt. That kind of thing. Though such *apports* aren't totally unheard of in the metaphysical literature, substantiated reports are pretty uncommon in modern times."

"He had a lot of junk in his house. Things that smelled like magick. Swords, jars of skeletons, charm bags . . . "

Ciro nodded sadly. "He hasn't changed much, then. He started getting into dealing magickal artifacts in the early eighties. Didn't care about the provenance or the background of the items, or who he sold them to. He was in it for the money. He brought some really ugly stuff around the bar. . . . Once, he brought a piece of armor he swore had come from a demon. Stuff that reeked of evil. I told him to quit, before he picked up something too big for him to handle."

"What did he say?"

"Said that he wasn't using the things he sold, had no attachment to them, so he was safe. He said that he was just the conduit. I told him that didn't matter. Sometimes things attach to you."

Anya's fingers fluttered to the collar around her neck. She understood that kind of attachment better than most.

Attachment wasn't necessarily a bad thing, Anya had decided. But she still trod carefully.

Too carefully, she knew, for Brian.

Brian pulled his van into the driveway of Anya's tiny one-story house. It was the same as every other house on her street, except for the huge, leafy maple tree in the front yard and the fact that the shutters were green. Everything else was identical as far as the eye could see down the block: fading siding and aging brick, curling roof shingles, and postage-stamp-sized lawns, illuminated by the glow of porch lights. Spring was summoning leaf buds from square-trimmed shrubs and the trees, though it was still too early for the grass to need cutting.

Anya had lived here, in the Detroit village of Hamtramck, since she was a child. Different houses, but all much the same . . . The house she'd lived in with her mother, the one she'd lived in with her aunt and uncle, and this one all had the same layout that she could navigate with her eyes shut. All stood in the comforting shadow of the massive St. Florian Roman Catholic church. But things were a bit different than she remembered as a child. More bits of trash blown up against chain-link fences and never removed. A few more fire hydrants marked OUT OF ORDER. No traffic going to or from the now-closed auto plant down the road. People left their porch lights on all night, as if the wan glow might keep some of the darkness at bay. When Anya was little, her mother would have called it a waste of electricity. But it seemed necessary, somehow, now. It was a futile hope, Anya knew, but still instinctive. Humans gathered around light, like campfires, to feel safe.

Brian's breath fogged the glass of the van. "Do you want me to come in?"

Anya weighed the question for a moment, and she knew that he felt her hesitation. The pulse in the collar she wore around her neck felt sluggish. Sparky was sleeping, so she said, "Sure."

She popped open the door and stepped onto the cracked driveway, pulling her keys from her jacket pocket.

Brian crossed to the back of the van and shuffled in the pile of wires and boxes of ghost-hunting gadgetry. He rounded the corner of the van with a cardboard box in his arms.

"Whatcha got?" she asked.

"A present." He balanced the box on his hip as she unlocked the door. "A little something for your house."

Anya frowned. She supposed that her decor could have used the improvement. Compared to Brian's usual milieu, a bird's nest of wires and electronarcanum, her house probably looked pretty spartan. Furnished in spotlessly clean used furniture, the living room was nearly perfect in its efficiency. Anya liked it that way. Most days, she came home from work covered in ash, and the hardwood floors were easy to clean. She was compulsive about keeping bits of her work out of her sanctuary, and the cleanliness managed to create the comforting illusion of order, much as her neighbors' porch lights created the illusion of safety.

Brian set the box down in front of the coffee table.

"What is it?" She sidled up beside him, and his arm wrapped around her waist.

"I've been spending a lot of time here, so . . . " His chin rested on the top of her head. "I took the liberty of getting you a television set."

Anya blinked. Thanks to Sparky, she kept very few electronic devices in her house. Hell, he blew up her last microwave and destroyed a can opener a week ago. "Um, I hope that Sparky doesn't . . . "

"If he blows it up, he blows it up. I thought it would

be fun to try, though." He kissed her cheek. "He's pretty much left us alone lately."

Anya smiled against Brian's chest. A petulant salamander could be a distraction in a relationship. Sparky's need to demand attention at inopportune moments had been a serious handicap in her previous relationships. It was very difficult to get in the mood with an invisible mewing salamander perched at the foot of one's bed. But Sparky seemed to be less needy now. Last week the salamander had allowed Brian and Anya to sleep spooned up on her worn velvet couch, without so much as a peep.

Anya still felt a twinge of reticence about becoming involved. Everyone she'd ever loved had disappeared from her life. And she didn't want that to happen to Brian. He was too important to her, and she was too afraid of screwing things up.

She felt Brian nuzzle the top of her head, felt his arms stiffen and his chin move back, almost imperceptibly. She realized that she still smelled like work: like death and magick and the grease stain on Bernie's floor. The psychic grime on her made her skin itch.

She pulled back, stood on tiptoe to kiss Brian's top lip. He had a tiny scar on the upper left side of his mouth; she'd never asked where it came from, but she loved the feel of it. "Let me get cleaned up."

"Only if you promise to come back."

She slipped away from him, down the dark hallway that smelled of lemon wood polish, to the cold white tile of the bathroom. A dozen yellow rubber duckies stared down at her with cartoon eyes from a shelf as she undressed. The salamander torque remained next to her skin; it always did. She'd never taken it off, even as a child.

Closing the door, she tugged her shirt over her head. Her nose wrinkled. Her clothes smelled like charred bacon. Absently, she ran her fingers over the scar on her chest, the remnants of a burn mark. White, shiny scar tissue spread over her heart in a star-shaped pattern that was slowly darkening. It wasn't a mark from an ordinary burn—this had been left by a demon, a demon she'd barely survived. It shouldn't have happened. An ordinary demon could not have done to her what Lilitu had. A Lantern could devour ghosts and demons at will, burning them up and destroying them. Lilitu had been the exception.

But a lot of things happened that shouldn't; unpredictable things like the grease stain that had been Jasper Bernard, reeking on his charred floor.

Anya cranked up the heat on the shower and stepped into the steam. She thrust her head under the hot water, trying to rinse the image from her mind. Her toes tickled the breast of a yellow rubber duck bobbing around the drain. This duck was a demon duck, looking sinister with red horns and a red plastic tail curving over his back.

She shut her eyes, feeling the water dribble over her lips. She rubbed the juicy tang of mandarin orange body scrub and a handful of salt over her skin, scouring it red. She might not be able to rinse the image away, but she could at least scrape away the smell. She could scrub herself clean of all the death and magick and pretend to be normal, to have a normal evening with a normal man.

A corner of her mouth tugged upward. That was what she loved most about Brian: He was ordinary. Stubbornly non-magickal and a skeptic to boot. While she smelled like unseen and intangible things, spirits and fire, Brian dealt with what was solid and could be touched. Circuits. Machines. The cold tang of metal and silicone. Everything reduced to ones and zeros, to binary code, on or off. There was something comforting about that knowledge, that he had a tight grip on things that were irrefutably *real*.

Somebody had to.

She towel-dried her hair. No matter how hard she scrubbed, she never was able to shampoo away a faint smell of burn. It wasn't an unpleasant smell; it smelled of wood smoke. She'd burned her hair off several months back in an encounter with one of Sparky's relatives, nearly burned to a cinder herself. It had grown back dark and straight, but it felt soft and fine as ash.

She shrugged into her robe, covered with cartoon yellow ducks. She padded out into the hallway with her death-stinky clothes balled under her arm, en route to the washing machine.

She paused in the doorway to her bedroom. Light from the street drenched the walls and floor. Her gaze picked out the stylized magick circle painted in black on the floor around her bed. It could be opened and closed with a simple gesture, to keep evil out and guarantee her a restful night's sleep. Or it could keep a salamander out for a restless one.

She felt eyes upon her, watching in the stillness. They were her eyes, captured in a painting hung on the south wall. The canvas was treated with mineral dust that sparkled in the low light, and there was some small part of Anya that thrilled to see it: Her image was dressed in a black corset dress, her back facing the viewer, and she was looking slightly over her shoulder. It was the most sensuous, powerful work of art she'd ever seen. It had been painted by a former lover of hers, Drake Ferrer. He was many things: painter, architect, arsonist. He was also the only other Lantern she'd ever met. And he was dead.

But he'd captured this strange, compelling part of Anya, this shadow self that she couldn't quite tear herself away from, looking out from black carbon and glittering mica. He'd called the painting *Ishtar*, after the Babylonian goddess of passion and war. It was the thing she most feared becoming, and she kept it close at hand to remind herself not to go there. Not to become a destroyer. Not to become like Drake.

The sound of voices startled her; she was too used to silence in her house. From the shadow of the hall, she could see Brian crouched over the flickering screen of the massive flat-screen television sitting on the floor, fiddling with the remote. Noiselessly, she padded down the hallway in her bare feet to his side.

She crouched next to him, wet hair dripping over her shoulder, feeling as oddly awed as a caveman hunkered down over a fire. The picture was clear as glass as Brian cycled through the channels: skinny fashion models bright as butterflies stalking a catwalk; a chef holding up a lobster; a woman speaking Japanese before a blue screen.

"Wow. Fancy." She gave a low whistle of approval.

"Glad you like it."

"Thanks. You didn't need to do that. Really." She chewed her bottom lip, afraid to ask: "But . . . where did all the channels come from? I don't have cable. . . . "

"Don't worry about that." He gave a sly grin. Brian did some strange and shady things with technology, some things she didn't understand and wasn't quite sure were legal: surveillance equipment; voice recorders; an insanely huge collection of techno music. Most of his toys wound up in the service of DAGR. But she never asked where he got his playthings, or exactly what sort of research he did for the university. None of them did.

She blinked at the image of a brutal nature show, a bloody seal pup barking as it tried to flee a polar bear across a white ice field. More than anything else she'd seen today, she knew that the seal pup would give her nightmares. "Um . . . could we watch something else?"

Brian clicked to the next channel. A woman paced a stage like a caged tiger on grainy homemade video holding a microphone. Anya guessed her to be in her early fifties. Dressed in a powder-blue pantsuit, she had bleached-blond hair that was meticulously teased in spiky fringes over burning blue eyes. Those eyes blazed with something more than fervor, but Anya couldn't define it. A glass vial was suspended from a golden chain around her neck. Her voice was larger than her petite frame suggested, ringing like a bell over the heads of the audience:

"Nothing is impossible, my friends. With enough will and imagination, your dreams can come true, too. The universe wants you to be happy. . . . "

Brian grimaced and turned the channel.

"Wait. Go back." Anya pressed her hand on his arm.

Brian clicked back, and Anya's attention was captured by the yellow banner scrolling at the bottom of the screen: *Miracles for the Masses.* She recognized the name: It was stamped on the check fragment from Bernie's fireplace.

"Who is she?" Anya asked.

Brian sighed. His god was pragmatism, and he had little patience for anything that didn't work. "Have you been living under a rock? That's Hope Solomon, head of some New Age pyramid scheme called Miracles for the Masses. She's on every night on local cable access. Good for a laugh, but I feel sorry for the poor morons who send her money."

Anya watched Hope smile beatifically at the camera. "She's local, then?"

"Yeah. Unfortunately."

". . . and visualize the destiny you want, the destiny the universe wants you to have. But also apply will to make your wishes come true. Will is key. Will means action. And you can take action today to manifest your dreams by calling the number at the bottom of your screen.

"Pay it forward. Pledge to make your dreams come true, and we'll pledge to help you on your journey. The Divine Intelligence will help your miracle come true for you, too. You just have to take that first step. Operators are standing by to take your call.

"Blessings and good night."

To a standing ovation and thunderous applause, Hope waved and exited stage left. The screen filled with Miracles for the Masses' phone number and address, then cut to a commercial.

Anya sat back on her heels. "She's got charisma. I'll give her that. I suppose some people might find her to be appealing."

Brian snorted. "Sheeple. Sheeple might think they need to be led."

Anya lifted an eyebrow. "That's kind of harsh, don't you think? People want to believe in a better future. I mean, the fact that I've had my issues with the Catholic Church doesn't mean I'd throw the baby out with the bathwater." She had to admit, though, that it was hard to believe in a better future for Detroit. If she lay in bed, sleepless in the early hours of the morning, she swore she could almost hear the brittle city rusting.

"Just because the rich lady talks a nice line and built a big building with other people's money doesn't give her moral authority. It's a sociological fact: People get stupid in groups."

"Maybe. But good things can happen when people get together, you know?"

Brian leaned over, sniffed her hair. He grasped the sleeve of her robe and tugged her down to sit on the floor beside him. "You smell like oranges."

Anya blushed. The change of subject wasn't unwelcome. Her attention was distracted as his fingers brushed aside the curtain of dark hair covering her jaw. He nibbled below her ear, sending ripples of anticipation through Anya's spine. She swung her legs into his lap, eager to touch and be touched by something real.

"Hmm. Taste like oranges, too."

His arm wrapped easily around her waist, and his lips began trailing up her jaw line to her lips. Anya sank into the kiss, tasting mint and heat in his mouth. Her fingers wound in his shirt. She could feel the quickening of his heartbeat under her palms as one hand slid under the collar of her robe, pressed against the bare flesh at the back of her neck. She yearned to feel his bare hands on more skin. . . .

Around her neck, she felt the salamander torque begin to yawn and stir.

Go back to sleep, Sparky, she pleaded in the back of her mind. *Not now . . .*

The phone rang. Reluctantly, Anya drew away. The universe was conspiring against her. She felt Sparky stretch and glide down her arm to the floor, where he watched Brian with half-lidded suspicious eyes.

Brian reached for her. His eyes were shadowed in dark. "Can't it wait?"

"No one ever calls me at home . . . not unless it's important."

She climbed up from the floor and plucked the receiver from the kitchen wall. The phone, an old-fashioned turquoise corded handset, had come with the house and was older than Anya. Thus far, like the 1972 Dodge Dart she drove, it had proven impervious to Sparky's tinkering.

"Hello." From the corner of her eye, she watched Sparky's tail lashing as he stalked around Brian. The salamander's attention was suddenly arrested as he looked past the man to the glowing rectangle of shiny new circuitry on the floor. Sparky leaned forward to lick the HDTV. *"Sparky,"* she snapped, and he looked over his shoulder at her as innocently as a Rottweiler-sized fire elemental could look.

"Kalinczyk?" the familiar voice on the other end of the line crackled with impatience.

Anya pressed the heel of her hand to her forehead. "Yeah."

"This is Marsh. There's been an incident at the Jasper Bernard scene."

"What kind of incident?" Her brows knit together as her mind flashed through the possibilities. It couldn't have caught fire again—the scene had been cool throughout.

"The house has been ransacked. The press is already here. Better put on your Wonder Woman boots and come down here ready to kick some ass."

CHAPTER THREE

JASPER BERNARD'S HOUSE WAS A hive wrapped in yellow fire line tape, surrounded by the buzz of voices. Anya elbowed her way through the throng of neighbors gawking behind the line in their pajamas and robes. The shellacked news reporter she'd seen earlier at the site was standing in front of the fire line tape, the lights from his news van illuminating the face of the house, a pump truck, a burned-out sedan, and two police cars at the entrance.

Anya flashed her badge and ducked below the line. The reporter reached over the line with his microphone: "Nick Sarvos from Channel 7 News. Is it true that a man was burned to death inside?"

Anya grimaced. She hated dealing with the press. Her mind froze under questioning, and she was always afraid of saying something monumentally stupid. There was nothing the press could do for her, so she didn't trade favors by leaking info. These things were best left to the Detroit Fire Department's public relations people. She held up her hand as she walked away, telling him, "No comment."

The reporter shouted after her, "The neighbors are saying this is a case of spontaneous human combustion. Is there any truth to that rumor?"

Anya walked briskly up the steps to Bernie's porch, pretending she hadn't heard him. Ignoring him would probably come back to bite her in the ass by looking damning on film, but she had nothing to give him. Hell, *she* didn't even know which end was up yet.

Cops milled around the porch, at the edge of the news van's mast light glare. Their shadows cast long over the peeling paint, the uniforms moved aside to let her pass. Marsh stood in the doorway, scribbling on a clipboard. He did not look happy.

"I thought the scene was secured." Anya frowned up at him. DFD didn't release a scene until the scene was deemed safe and all evidence of arson had been collected . . . and they were a long way from that point. Leaving at least one firefighter at the scene allowed DFD to come and go without a warrant. It was a handy facet of the law that allowed DFD a good deal of latitude in investigating . . . all in the name of public safety. "How in the hell did anybody get in?"

"Yeah. It was supposed to be secured." Marsh glowered. "I posted a guy on the curb. His car apparently caught fire. When he got it extinguished, he saw lights inside the house."

"Lights? What kind of lights?"

"Not flashlights . . . the guy posted to guard the scene described it as a flickering orange glow. He thought the place had caught fire again, went in to investigate. Found the place tossed."

"Excellent."

"Yeah, well, DPD is taking a report, but can't tell if anything is missing."

Anya pinched the bridge of her nose. "Let me guess. . . ."

"Yup. Figuring out what's gone is your job. You took pix of the scene before it was tampered with."

"It's not as if I had time to do a thorough inventory. . . ."

"Congrats. It's your baby now."

Anya's shoulders slumped. She trudged past Marsh through the kitchen door.

It was not a pretty baby.

The kitchen had been thoroughly ransacked. Boxes of cereal had been ripped from the cupboards, spewing rice puffs on the floor that crunched underfoot. The kitchen table had been overturned, a leg broken in the fall. Pots and pans littered the floor, mixed with newspapers and the contents of the refrigerator. The refrigerator door stood open, light on. Lids had been torn off dozens of plastic containers, leaving their contents cast aside. A bottle of ketchup leaked out onto the floor. Anya smelled the remains of Kung Pao chicken, the sickly sourness of melting ice cream. She tugged her jacket more tightly around her against the chill.

How the hell had the firefighter posted outside not heard this shit going on and put a stop to it? she wondered. *It had to have sounded like a frat party in here.*

Reluctantly, she shoved the door to the living room ajar. Unbelievably, Bernie's living room was even more of a mess than before. The couch had been overturned, the stuffing slashed out of it. Bookcases had been ripped apart, their contents spilled among the black shards of broken vinyl LPs. Ashes from the fireplace were smeared along the carpet, almost obliterating the stain that had been Bernie.

Anya's eyes narrowed. This was no random burglary. Someone was looking for something specific.

Her eye turned to the fireplace mantel. It had been stripped clean: no bottles, no sword, no talismans. She inhaled deeply. For all the chaos, one thing was clearly different here: She could smell no magick. None at all.

She orbited the room, nostrils flaring. None of the objects she'd identified as magickal seemed to have been left behind. All she could detect was a dull, background smell of ozone she'd detected on her first visit here.

Staring at the fireplace, Anya drummed her fingers on her lower lip. Someone had been digging around in the ashes. Perhaps someone who'd been after the fragments of the magick-stained geode bottle she'd found. At least that had been safely packed away in the evidence locker. She hoped Forensics might be able to lift some prints from it.

She retraced her steps out of the room, careful not to touch anything. She'd get her camera and the rest of her gear, and would likely spend forever comparing these photos with her previous set. Cataloging the scene was shaping up to be a perfect nightmare.

Anya sidled through the kitchen, through the knot of

cops gossiping. She heard Marsh growling at the petrified fire cadet who was supposed to keep watch. His voice was too low for the press at the street to hear, but his tone had reduced the cadet to Jell-O:

". . . what the hell you were thinking. You've compromised the scene of an active investigation. I'll have your badge on my desk by morning, understand?"

The firefighter stood there, hands jammed in his pockets, staring at the floor. "Yes, sir. I don't know what happened. My back was turned for just a few minutes."

"Were you sleeping on the job?"

"No, sir."

"You been drinking?"

"No, sir."

"Drugs?"

"No, sir."

"Your ass is going over to the ER for a drug test. Now."

Anya slipped past them, stopped. Her nose twitched, and she turned toward the hapless firefighter.

He smelled like magick. The odor of ozone clung faintly to his coat. Anya sized him up. He was a regular guy—nothing outstanding about him: young man in his twenties with a buzz cut, shaking in his boots as Marsh chewed him out. Seemed earnest enough . . . not like a closet magick worker.

"Hey," she said, interrupting the ass-chewing. "Tell me what happened. What did you see?"

The firefighter rubbed the back of his head. "I was watching the house, just like Captain Marsh told me to.

I was listening to the radio, when I heard it get staticky. I tried to adjust it, but then I saw smoke rolling out from under the hood of the car. I popped the hood, thinking maybe it was steam from the radiator. But it was smoke."

"What color was it?"

"White. I think. That's why I thought it was steam. But I'm not sure."

Anya frowned. An engine fire fueled by motor oil would have emitted black or blue smoke. Maybe it had been an electrical fire, or an ignition of battery acid.

The firefighter continued. "I got the fire extinguisher out of the trunk. By that time, the whole front of the car was in flames. I was afraid that the gas tank would ignite, and I called for backup."

"When did you notice there was movement in the house?"

"I saw light in the house after the guys from the ladder company showed up to put the car out. Like I told Marsh, it wasn't flashlights . . . it was golden orange. I ran up the steps, and when I opened the door, the lights went out."

"Did you see anyone?"

"No. And I don't get that." The firefighter shook his head. "I don't see how they could have gotten past me."

Anya's eyes narrowed. "No one rushed past you?" There was only one door, the front one. Well, it was fairer to say that there was only one door that was accessible. The back door was blocked with crap; no one could've gotten out through there. And she'd seen no signs of forced entry yet.

Anya's eyes slid past him to the car he'd been sitting

in by the curb. It was a charred hulk, the front end burned black and the hood gaping open like the mouth of a monster. The glass was still intact, suggesting that the fire hadn't reached peak temperature. Car fires could get hot, over a thousand degrees, sometimes up to two. Perhaps opening the hood had dispersed some of that heat. Dodging through the police line and onlookers, she reached for the door handle . . .

. . . and was almost knocked over by the stench of magick that rolled out of the car. It was as if someone had been in the car with the windows rolled up, smoking pages from a witch's Book of Shadows for the last twelve hours.

Anya coughed. Her eyes watered, and she felt the remnants of magick seep into her clothes and her skin. She felt the salamander collar move around her neck as she stumbled back. Sparky leapt lightly on the ground. He grasped her coat in his teeth and hauled her back, back into the fresh air.

She breathed it deeply, forcing the heavy, still magick air out of her lungs. Sparky's head swiveled toward the car, and he growled.

Someone who knew how to use magick had started that fire to distract the firefighter. They'd broken into the house and lifted Bernie's magickal inventory right under their noses.

And she had no idea of what that all included. For all she knew, Bernie had the goddamn philosopher's stone or fucking Excalibur buried under his stacks of newspapers.

Shit.

———

Anya's office wasn't much, but it was a pretty damn good sanctuary.

Hidden in the labyrinthine bowels of Detroit Fire Department HQ, it tended to be forgotten. The basement office, with its old black-and-white tiled floor, broken transom window above the door, and beat-up 1960s office furniture, smelled like mildew and stale coffee. The overhead fluorescent light buzzed and flickered. But it was home away from home. And people rarely bothered her here. She appreciated not being in the upstairs cubicle farm; Anya didn't care about seeing or being seen. She wanted space to think. Even if it smelled.

Anya sat cross-legged on the floor, surrounded by stacks of eight-by-ten photographs. She'd spent all night logging the newly contaminated fire scene with her camera, and was comparing these shots to the ones she'd taken the previous day. The squeaky ink-jet printer on her desk grudgingly coughed them out, one at a time, before capriciously succumbing to paper jams. Anya perched over the photos with a red Magic Marker, circling things that should be there but weren't. It was like playing a giant game of Where's Fucking Waldo? and it made her head hurt.

So far, Bernie's place was missing six swords, twenty-six bottles of various descriptions, crystals and stones, a few statues, a carved wood skull, and a bag of marbles. And that was just what she could discern from an initial inventory and review of the photos. There was likely to be much, much more missing that she'd never know about. She'd tried tracking down Bernie's relatives to see if they might be able to shed light on either his death or the missing items, but his only living relative was a nephew he hadn't spoken to in twenty years. The nephew had the good sense to move out of Detroit. When Anya asked him what he wanted done with his uncle's remaining things, the nephew told her, "Torch it. Can't you use it for fire-fighter training or something?"

Anya chewed the pen cap, staring at the pictures. This would take months to unravel. Years.

The phone on the top of her desk rang, jolting her. She reached up and snagged the receiver. "Kalinczyk."

"What the hell is this thing you sent me? A goddamn foot?" the county medical examiner squawked on the other end of the line. The rustling of a plastic bag could be heard. "What, two feet?"

"It's a body, Gina."

"Where's the rest of it?"

"That *is* the rest of it."

"Explain this to me, please."

"It was found at a burn site. Scorch marks on the couch, floor, and the feet were found at the margin of the burn."

"You got photos?"

"Yeah. I'll send them over interoffice—"

"Bring 'em to me if you want a report. Otherwise, these feet can stay in the fridge until Christmas." Gina hung up.

Anya sighed, plucked the photos off the floor that included shots of Bernie's remains and jammed them into a manila file folder.

She hated going to the morgue, but there was no defying the will of Gina the Ghoul.

Folder tucked under her arm and muttering under her breath, Anya turned off her office lights and headed upstairs. Detroit Fire Department Headquarters had been built in 1929 in what was now known as the Washington Boulevard Historical District. The lobby and upper floors, which were open to the public, had been remodeled and refurbished several times, but the exterior still retained the original facade with high arches reaching over doorways.

The spell the 1920s cast ended when she hit the street. Directly across from DFD HQ was the modern Cobo Center. Built in 1960, the modernist cubic structure sprawled over city blocks and even reached over the Lodge Freeway below. The disconnect between new and old still jarred her, no matter how often she stepped out of the cool shadow of HQ into the bright sun of the street.

Anya dawdled getting the Dart out of parking. She took her time, pulling out and driving by the river district, intending to pick up I-75. She drove north to the morgue, hoping for traffic delays to postpone her visit there.

The glossy columns of the GM Renaissance Center reached up to a clear blue sky, sharply contrasting with some of the older buildings in the downtown area. In the late 1800s and early 1900s, Detroit had been known as the "Paris of the West" for its dazzling architecture.

The Great Depression put an end to that building boom. Construction had sputtered in fits and starts since then, but seemed to have burned out completely.

The Wayne County Medical Examiner's Office had been built a handy stone's throw away from Detroit Receiving Hospital and the VA Medical Center. Trees planted along the sidewalk served to visually insulate the nondescript brick building from prying eyes at street level.

Anya pulled the Dart into the parking lot. She sat behind the wheel, staring at the building. There were certain places mediums hated to go: hospitals, funeral homes, cemeteries . . . any place the dead congregated. The freshly dead were often confused and angry. The stale dead, those who chose to hang around the physical world, tended to be manipulative and malicious. Many mediums refused to set foot into those chaotic environments. Though they seemed quiet and peaceful to ordinary people, to a medium, they were the equivalent of taking a walk in an asylum after lights-out.

Sucking in her breath, she popped the car door. Warily, she advanced upon the morgue's glass doors. The salamander collar around her neck shivered and rolled, and Sparky slithered down her back, roiling around her feet.

"Behave," she warned him.

Sparky blinked up at her, then trotted through the motion-activated doors. He gave a squeal of delight that the doors registered his presence and opened. He circled back behind her and activated them three more times before settling down at her heels.

Anya put her head down, jammed her hands in her pockets, and briskly walked down the industrial-green tiled hallways. Her shoes echoed loudly on the floor. The place reeked of disinfectant and some type of preservative that smelled suspiciously of Italian sausage. She tried to ignore the ghost of the old woman dressed in a housecoat, screaming at the vending machine. She looked away from the translucent figure of the teenager sitting in the hall, cutting her wrists. The girl looked puzzled when no blood came out. A car-crash victim still wore his seat belt, embedded in his torso, as he drifted through the walls, oblivious to his surroundings. Sparky rubbernecked, snapping at any ghost who came within reach.

These were not her concern. Anya didn't know what she believed about an afterlife. She fervently hoped these people went somewhere, that some merciful angel swooped down and collected their confused souls, took them away to a bright and shiny place.

But she doubted it.

"No . . . leave me alone."

A thready feminine voice leaked from under a door, breaking Anya's step. Sparky turned, growled. Anya paused, leaning toward the stainless-steel door of the refrigeration unit. Another, deeper voice rolled over the small one:

"No one can hear you scream, girl."

Anya ripped open the latch to the cooler, reached inside for the light.

The refrigeration unit was packed. Flickering

fluorescent light illuminated body bags placed on open shelves, gurneys, and stacked in place. Something dark and sticky trailed on the concrete floor down toward the floor drain, and the room smelled like a butcher shop.

The ghost of a tall, thin man grasped the throat of a young woman spirit, pinning her to the wall. The harsh light played through bullet holes in his chest, but Anya could see no mark on the girl. Tears streamed down her cheeks.

"Get the fuck off of her." Rage boiled in Anya's chest.

The man turned, sneered at her. *"Mind your own business."* Perhaps he was used to no one seeing him. Perhaps he was used to scaring humans, both in life and in death. But Anya was having none of it.

Sparky lunged for him. His teeth grabbed the back of his hooded jacket, ripped him down from the wall. The salamander mauled him, growling, tail lashing, teeth tearing into his ectoplasmic throat. Anya had never seen him this violent, but she'd never seen him defending a child, either.

"Get back," Anya told the girl, and she shrank back between the bars of a set of shelves.

Anya felt the power of the Lantern burning in her chest. She could feel the fire expanding into her aura, reaching outward through her palms, hungry for that terrible ghost. A Lantern was different from other mediums in one critical aspect: A Lantern attracted ghosts like insects to a bug zapper . . . and could devour them.

"Sparky," she warned, and the salamander clambered

out of the way. Anya reached toward the ghost, writhing on the floor. She breathed him in, drawing him into the black void in her chest. She could taste the metallic frost of the ghost as she swallowed him, the ash in the back of her mouth as the fire in her chest immolated him. She stepped back, gasping, feeling the burn of it bubbling on her chest. That might leave a scar on her physical body, but it would heal.

She turned to the girl. The ghost of the girl cowered behind the racks, terrified.

Anya stuffed down the fire in her heart, tried to reach out with hands that didn't scald. She struggled to let the wrath drain down through her feet, into the ground. "It's okay . . . he's gone now."

The face of the girl peeped behind a body bag. *"He's not coming back?"*

Anya swallowed, shaking her head. "No." She didn't know for certain where the ghosts she devoured went. Someone had once told her that they went to feed powerful fire elementals, but she wasn't entirely sure. "You're safe now."

Sparky growled. Anya turned to see a man-shaped shadow forming on the wall. The black mass resolved to the translucent shape of a man in a black coat and jeans. Cold blue eyes stared out of a chiseled face, the kind of face that might have belonged on an album cover in the 1980s. A shock of blond hair was ruffled over his skull in some kind of butchered punk tribute hairstyle.

"Get the hell away from the girl," she snarled. "I've had enough of you fucking perverts."

The ghost held up his hands. *"I'm not here to harm anyone."*

"What are you here for? Hanging out, waiting for the apocalypse?"

A smile played over his mouth. *"I'm here for the girl."*

Anya bristled. She lifted her hand, feeling the heat gathering in her fingertips. She'd devour this one as easily as the last.

"I'm here to take her to the Afterworld."

Cold trickled down Anya's spine. "Who are you?" she asked, suspicious. Ghosts were inveterate liars, no matter how smooth their manner.

He turned toward the girl, making Anya bristle. *"Trina, my name is Charon. I'm here to take you on a trip."* He extended his hand toward the shelves.

"How do you know my name?" The girl watched him, her arms wrapped around her sides.

"Your grandmother told me. She would like for you to come visit her."

"Can you take me out of here?" Trina shivered, and looked up at the ceiling.

"Yes." When Charon smiled, it was with the beatific smile of an angel. Sparky waddled up to him and sniffed. His gill-fronds reached out, sensing the ghost's aura. The ghost let him, offering no sudden moves or resistance.

Sparky might be on the fence, but Anya didn't trust him. At all. "You aren't taking anyone anywhere."

Charon's eyebrow lifted. *"That's not up to you, Lantern."* He straightened to stare Anya in the face. When he spoke within the reach of her aura, Anya felt the cold radiating from him. He was powerful; she could sense the stillness of time dragging on him. His breath steamed in the air. *"It's the girl's time to go. You've done her a service by protecting her. But what would you do? You can't take her from this place."*

Anya's jaw hardened. Charon was right. Ghosts were anchored to physical locations, to people, or to things. As much as she wanted to, she couldn't take the girl-ghost into protective custody. The only way she could break that bond would be to devour the girl. Or she could leave her at the mercy of the other spirits in the morgue.

"What exactly are you?" Anya asked.

Charon shrugged. *"I'm a guide, that's all. I take ghosts back and forth . . . a cabdriver for the Afterworld. The morgue is . . . one of the stops on my route."*

Trina peered out from behind the racks. *"I want to go with him."*

Anya's hot fists clenched. All she could offer the ghost was oblivion.

She said nothing as Charon took the girl's hand. They walked through the wall of the cooler and vanished.

CHAPTER FOUR

"I CAN'T EVEN SAY THAT he's dead, for sure."

Gina stared through her bifocals and poked at Bernie's remains. The slippers had been removed from Bernie's feet, and the diminutive medical examiner fussed over them with tweezers. Ash drifted in tiny dunes around the feet on the stainless-steel coroner's slab. Anya wasn't sure how much of that was Bernie's, and how much of it had come from the cigarette dangling from the octogenarian's latex-covered fingers.

Anya must have grimaced, because Gina stuck her wrinkly face in hers. Gina had a face like a caramel candy stuck between the seats of a car on a hot summer day: "The dead don't give a rat's ass if I smoke. You shouldn't, either." The ME then shuffled over to her desk, where Anya's photos were laid out. Gina was so short that she had to roll up the sleeves of her standard-issue lab coat, and the hem brushed her ankles. With her frizzy gray hair, the result was very Bride of Frankenstein at the Nursing Home.

"Look, I'm a hundred percent sure the guy's dead," Anya said. She wasn't going to tell Gina about seeing his ghost. "Nobody's seen him, and the guy's not driving or walking around without his feet."

Gina looked through the bottom of her bifocals as she appraised the photos. "Very cool." Gina had called Anya down just to see the pictures. The old lady was an unapologetic ghoul, and this case had captured her imagination.

"Am I not gonna get a death certificate issued?" That had never happened before.

Gina rolled her eyes. "There aren't any tool marks on the bone that suggest his feet were sawed off, so I called around to some of my mortuary friends. They think that there's probably enough volume of ash to suggest the guy burned up. But—"

"That can't happen outside of a crematorium. Yeah, I know."

"Crematoriums have to bake the bodies at a temperature of at least sixteen hundred degrees, overnight, and then the bones are pulverized in a machine to make the ash. It's like putting a body in a giant clothes dryer with bowling balls for a few hours."

"We don't have a day or more in the timeline for that process to have taken place," Anya said. "The victim picked up his mail and took it inside, sometime after it was delivered, at 1600. Phone records show he called the local pharmacy for a refill on his sleeping pills at 1923 . . . and the body was found in this condition around 0600 the following morning."

Gina flipped through her papers. "There wasn't enough left to do a toxicology report on the findings, but the sleeping pills you found in his bathroom might be significant. Statistically, most cases of reported spontaneous human combustion involve the subjects being under the influence of alcohol. The theory is that the subject drinks himself into a stupor or takes some pills, passes out in front of a roaring fire, and fails to wake up when a spark lights on his sexy flammable jammies."

Anya squeezed her eyes shut, trying to drive out any mental image of what Gina might consider to be "sexy." "But we've established that a spark from the fireplace wouldn't have been hot enough to cause him to burn completely to ash like that. I've got the lab checking for high-temperature accelerants." Anya thought back to the contents of Bernie's fridge. "He did have a nice stock of wine."

"Any evidence of electrical fire?"

"No evidence of electrical faults in the house has been uncovered so far. The breaker box didn't even trip, so no surges."

"What about lightning? It's not common, but people do occasionally get struck indoors. Usually through phone lines or contact with wiring, though."

Anya shook her head. "I was hoping for that explanation. I checked with the National Weather Service. There were no storms that night, and no reported lightning strikes within eighty miles. His windows were shut when the cops found him, so that rules out any really weird atmospheric phenomena, like ball lightning, drifting in through an open window."

"Well, while we're getting weird and kinky with science . . . there's the wick effect theory. I saw a guy demonstrate that on TV once with a pig corpse. Pretty impressive stuff."

"Yeah. The idea is that fat from the human body can burn for hours, like candle wax. There was a great deal of fatty residue left on surfaces in the room in which he died, and even in the surrounding rooms."

Gina poked at the feet. "The subject has a nice set of cankles on him. I'm betting that he was overweight?"

"Yes. More fuel for the fire?"

"More fuel for the fire. There's also the possibility of the phospheinic fart."

Anya blinked. "The what?"

"That's another theory . . . that abnormal digestive processes can generate phosphines, which, under the right conditions, can spontaneously combust."

Anya pinched the bridge of her nose, picturing flames shooting out of poor Bernie's ass. And his sexy flammable jammies. "I'm not sure I want to imagine that."

"Hey, I'm just suggesting possibilities."

"You are one seriously morbid lady." Anya crossed her arms. "Why are you so interested in this case?"

"It's what I do best." Gina tapped her cigarette into an ashtray on her desk. "Actually, this is not the only weird burn victim I've seen in the last few weeks. Check this out." The coroner pulled an accordion file folder out of her desk. "An anonymous tip to nine-one-one brought the cops to the old train station."

Anya dredged her memory. "The one on Fifteenth Street? That's been closed since the eighties."

"That's the one. The homeless have pretty much taken it over since it was closed to rail passengers."

Anya pulled out a sheaf of photographs. Taken under the cold, clear fluorescent light, the first shot showed a body of a grizzled old man in a filthy coat on the coroner's slab. He looked like a bum asleep, except that the bottom of his gray beard and the front of his coat were charred black. The next photo showed the coat open, and it was apparent that nearly the entirety of his torso was sunken in and burned away. Bits of ribs could be seen curling around the remains of his flannel shirt, like bony fingers blackened at the tips.

"What the hell?" Anya muttered, flipping through the shots of the body, washed clean, but exhibiting a gaping black hole where the abdomen should have been. It looked like the spirit-devouring black hole in her own chest felt, but this was splayed open for all to see.

"Police report's in there, too. Beat cops found this guy curled up under the ticket window. Nobody had seen or heard anything. They fished him out and sent him here. No identification on him. The other homeless guys called him George."

"Where's the body?"

"Nobody claimed him, so the county cremated him." Gina shrugged. "Ironic, I know. But this one was just weird enough to put into my collection of bizarre forensic files."

Anya's brow wrinkled. "You have a collection?"

"Hell, yeah." Gina planted her fists on her hips. "I'm gonna write a book when I retire."

Anya snorted. Gina the Ghoul would never retire. "Can I borrow this file?"

"Sure. Gina's collection of forensic mysteries is a lending library." Gina stuck her thumb over her shoulder at Bernie's remains. "I'll lean on the lab to get you the test results back on this guy. But it's anyone's guess what you're gonna find in that mess."

Anya's gaze flicked between the photo of the dead bum and Bernie. Was this a fluke, or could these really be connected? She frowned at the lumps of ashes and flesh on the table.

They were both impossible. How could they *not* be related?

No one cared very much about the homeless. In Detroit, they lived generally underneath the public radar, more visible in summer months and hidden away from the cold in shelters and abandoned buildings and alleys in the winter. They were often invisible, as much a part of the landscape as any other eyesore. Since no one cared, no one bothered much to investigate the death of a bum who'd passed out and probably dropped a cigarette on himself. A few perfunctory forms were filled out, filed, and promptly forgotten.

Its Beaux Arts bones still beautiful, Michigan Central Station loomed like a battered spider, reaching over a dozen bent and twisted railroad tracks. Built in 1913 with generous arches and graceful columns to ferry passengers from to and from their destinations, the train station itself was backed by an eighteen-story tower. The grand old building was now surrounded by a tall fence crowned with spirals of ribbon razor wire. Most of the glass in the windows had been struck out; years of acid rain and lack of maintenance had blackened the exterior.

Anya stared up at the looming station, Sparky perched on her shoulder. The Dart sat behind her in a parking lot, its asphalt shattered with cracks and speckled with grass. She could see how someone could easily get lost in such a huge place, burn to death and not be found. The building had been alternately slated for revitalization and destruction for as long as Anya could remember. She couldn't remember whether its latest destiny was to become a casino or be turned into a parking lot.

She paced along the chain-link fence, searching for a way to get in. If the street people could easily get in, she could, too. Anya was rewarded for her efforts by a pair of fence posts that didn't quite fit snugly together. Squeezing between them, she scraped her arms on the raw edges of fence, wriggled through onto the property. Picking her way through weeds and trash, she climbed the short steps to the arched entrance. A piece of plywood leaned against a broken door. Anya nudged it aside and ducked in.

It took a moment for her eyes to adjust to the

darkness of the interior. As her vision cleared, she found herself in the main-floor waiting room. Huge vaulted ceilings reached skyward, more than fifty feet, into black, flanked by an arcade of Doric columns and broken marble walls. Sunlight streamed in from the broken windows. Somewhere above, she could hear the warble of doves in their nests. Graffiti was scrawled on the walls as high as a man could reach, and higher. Bits of rebar protruded from the walls where remnants of wires and copper pipe had long since been torn out. Rusted-out barrels stood on the open floor. Newspaper and rags were strewn throughout. Shopping carts were turned over piles of burned trash to create makeshift barbecues. The place smelled overwhelmingly like stale piss. Someone was definitely living here.

Movement caught her eye. As her vision adjusted, she could make out shadows writhing in the darkness, black silhouettes moving down the waiting room to the bricked concourse by the dozen.

Her neck prickled, and Sparky growled. His gill-fronds twitched and extended forward.

Anya switched on her flashlight, swept it in the seething darkness. The shadows scuttled away, as if the presence of light was caustic.

"Hello?" she called out, heart hammering behind her sternum.

The shadows flitted away. Anya's grip on the flashlight was slick with sweat. Perhaps coming here alone had not been a good idea.

The police report had said that the bum's body had been found in one of the old ticket offices. Anya resolutely put one foot in front of the other to peer inside the cracked remains of the box office. Her light swept the dented counter, through the scarred mouth of the ticket window. There had not been glass here for decades.

Sparky hopped through the window onto the counter. Anya clumsily followed, sticking one leg and then the other through the frame. She scooted down the counter until she could set her feet on the floor . . . in what smelled like human excrement.

"Ugh," she groaned, wiping her shoe on the wall.

She shone her light around the litter-strewn office, which smelled like a sewer. A rat scuttled across the cracked floor into a nest of newspaper, startling her. The light picked out a scorch mark on the floor underneath the counter. Anya bent to get a better look.

This must have been where the homeless man was found. Though no usable evidence remained today, weeks later, Anya had wanted to see it for herself. The perfunctory photos taken of the scene by DPD had shown much the same scene of refuse, with a pair of feet extending from the bottom of the counter. Anya's light picked out the scorch mark on the floor, and a matching one on the filthy underside of the counter where a roach zipped past. If the fire had started while the man was on the floor, smoke surely would have burned up the entire counter . . . and the intense heat required to do that would certainly have spread to the nearby trash. Yet, as in Bernie's house, there was only a black mark remaining, very little evidence to suggest such a dramatic end.

Anya straightened, chewing her lip. There were glass bottles strewn around, some of them liquor bottles. Perhaps there was something to the theory about heavy drinking creating a stupor that would make the victim impervious to a cigarette burn. But that felt like too much of a reach. Wouldn't the homeless man have woken up at some point, regardless of how much Two Buck Chuck he'd managed to down?

Anya slithered back through the ticket window. Shadows wildly chased one another in the flashlight glare as she found her footing.

She squinted into the half-darkness. Someone was here. And someone had seen something.

"Hello?" she called out. Her voice scraped the roof of the waiting room. "I'm looking for anyone who knew George. I'm not a cop. I just want to talk."

Shadows seethed. A voice squeaked from behind a Doric column: "You ain't no cop? You a social worker?"

"No. I'm a firefighter."

A silhouette slipped around the edge of the column. Anya shone her light before her, picking out a bearded man wearing an olive green military jacket and a ball cap. A backpack was slung over his right shoulder, and his left hand held a brightly colored bag of donations from a local supermarket known for charitable works. The man looked her up and down, and Anya's skin crawled. Sparky parked himself between Anya and the man, hackles raised.

"You don't look like no fireman. You look like a social worker. And you've got shit on your shoes."

"I'm not a social worker. And yeah, I've got shit on my shoes. I'm pretty sure it's not mine."

The man cracked a toothless smile. "You got money?"

"I've got money if you've got information." Anya didn't step closer; she didn't want to spook him. Nor did she want to get much closer to this man who smelled like he hadn't showered in a year. "Did you know George?"

"Yeah. He's dead."

"I know. Did he usually sleep back there, in the ticket office?"

"Yeah. That was his favorite hidey-hole."

"Did you ever see any signs of a fire?"

"The night before he disappeared, he damn near caused a fight. He was cookin' something in there, something that smelled good, and he wasn't sharing." The homeless man frowned and rubbed the scabs on his chin. "Turned out it was him cooking."

Anya's stomach turned, remembering the bacon smell from Bernie's house. She couldn't imagine what it would be like to be that hungry.

"Things burn in here a lot," he said.

"What kinds of things?"

"George wasn't the first person caught fire since I been here. One dude caught fire while walking the tracks . . . his bag went up like a sack of firecrackers. 'Nother time, a preacher-man came down to 'save' us." The man made air quotes around the word and giggled. "He brought some candy bars, so we listened to him sermonizing. Didn't have anything else to do. His jacket caught fire and he ran out, swearing like a sailor about hellfire and Satan."

"Do you remember their names?"

"I'm not good with names."

So much for interviewing additional witnesses. "What do you think happened?" Anya tried another approach.

The man shrugged, spat some noisome phlegm on the ground. "I think this place is haunted. I think the ghosts burn shit every once in a while."

Anya looked up at the dark ceiling. "I could see this place being haunted."

"There's always strange sounds here. Things moving in the shadows, to and from the tracks. Sometimes you can still hear the trains at night." His eyes burned. "It's like this decrepit old joint is still alive, you know what I mean?"

"Yeah. I do know."

"At least the lady in pink is getting rid of some of 'em."

"Lady in pink?" she echoed.

"There's a woman that comes around here once every couple of weeks. She brings a lot of bottles and jars. The ghosts disappear into the bottles and jars."

Anya's heart quickened. "Can you describe her?"

"She's short, got some meat on her bones. Early fifties, blond hair. Always wears a pink suit and minces around in ridiculous high heels." The man glanced at Anya's feet. "She manages to keep the shit off her shoes, though."

Anya blinked. That sounded like Hope Solomon. "Did she ever tell you her name?"

"She acts like she's too good to talk to us, but she talks to the ghosts. Sweet-talks 'em until they get close enough to the bottle. Then . . . whoosh! In they go." The homeless man pursed his lips, extended a filthy hand. "I gave you all the information I got. Hold up your end of the bargain."

"Thanks," she said awkwardly. She reached in her pocket, fished out a twenty-dollar bill. It was all she had in cash, but it felt like a pathetically small amount.

The man snatched at it, his hand as fast as a cobra striking. He plucked the money from her fingers and melted back into the shadows.

Anya sighed. Maybe it would be for the best if this place was torn down. She spun on her heel, scanning for more evidence of scorch marks. Her flashlight shone on graffiti, some crude and some elaborate. In several places, she saw red depictions of flames, and one rudimentary sketch of a devil with horns.

For people like the homeless man, this could very well be hell.

Shadows boiled in her peripheral vision. They seemed to flow in an unusually ordered fashion, like water. She reached out with her Lantern senses, could sense the shapes and movement of something otherworldly—of ghosts.

"Hello?" she breathed.

But they ignored her. Anya suspected they were part of some subtle, residual haunting, some darkness playing over and over again like a stuck record. Perhaps the images of passengers were indelibly recorded in the bones of this grand old structure, moving toward their destinations as they had in life.

She walked through a puddle on the floor, lit from above by the copper frame of a ruined skylight. She followed the flow of the shadows, moving down through a tunnel to the broad brick expanse of the train platform. Her shoes rang loudly against the brick, and Sparky scuttled on point before her. His glowing amber light cast some relief from the gloom.

The platform itself was crumbling onto the tracks, exposing rusted rebar like teeth. Here, without the meager benefit of broken windows, the darkness was nearly total. She could hear water dripping and the movement of air swirling around her, much like standing on a train platform in any major city. Instead of people, spirits stirred around her, moving back and forth in lines like ants. She could see only silhouettes, snatches of hats or briefcases or shoes. She glimpsed men and women in modern dress, a teenager with a cell phone, and a woman wearing a poodle skirt and bobby socks. But the images flowed past her in a cacophony of rising voices, parting around her as if she were a stone in a river.

A dull roar came from the distance, growing closer. The wind picked up, lashing her hair around her face. Sparky dug his toes into the brick. Anya leaned backward as the sound of a train whooshed down the tunnel, tearing at her with a terrible vortex of wind. She threw up her arms to shield her face from flying debris and the terrible light washing through the tunnel.

The sound and light receded. Anya removed her arms from her face and opened her eyes.

Except for her and Sparky, the platform was empty. Every single ghost was gone, sucked away by that terrible wind.

Witches were often willing to do things other people were squeamish about, and were known to keep the strictest levels of confidence.

Those were some of the reasons Anya went to Katie for odd magickal jobs.

Those, and Katie's baking skills.

Anya sat at Katie's kitchen counter, plucking a hot oatmeal chocolate-chip cookie off a baking rack. She juggled the cookie, trying to keep it from scalding her fingers as she crammed it in her mouth.

Barefoot, Katie swished around the kitchen in a long, crinkled skirt. She'd picked up a polka-dotted apron from a vintage shop that clashed with her plaid pot holders. She looked like Betty Crocker's demented little sister. The felt kitchen witch strung over the kitchen window jiggled in the breeze, seeming to chuckle at her bizarre fashion sense.

"I could live on these," Anya muttered in gooey happiness.

"Glad to share." Katie leaned over the sink to lick the dough from beaters. Witches did not fear food poisoning from raw eggs.

Katie's cats, Vern and Fay, tore through the kitchen,

dodging between the bar-stool legs. Vern, a gray tabby, got hung up around the kitchen table leg, spun out, and scrambled for purchase on the freshly waxed linoleum. He bumped Katie's leg, causing her to drip dough on the front of her apron. Sparky plowed into the kitchen, feet churning and tail kinked in delight at having someone to play chase with. He chased Vern into the hallway. A faint yelp sounded from the back of the house.

Katie shook her head, dabbing at the dough on her chest. "I really wish I could see Sparky play with them."

Anya spread her hands. Cats could see him. So could dogs and other ghosts. And Anya. The only other person Anya had met who could see Sparky was another Lantern she'd encountered, months before. Her thoughts darkened, remembering: Drake had been her enemy and her lover. He was probably the only other person who really understood her. And now he was dead. Anya felt only a small twinge of grief at that; it had to happen, but she wished she'd had more time with him, to ask him more about what their kind was supposed to do in the world.

"You said you needed a favor." Katie stripped off her pot holders, and her fingers glistened with silver rings.

"I need to talk to Bernie." Anya said it without preamble. She rested her chin in her hand, staring across the bar at Katie.

Katie raised her eyebrow, and a teasing smile played around the corners of her bow mouth. "You didn't ask Ciro. Or Jules."

"It's not DAGR's case. And neither one of them is my

father." It sounded petulant when she said it, but it was the truth. Ciro had forgotten more things about metaphysics than Aleister Crowley had ever known, but was very sparing and particular in its usage. He would never tell Anya how to get in touch with Bernie. And Jules . . . Anya was certain that talking with the dead violated Jules's ethics. No use provoking him.

Katie shrugged. "Well . . . we could always try to summon him."

"How do we do that?"

"We could hold a séance. But we'd have to rustle up at least four people."

Anya made a face. She could probably rope Brian into it, but Max would blab to Jules.

"Or we could run down to the toy store and pick up a Ouija board. But I don't advise it."

"Why not?" Anya was genuinely curious. DAGR had gone on a number of runs in which a Ouija board had allowed a ghost or demon into a house, but she didn't know what made that method better or worse than any other.

Katie picked up a cookie. "A spirit board is neither good nor bad, in and of itself. It's just a tool. But modern spirit boards have become too intertwined with the idea of a game. No one takes them seriously, and rarely do people take the necessary precautions. Bad stuff gets in, and most people lack the ability to test the veracity of the spirits they've summoned."

"There's no off switch?"

"They've not been trained to break the connection or protect themselves. No magic circle's drawn, no protective elements are invoked. It's the metaphysical equivalent of allowing a hitchhiker to ride in your car, and then asking him nicely to get out when you're done driving."

Anya stifled a shudder. She'd had a hitchhiker before, a demon. Picked it up like a bad cold from a teenager who had been playing with a Ouija board. She remembered what it was like, feeling the demon working beneath her skin, controlling her hands and her voice. She would never, ever allow that to happen again.

"So . . . where is Bernie now? Is there any way to know?" Anya asked, changing the subject. Her curiosity had been piqued. Had Bernie been sucked into the afterlife? Had he gone to the same place Charon had taken the little girl?

"I don't know where he is." Katie dusted crumbs off her apron. "I don't think anyone really has the authoritative answer on what happens after we die. But we can still try to summon his ass and see if he responds."

She rummaged through her cabinets for a glass water goblet, a container of salt, a dish towel, and a notepad. Katie poured lemon oil on the dish towel and polished the scarred kitchen table to a high, slick shine.

"I'll need to dust off your aura, too," she said.

Anya nodded. "What do you need for me to do?"

"Just stand over here beside the table and think pure thoughts."

Anya screwed up her forehead. "I spent half the day

at the morgue and the other half at a haunted train station covered in shit. I don't know any pure thoughts."

"Then think happy thoughts. Think about sunshine. Puppies. Or getting laid. Just not all at the same time, or you'll confuse the Goddess."

Katie lit a bundle of sage and fanned the smoke over Anya's body, head to toe. She paused when she fanned the smoke over Anya's heart.

"Interesting," she murmured.

Anya's nose twitched. Sage always made her sneeze. "What?"

Katie squinted. She didn't squint exactly *at* her, but *through* her. "Your aura," she said. "It's changed color."

"What do you mean?" Anya asked. Katie had graciously scrubbed Anya's aura on many occasions, but hadn't noted any abnormalities in it, except when she was hosting a demon. Alarm prickled over her. Perhaps the demon had left something behind. . . .

Katie shook her head, sending blond wisps of hair over her shoulders. "I don't think it's anything bad. Your aura usually appears to me to be amber, like fire. It just feels darker, blacker. Solid. Like obsidian."

"How is that not bad?"

"Sometimes, when black reaches into an aura, it's a sign of transformation. It's not necessarily negative, so just try to suspend judgment about it."

Anya's mouth turned down, dubious.

Katie fanned the smudge stick over herself and stuck it in the soap dish on the edge of the sink. A wisp of smoke reached upward, tickling the kitchen witch's bloomers.

Attracted by the smell of sage, Sparky trotted into the kitchen. He paused, gill-fronds twitching. Fay and Vern hopped up on the counter near the sink, pressing their paws into bits of flour left behind from the mixing. Sparky sauntered beside Anya and looked soulfully up at her.

"Can Sparky come play?" Anya asked.

"Sure." Katie was pouring salt in a circle around the kitchen table, muttering invocations to the four elements. She lit a jar candle in each cardinal direction on the floor: north, south, east, and west. An extra candle in the center of the table was lit, for spirit. "Just keep him in or out of the circle. Doesn't matter to me which."

Anya pulled Sparky into the circle Katie drew around her heels. Katie closed the circle, and Anya pulled out a chair. Sparky arranged himself in her lap, looking at his reflection on the glossy table surface.

Katie sat opposite Anya. She took a plain stack of recipe cards and marked each one with a letter of the alphabet in Magic Marker. She arranged the cards in a semicircle around the table, and made three more cards that read YES, NO, and GOODBYE.

"That looks suspiciously like a Ouija board."

"One of its forebearers. This type of spirit contact was in vogue when table-tipping, cabinet-knocking, and the like were parlor games in the late 1900s. The difference is, these tools are all consecrated and we're within the safety of a magic circle. And since we're not wearing corsets, we're unlikely to faint." Katie turned the glass goblet upside down on the center of the table. "May Goddess bless and guard our efforts."

She placed her fingertips on the base of the glass, motioning for Anya to do the same. Her rings sparkled in the candlelight. Anya reached around the salamander's head and mimicked her. "Now what?"

"We summon the spirit of Jasper Bernard to speak with us."

"That sounds like a grand, ceremonial magick gesture." Katie was a kitchen witch—she improvised with whatever was at hand. Anya had seen her do high magick, but the witch's distinct preference was for enchanting the mundane.

"It is. It goes something like this: Jasper Bernard, are you here?"

Nothing happened. Anya and Katie stared at the goblet for a good five minutes. Sparky yawned and placed his head on the table.

"Jasper," Katie said, in a more authoritative voice. "Please come to us."

Anya whispered, "I think he responds better to 'Bernie.'"

The glass jerked under her hands. It orbited in an agitated circle, moving faster and faster. Anya had difficulty keeping up with it. From her lap, Sparky sat up and pushed his gill-fronds toward the tabletop.

"Bernie, is that you?"

The makeshift planchette curled its way over to the recipe card marked YES. It stopped below it, circling like a beetle caught in the bottom of a jar.

Katie whispered to Anya, "Ask it something to verify its identity. Something that no random spirit would know."

"Bernie, we know you knew Ciro. Tell us about your time with him."

The glass hesitated. For a moment, Anya was sure they'd caught a voyeur spirit toying with them, and her thoughts raced on plans to banish it. But the glass deliberately spiraled over to the alphabet of recipe cards. It spelled out: B-O-W-L-I-N-G.

Katie nodded. "Very good."

"Where are you, Bernie?" Anya couldn't help but ask. After seeing the spirit violently sucked out of the house like lint in a vacuum cleaner, she wanted to know.

The glass turned in a figure-eight pattern, spelled out: V-E-S-S-E-L.

"What kind of vessel? A boat?"

The goblet curled around NO. Its motion became jerky, erratic, and it zinged around the table, scraping random letters.

"I think we're losing him," Katie muttered. "It feels like the communication is being interfered with."

Anya leaned forward, knuckles white on the goblet base. "Bernie, what happened to you? We need to find out."

The glass spun out of Anya and Katie's grip. It spelled

out H-O-P-E before sliding off the edge of the table and shattering on the floor. Katie's cats fled the kitchen in a flurry of fur. Sparky climbed down to the floor and sniffed the glass shards, growling.

Katie looked across the table at Anya. "Hope. Does that mean anything to you?"

Anya smiled grimly. "It gives me a place to begin looking."

CHAPTER FIVE

THE MORNING PAPER INCLUDED A headline in large type on the front page of the Metro section: DFD INVESTIGATES SUSPECTED CASE OF SPONTANEOUS HUMAN COMBUSTION. The article went on to quote an unidentified source about the grisly details of the Jasper Bernard crime scene and discuss how DFD was "stymied" by the case. Mention was also made about the crime scene being "mishandled" and a break-in occurring, calling any evidence in the case suspect.

Anya rolled her eyes. She was certain that some letters to the editor would be forthcoming about DFD's incompetence. She flipped the page, scanning for the continuation of the article. Her attention paused on an article discussing the possibility that the Detroit Tigers weren't generating sufficient sales tax revenue for the city during baseball season. The Detroit Institute of Arts had a nice full-color spread about a forthcoming exhibit on ancient Greek art that piqued her curiosity. The photos showed faded urns and amphorae decorated with the shapes of gods and beasts. One of them was even nick-named "Pandora's Jar." The massive pithos was painted with images from the myth. Scholars speculated that the age of the jar surpassed the age of the decoration, giving rise to debates about forgery and the provenance of the item. One set of experts suggested the jar could have been Pandora's Jar from myth. Another insisted the jar had been used for entirely different purposes, as a burial urn. A third argued it was merely a piece of art, carved from unusual stone.

"Ms. Kalinczyk?"

Anya looked up, tucked the paper under her arm. The waiting area in which she sat was worthy of GM Head-quarters: potted plants, sleek chrome furniture, pastel watercolor art. Not prints—originals. A massive arrange-ment of fresh stargazer lilies bloomed on the coffee table, though they were curiously sapped of fragrance. The re-ceptionist who stood before her was impeccably attired in a designer suit, displaying two-inch airbrushed fingernails that had clearly never been used for typing. The posh set-ting was completely incongruous for a nonprofit organiza-tion, housed in a nondescript building in the warehouse district with weeds sprouting between the cracks in the sidewalk. Miracles for the Masses put on a nice front of virtuous poverty, but the inside lining of the cloud was flush. The air-conditioning was turned way up, practically spewing cash from the vents.

"Yes?" Anya responded, with a slight degree of ir-ritation. She'd been waiting more than an hour for Hope

Solomon to finish her coffee and decide to start taking visitors.

"Ms. Solomon will see you now."

"Fantastic." She rose to follow the receptionist down a peach-painted hallway lit with broad-spectrum bulbs to mimic sunshine. In this pastel palace, Anya felt as out of place as a crow at a garden party.

The receptionist opened a door and gestured for Anya to go inside. Anya's shoes sank into the plush white carpeting. A skylight overhead poured a dazzling amount of sunlight into the room. When her eyes adjusted, Anya fixed on a short blond woman sitting on the other side of a glass desk. She was wearing a pink pantsuit.

"Ms. Kalinczyk." The woman stood and extended a hand that clinked with gold bracelets. She smiled warmly. "I'm Hope Solomon."

"Pleased to meet you." Anya grasped her hand. Hope's hand was cold as a corpse's.

And she reeked of magick. She stank of sour, dark magick the way some women emanated cheap perfume. It wasn't the pleasant, white-magick herbal whiff that surrounded Katie. This was the metallic tang of ozone, the smell in the air after a lightning strike. And all the Chanel in the world couldn't cover it up.

Hope's eyes narrowed almost imperceptibly when she grasped Anya's hand. Her blue eyes flickered to the salamander torque around Anya's neck. Anya could feel the collar growing hot as Sparky stirred. Hope dropped Anya's hand a beat too quickly; Anya wondered what

Hope sensed. Could she smell some of the char of a Lantern about her?

Hope nodded and retreated back behind her desk. Anya looked at the glass vial dangling around her neck as a pendant with interest. It appeared to be opaque glass, but it exuded the pungent fetor of magick. She sat in her chair, motioning for Anya to sit in an armchair in front of the desk, placing the barrier of chrome and glass between them. "I'm told that you're conducting an investigation." Her voice was the controlled purr Anya had heard from television.

"Yes." Anya settled into the chair, feeling Sparky pacing around her throat. A tongue flickered in her hair. "Some correspondence from you was found in the home of Jasper Bernard." She didn't tip her hand just yet. She wanted Hope to wonder what kind of material she possessed; there was nothing to be gained by divulging that it was only the scrap of an envelope and the corner of a check.

"The name doesn't ring a bell. Does Mr. Bernard need help?"

"He's dead." Anya watched Hope. Hope didn't twitch or flinch at that knowledge; she knew. Perhaps she read the paper. Or she had known before.

Hope touched her fingers to her chin in an expression of concern. "Oh, dear."

Anya wasn't buying it. "Bernard's bank records show that he received several checks from you over the past five years, ranging in amounts from five hundred to ten thousand dollars."

"I can check with our accounting department and see what they have. I'm afraid that I simply can't remember every detail in the budget for an operation this large." Her fingers sketched the office and world beyond them. "I'm sure you understand."

Anya felt Sparky peel off her neck and drop to the floor. The salamander padded through the plush carpet, pacing around the office. His tongue flickered over the bookshelves holding a wide-screen television, the potted plants. He reached up on his hind legs to analyze the knickknacks on the shelves.

"I'll look forward to receiving your records, then," Anya said mildly. She didn't want to have to force a subpoena, but she would if the information wasn't forthcoming. "Perhaps it would help me understand more about Mr. Bernard if you would explain what it is exactly that your organization does."

As easily as if she were shrugging on a coat made from the skins of dozens of PR people, Hope assumed the sunshiney persona from her television program. "Miracles for the Masses is dedicated to serving the greater Detroit area by granting wishes to deserving citizens. We provide training on aligning one's goals with the universe, and harvesting the rewards."

"Are you a church, then?"

"No. We don't like to pigeonhole ourselves that way."

Anya looked around the well-appointed room. Sparky sauntered back to the center of the room and began sniffing Hope's desk. "I'm afraid I don't see what you're selling."

"We are a nonprofit organization incorporated under the laws of this state, operated for charitable and educational purposes." Hope's mouth tightened. "We provide seminars on self-actualization to help people realize their true purpose."

"How much do the seminars cost?" Anya sat back in her chair.

"We have a sliding-scale fee structure. Members are charged based on ability to pay."

"So . . . " Anya leaned forward. "Tell me about the miracles." Sparky reached up to nose the telephone on the desk. It burped out a bleep, startling Hope.

This was more comfortable territory for Hope. "Our testimonials are impressive. While we can't guarantee a miracle, our members' experiences run the gamut from cured terminal cancer to two lottery winners. Our seminars have allowed people to harness the power of their own wishes to gain new employment, repair marriages, and get their children off drugs. Wishing is a powerful process. We're simply here to facilitate it."

Sparky reached up to the desk and licked Hope's business-card holder. He made a face and turned his attention to a cloisonné ginger jar decorated with a branch of cherry blossoms wrapping around the body and closed with a porcelain cap. It looked very old; the enamel had crazed in a few places. Sparky batted at it but was unable to make the container move. He turned his head to look at it, this way and that, fascinated.

"I'd appreciate it if your accounting department would

send over a copy of your annual report as well," Anya murmured.

"Our finances are not open to the Detroit Fire Department for audit," Hope replied, her taut skin near to cracking like the enamel on the ginger jar.

"You're a public charity. I'll get them from you, or I'll get them from the IRS with a subpoena," Anya said, lacing her hands primly together in her lap. "And the scope of the investigation is not for you to decide." She might not be able to stop Hope from taking money from desperate people, but she could sure try to make her squirm. Out of the corner of her eye, she watched Sparky bat at the lid of the ginger jar. She thought she heard something tapping inside it, like a bird pecking.

Hope abruptly stood up. "I'm afraid that I have another meeting. My accounting department will be in touch with you to give you the information you're legally entitled to."

"Thank you for your cooperation." Anya glanced down at Sparky, who was still determinedly fiddling with the ginger jar.

Anya reached out over the desk to shake Hope's hand. She allowed the hem of her coat to brush over the glass and bump the ginger jar. The jar tipped over on its side, rolling across the desk. Hope lunged for it, but too late. The cap rattled off the jar, and a ghost roared out of the open mouth in a burst of cold air. In a flurry of white ether, it soared up to the skylight and vanished.

Covering her shock, Anya bent down to pick up the cap of the jar on the floor. Her fingers brushed its sharp interior: A surface like a geode glittered on the inside. Identical to the surface of the bottle Anya had found in Bernie's fire grate.

Anya set the cap delicately back on the desk, sparkling side up. Hope had snatched up the container and wrapped her arms around it like a child with a firefly jar. Her look was one of barely concealed fury.

"I hope I didn't damage your . . . antique," Anya said mildly.

Hope's face contorted, settled. She placed the jar back down on her desk. "It's fine." Her narrowed eyes raked over Anya, and Anya guessed that Hope had known what was in the jar. With the ghost gone, Anya felt Sparky crawling back up her sleeve to her collar. And she watched Hope's eyes follow him. She *saw.*

"Speaking of antiques . . . that's an interesting necklace, Ms. Kalinczyk."

Anya's fingers fluttered protectively up to her torque. It was so much a part of her that she assumed it was invisible to other people—like Sparky. "Thank you."

Hope eyed it like a gemologist staring at a diamond, and the threat was heavy in her words: "I'd keep a close eye on a valuable piece like that. Those kinds of things can disappear very easily."

Anya's eyes narrowed, but her fingers remained wound in the torque, even when she walked out of the building into the sunlight that failed to chase Hope's chill from her skin.

The Detroit Crime Lab had been shut down for several years after an audit had unearthed gross mishandling of evidence. Recently resurrected, the lab hadn't yet escaped the shadow of its earlier reputation. The newly hired lab workers were touchy and sensitive to criticism, but determined to prove themselves.

Housed on the upper floors of DPD Headquarters, in a 1920s-era building just north of Greektown, the crime lab seemed a shiny anachronism. Computer monitors gleamed on stainless-steel tables, where paper evidence bags were neatly labeled. Microscopes, glass test tubes, and rolls of adhesive tape were arranged at workstations. Fluorescent light overhead shone on the yellow metal cabinets containing arcane tools for DNA analysis, fiber collection, and ballistics.

Sparky found the machines to be irresistible, so Anya kept her visits to the lab short. As soon as she stepped through the glass doors, she could feel the salamander moving around her neck.

"Lieutneant Kalinczyk." The shift supervisor, Jenna Bentham, approached her with a clipboard. Her white coat was immaculately pressed, the braids of her hair tied severely away from her face. Anya could see the thick files stacked up on the desk behind her. Despite their efforts, the lab had a huge backlog; whatever Gina had said to them had clearly put Anya's evidence at the front of the line.

"What've you got for me?"

"Some pretty interesting stuff. Shall I start with the tame stuff and work my way up to the unusual?"

"Sure." Anya felt Sparky creeping down her back. He padded toward a counter and slithered up a stool. He started playing with the knobs on a hot plate. No evidence was currently cooking in glass beakers on its surface. Figuring that was the least problematic thing he could get into, Anya let him, turning her attention to Jenna and the lab results.

"Let's talk about the remains. The ash and tissue samples sent over by the coroner's office were chemically unremarkable. The gas spectrometer didn't register the presence of standard flammable compounds in either the victim's remains or in the couch fibers you sent. No chemical signatures of gasoline, kerosene, or the like."

"What about high-temperature accelerants? The exotic stuff, like fireworks compounds, fertilizers, thermite compositions?" Anya still held a flicker of hope that a conventional explanation could be found.

Jenna frowned. "That was what we expected to find, frankly . . . but no HTAs were detected. And it doesn't fit with the scene. HTAs, at four thousand degrees, would decimate that room. And the damage just doesn't support that conclusion."

"So we're assuming the body smoldered at low temperature for an extended time?" Anya frowned. That didn't fit the timetable.

"That's all I've got now." Jenna flipped through her clipboard. "The only other unusual thing we found, chemically speaking, was a residue of silicon dioxide on the slippers."

"Silicon dioxide? Quartz crystal?"

"It's not a byproduct of any combustion process. The particles are very small, less than a millimeter in length." Jenna peered through her glasses. "If this were an HTA situation, I might expect to see some turquoise glassiness that mimics a natural mineral if, say, a jet plane burned up on a concrete runway. It's structurally similar. But this is not that kind of situation."

Anya shook her head. "I just don't see how this is possible."

Jenna gave her a sharp look. "I rechecked the results myself."

Anya put up her hands. "Look, I'm not questioning you. At all. This investigation is just . . . weird. I can't see how it fits together . . . in a scientific sense." Never mind the nonscientific puzzles.

Jenna shrugged. "I'm gonna leave the significance of that up to you, as the investigating officer, to interpret. I'm just giving you the facts."

Anya frowned. "You said we were progressing from the least weird evidence to the most weird."

"Yes. We analyzed the fragments of the bottle you brought in." Jenna held up a plastic bag containing the bottle shards. "Silicon dioxide—quartz—is the crystal inside the bottle. But it's structurally odd. In the natural world, a geode is formed in sedimentary or igneous rock. Dissolved silicates are deposited in the interior in layers, forming the geode. However, these silicates are bonded to glass in a crystal latticework structure. The glass isn't much more than fifty years old—a wine bottle, judging by the stamping on the base. It's simply not possible for a geode to form in that environment over that short a period of time."

She gave the plastic-packaged shards to Anya. Jenna had told her how a geode is formed in the natural world, but Anya wondered how it had formed in the unnatural world. . . and if there had been a ghost in this bottle, like the ginger jar on Hope's desk.

"Is that the weirdest thing you've got for me?"

"No. I've still got one scandalous thing and one just plain bizarre thing."

"Hit me with the scandal first. I'm all full up of bizarre."

Jenna handed her a plastic bag containing the corner of the envelope and piece of green check Anya had found in Bernie's firebox. "We got a partial print on this. You'll never guess who it belongs to."

"Wild guess . . . Hope Solomon, the late-night television miracle worker?"

"No . . . Christina Modin, con artist." Jenna gestured for Anya to follow her to a computer terminal. She summoned up a mug shot of a smiling blond woman with smudged blue eyeliner. The woman looked like a version of Hope, twenty years ago. Her rap sheet scrolled down the side of the page: extortion, fraud, bad checks, forgery.

"That's her. That's Hope Solomon."

Jenna lifted her eyebrows. "Maybe. But we can't really prove it yet. Christina Modin was involved in some seriously bad real-estate deals in Florida. Predatory lend-ing and the like. She's served her time. Even if you proved Hope and Christina are the same person, you can't arrest her for just being a weasel."

Anya crossed her arms. "Damn. You're good."

Jenna hid a smile, but Anya could see her glowing. "One last thing . . . There were latent prints in the carbon around the fireplace. They made absolutely gorgeous fin-gerprints. Just textbook." Jenna flipped a folder open to a page displaying prints fixed on paper with adhesive tape.

"Nice," Anya agreed. Those were the prints taken after Bernie's house had been tossed. "Are any of them Bernie's?"

"Some of them we were able to match with his military records. We found five other sets of prints, though, that were not his."

"Neighbors? Family?"

She shook her head. "One set didn't match anyone in the National Crime Information Center database. The other four belong to a former waitress, a retired postmas-ter, a landscaper, and a college student at Michigan State."

"Great. Do you have a list of names?"

"I do, but it won't help you much. All of them are dead."

Anya blinked. "Dead? Like, recently dead?"

"The postmaster's been dead for twenty years. The college kid's been dead for two. Four years for the wait-ress, and ten for the landscaper."

Anya's thoughts churned. What the hell were dead peo-ple doing at Bernie's place? Bernie was a shitty housekeeper, but there was no reason for latent prints to have stuck around for twenty years before being cleaned off.

"Can you tell how fresh they are?"

"I thought you'd ask that. We estimate that the carbon they were formed in is no older than six months."

Anya chewed on her lip. Dead people leaving fingerprints all over Bernie's house? She knew that ghosts could sometimes affect the physical world, but she'd never heard of them leaving prints behind. What kind of weird shit had Bernie been messing with?

Jenna looked at her with a smile. "You really get all the interesting cases, don't you?"

Anya opened her mouth to respond but smelled something burning.

She swung around to see Sparky gleefully sitting on the lab counter before the hot plate, warming his rounded belly before a foot-tall yellow flame shooting from the device. She lunged for the hot plate, unplugged the cord.

But too late. The smoke alarm wailed overhead, and the sprinkler system kicked in.

Jenna shrieked and tried to cover her samples with a file folder. Anya ran into the hallway to find the main override. By the time she'd grabbed the emergency phone and convinced the alarm company to shut off the sprinkler system, people had poured out of the building onto the sidewalk. The lab lay in soggy ruins, puddles on the tile floor, glass vials full of water, and an electron microscope sitting in a pool. Papers and soaked evidence bags were plastered to desks and tables.

In the middle of it all, Jenna sat on the stool with her face in her hands, sobbing. "We're never going to get our certification back," she hiccuped.

All Anya could do was ineffectually pat her shoulder. She ignored Sparky as he crawled up her pant leg, slinked over her shoulders. He tentatively licked at the water droplets on Anya's ear, seeking forgiveness. She didn't respond.

He'd fucked up big time, and he knew it.

Sparky curled around her neck and melted into the collar, his paws wrapped tightly over his head.

CHAPTER SIX

ANYA DIDN'T TELL DAGR ABOUT Sparky's incident at the lab. She muttered indifferent noises at the evening news when it reported an accident at the Detroit Crime Lab had destroyed evidence for more than thirty pending cases. The media had taken the story and run with it, with city officials decrying the lab's incompetence and calling for another audit. Anya slunk lower in her seat as she watched the story on the television suspended over the Devil's Bathtub bar. Sparky hugged her neck and didn't look up.

Jules jabbed a thumb over his shoulder at the television. "Did that screw up any of your cases?"

"Probably," she said. Most of the evidence from her spontaneous human combustion case had been compromised, and there was no telling if what was left would stand up in court. But she sure as hell wasn't going to tell Jules that Sparky had a paw in it.

Jules leaned against the bar. "That's a crying shame. You think a city this size would be able to get some competent people."

Anya stared at the bar top, listening to the ice crack in her Diet Coke. "They're very competent people, Jules. Sometimes bad luck just happens."

Jules snorted. "Bad luck doesn't just happen. It feeds on carelessness."

"I don't think anything careless happened, Jules." But she didn't believe it. She'd been careless in watching Sparky. Sparky just did what he did, following his elemental nose . . . and she'd failed to monitor him. It was more her fault than his.

"The news says it was a fire. You've said yourself that ninety percent of fires are caused by human idiocy."

Anya's jaw tightened. That struck too close to home. "Unless you've survived a fire, Jules, leave it alone," she snapped.

"Break it up, you two," Brian said. His well-muscled arms held two black duffel bags clinking with equipment, and an orange extension cord was looped around his shoulder. "It's time to roll out."

Anya hung back until Jules, Max, and Katie headed out the door. Ciro's wheelchair wheels squeaked softly across the floor, and he reached up to pat her hand. He was dressed in his pajamas. Ciro rarely went out on runs anymore. He was too short of breath too often, and rarely left the Devil's Bathtub. Max brought him groceries, and he had everything he needed here. Somewhere upstairs, Anya could hear a record album playing old jazz tunes. A voice warbled like a canary. Anya knew that it wasn't the record; Ciro was never alone. Renee, the spirit of a flapper, had come with the bar, and she did her best to look after the old man. She was one of the few ghosts who actually enjoyed being seen and heard.

"Don't let Jules get under your skin."

"We're oil and water, Ciro. I try to stay out of his way, but . . . " She shrugged her shoulders. "I don't know how much longer this is going to last."

There. She'd finally admitted it. She'd tried to leave DAGR before but had come back. The city needed them, and DAGR needed her. But they all knew Ciro was the force that bound the group together.

Ciro's rheumy eyes crinkled. "Child, I've got plenty of time left."

"That's not what I meant." She blew out her breath. "I meant Jules and I . . . arguing."

"Jules is a good man."

"He is." There was no disputing that. Jules meant well. "But I feel like he won't look outside the box—the box where everything's good or evil, right or wrong. It feels like there's just too much gray out there, and he won't acknowledge it."

"The two of you need to put your differences aside long enough to get the job done." Ciro squeezed her hand. "Please."

She could never say no to the old man. She squeezed back. "I'll try."

"Good. Now, go run with the rest of the team." Ciro looked upstairs, where the angelic voice trilled. "I've got a date with an angel." He winked, straightened the lapels of his pajamas, and rolled back to the elevator behind the bar.

Anya put on her coat and headed for the front door, smiling. She imagined Ciro being quite the ladies' man in his youth. She waited for the elevator doors to creak shut, and she called upstairs:

"Renee?"

A beautiful face, framed by a glossy bob, phased down through the ceiling, like a woman peering through the surface of water. Thick eyelashes framed doe-like Cleopatra eyes, and a string of ghostly beads dangled down from space. *"Hi, baby."*

"How's Ciro doing?" Renee would tell her the truth.

The ghost's flawless skin creased over her penciled brows. *"He's weak. Weaker than I'd like to see him. Weaker than he'll admit."*

Anya frowned. "Thank you for watching over him, Renee."

"I'll keep him out of the giggle water. But there's only so much I can do." Renee's fingers passed helplessly through the plaster, and Anya could hear the frustration in her voice. *"I can't touch him. I can't dial the telephone for help."*

Anya nodded. Ghosts could sometimes affect things in the physical world. Poltergeists were notorious for breaking objects and harming humans. They could do that because they were powerful; most ghosts weren't. Some ghosts could move objects with great concentration, but it exhausted them. Renee wasn't a powerful spirit; in all the time she'd haunted the Devil's Bathtub, the most she'd managed to do was break a few bottles as pranks.

A horn sounded insistently outside at the curb, and Anya flinched. Upstairs, the bell sounded as the elevator doors grated open.

Renee made a shooing gesture. *"You go on. We'll talk later."*

She disappeared into the shadowed ceiling, and Anya reached for the doorknob. Sighing, she stepped out into the dark.

Anya sat in Brian's van, flipping through his case files. She'd missed the team meeting earlier in the evening, and didn't know if they were going to be drowning demons in holy water or playing patty-cake with poltergeists.

"Can you give me the Cliffs Notes version?" she asked.

"This is the full-body apparition case I mentioned the other day." If Brian was irritated by her lack of involvement in the case, he didn't show it. He gripped the steering wheel with one hand and fiddled with his iPhone with the other. Multitasking while driving made Anya nervous, but she bit her tongue. "The figure of a woman has been seen walking through the house. She doesn't speak or interact with the house's inhabitants, so the preliminary theory is that it's a residual haunting. But she's wearing modern clothes, so that's a stumper. No Lizzie Bordens in petticoats here."

"Who lives in the house?"

"Mom and two boys, ages eight and twelve, and a grandfather."

"Who's been seeing the apparition?"

"It started with the grandfather. He thought his daughter was home early from work, tried to talk to the ghost." Brian glanced sidelong at Anya. "His eyesight's not too good. Both kids have seen the apparition. Mom works nights, and the ghost evidently prefers evening strolls, so she hasn't seen it."

"How long has this been going on?"

"That's the weird thing. The house has been in the family for forty years. Not a peep of anything supernatural until two weeks ago. The ghost's been seen almost every night since then."

Anya chewed on her lip. "I wonder what changed."

"It's rare in the literature, but it's not unheard of for construction or environmental changes to 'wake up' a ghost. I've never seen it happen myself, but there are at least two other ghost-hunting groups that have documented cases in which a ghost became more active when something in the house irritated it. In one situation, a family was doing extensive remodeling and disturbed the location of a hidden grave. In another, a ghost didn't like the new owners' taste in decorating. The ghost preferred pink carpeting and striped wallpaper to the industrial-loft look. It kept leaving handprints and nasty messages scribbled on the stainless-steel appliances."

"That's assuming it's a ghost." Most hauntings that were proven to be more than figments of the owners' imaginations were benign ghosts. But DAGR had seen an uptick in cases involving hostile ghosts and demons. And Anya had a run-in with the king of salamanders some months ago, nesting in the salt mine beneath the city. It was enough to cause her not to make any assumptions about the nature of the creatures they faced.

"We won't know for sure until we get our feet on the ground."

The van tooled through Islandview, east of downtown. Apartment buildings were interspersed with row houses and single-family homes. Real-estate and FOR RENT signs peppered thin yards. Some attempts at urban revitalization had been made in this area, but the reach didn't extend far into the west side, where brick apartment buildings decorated with graffiti sat next to dilapidated homes on trash-strewn lots.

Brian parked beside the curb before an unremarkable house: faded yellow siding and bars on the street-level windows. Striped green-and-white awnings shaded the interior. Dogs barked somewhere in the backyard. Anya climbed out of the van, scanning the street. A group of kids comparing bikes on the other side of the sidewalk glanced at the strangers with interest. Anya waved at them, and one tentatively wiggled his fingers back before stuffing his hands in his pockets and trying to be cool.

The house just east of the subject house appeared to be abandoned, the front screen door decorated with various neon-colored shutoff notices from the gas and water companies. Weeds sprouted up through cracks in the porch cement. Even though it was apparently trash night, as evidenced by the green trash cans piled curbside in front of the other houses, this driveway was empty. The house on the west side, however, showed signs of life. A SOLD real-estate sign leaned up against the side of the house, and boxes could be seen through the front window, where a sheet was making do as curtains for the new inhabitants. Lights burned in every room, and the lawn smelled of fresh-cut grass. The haunted house seemed caught between the living house and the dead one.

Anya slung a bag of gear over her shoulder and followed Brian to the doorstep. Jules, Max, and Katie had arrived in Jules's minivan and were chatting with the homeowner, who had opened the screen door. The grandfather, Anya guessed. He was dressed for company, in a fresh-pressed shirt and knife-creased slacks. The sharp creases contrasted with the curve of his bowed spine and the spiderweb of wrinkles crossing his face. He leaned on a cane with a white tip. Anya noted how his eyes seemed to follow the motion of people moving past him, but she was uncertain how much he could actually see.

"Thank you for coming." He led them into the living room. All the furniture had been pushed back to the walls, no doubt to help accommodate the old man's slow navigation. A video-game system was connected to the television, and kids' backpacks sprawled in the corner. A curio cabinet full of Hummel figurines and a wall of family photographs had been recently dusted. A basket of freshly folded laundry sat beside the couch, containing women's pink hospital scrubs. "We'll try to stay out of your way. I've put the boys to bed, and Sara doesn't get off work until seven tomorrow morning."

Anya caught the trace of a frown around Jules's mouth. He didn't like to work with the homeowners present. None of them did—it constrained what they could say and do. But sometimes it couldn't be helped. They'd simply have to be on their best behavior.

"Tell us about your ghost," Jules said, pulling a yellow legal pad and pen out of his bag.

"I haven't seen much of her," the old man said with a chuckle. "But the boys say she comes every night, around two. She wanders through the house, wearing white. The oldest one, Tim, tried to talk to her, but she never answers.

"She's not anyone you know?" Anya's attention drifted to the family photographs. Many were old and yellowed with age.

The old man shook his head. "No."

"Has anyone in the house ever been involved in the occult? Ouija boards, séances, that kind of thing?"

Katie slid a glance to Anya, rolled her eyes. Anya noticed that she'd tucked her pentacle pendant into her blouse, so as not to alarm the old man.

The old man frowned. "The boys know that they'd get an ass-blistering if they ever brought anything like that into this house."

Anya drifted away, pacing through the house. She liked to get a feel for the geography of the place before the lights went out and she started tripping over the furniture.

The house was absolutely ordinary—kids' report cards and Mom's work schedule stuck up on the olive-colored refrigerator, cereal boxes and bowls set out for morning breakfast. Four bowls were placed around the kitchen table, suggesting that Mom joined the boys and Gramps for breakfast before school.

"I think this one might be a bust," Katie murmured, peering through ruffled curtains at the darkness in the backyard.

"You don't smell any magick here, either?" The salamander collar had remained still. Either Sparky was still cowering from Anya's wrath, or there was nothing supernatural here that interested him.

Katie shook her head. "Nope. And this place doesn't have the oppressive atmosphere I feel at most serious hauntings."

"Your best guess?"

"I think the boys have watched too many scary movies, and Gramps can't see well enough to distinguish headlights washing through the windows from a real spirit." Katie shrugged. "I'm betting on an uneventful night."

Anya wrapped her hands around her elbows. "I hope you're right."

Sparky slept for hours, curled tightly around Anya's neck.

Anya thought he had the right idea.

Sitting at the kitchen table with Brian, she watched the night-vision camera feed on the computers he'd set up. Computer and electrical cables snaked across the floor, feeding images of the upstairs hallway, basement, bedrooms, and living room into the flat-panel monitors. Nothing had moved in hours. The boys were asleep in their beds, Gramps in his. Katie was sitting at the end of the hallway, staring blearily at a temperature gauge that didn't budge. Max and Jules were poking through Christmas decorations in the basement, scanning for electrical interference on their ohmmeters.

Anya drummed her fingers on her headphones. The voice recorders were only picking up snatches of the conversation between Max and Jules, the sound of the refrigerator compressor cycling off and on. Somebody farted in their sleep.

All was quiet.

She glanced over at Brian. He was fiddling with a laptop that was displaying bewilderingly obscure strings of text and numbers on a black screen. The white text was reflected in his glasses, rendering his appearance inhuman.

Anya sidled next to him, pulled off her headphones. "Whatcha doin'?"

"Side project." His lips pursed.

Anya put her chin in her hand. Brian did contract work for the government in his free time. She never knew exactly what he was working on, but some of the tech was creepy: biometric tracking; anti-hacker algorithms; high-tech surveillance. And that was just the stuff she knew about. "You allowed to tell me?"

"Probably not. I'm working on an artificial intelligence simulator."

"Like HAL from *2001*?"

"Hopefully something less homicidal. I'm mapping artificial neural networks to resemble those of a test subject. I'm trying to mimic human brain function to allow for pattern recognition and data storage."

"That sounds very sci-fi."

"Not really." Brian shrugged. "The technology to do it has been around for a while. People just get squeamish in its application."

Anya's brow wrinkled. "What do you mean?"

"Well . . . I'm modeling this neural network on an existing human's recurrent biological neural network. Scientists previously mapped the brains of simple organisms, like worms. A microscopic worm, *C. elegans*, for example, has about three hundred neurons. Easy-peasy. Humans, however, have around a hundred billion neurons and a hundred trillion synapses to model."

"Wow. How the hell are you doing that?"

"Very slowly. I'm doing it, piece by piece, by using something similar to a self-replicating computer virus to test the multitude of connections possible. I basically sit back and let the program explore the brain and do all the work."

"Whose brain are you using?" Anya wondered if the process hurt. Thinking about it gave her a headache.

"Strange things happen when you leave your body to science. We got a nearly perfect specimen sent to the university not long ago. We keep the brain on ice in a nice jar, give it a jolt of electricity every once in a while to light up the neurons. The modeling program does the rest."

Anya's mouth twisted down. "Is that really what the donor had in mind? Don't most donors envision leaving their bodies to the medical school, for students to mutilate in gross anatomy class?"

"Maybe. But lack of specifics can kick you in the ass." Brian seemed unconcerned. "Eventually, you'll be able to ask Allen what he thinks."

"Who is Allen?"

"A-L-A-N-N. ALANN: Advanced Linear Artificial Neural Network. Homage to Alan Turing, the father of computer science."

"I've heard of him, I think. Wasn't he a code-breaker of some sort?"

"He did a lot of work on breaking the Nazi Enigma code during World War Two, though he's probably just as well known for the Turing Test. The test measures a machine's intelligence and ability to mimic human behavior by having a judge converse with a machine and another human in isolated locations. Each attempts to appear human. If the judge can't determine which one is the machine, the test is considered a success."

"I can't imagine a machine being able to fool an observer like that."

"That's the gist of my research, a variation of the Turing Test called the Immortality Test. The Immortality Test determines whether a person's responses and behavior is reproduced accurately enough to render it indistinguishable from the original subject. ALANN is patterned after a once-living brain, and I'm curious to see how closely it can match that brain's responses." Brian swiveled the laptop over to Anya, typed in a command at the interface line. "Go ahead and say hello."

"Are you using me as a guinea pig?"

"Not really. I've already told you about the Turing Test, so you know ALANN is a machine."

Anya swallowed. Brian's "not really" response was less than reassuring. She leaned forward, into the microphone attached to the webcam. "Hello."

The cursor on the screen winked, then letters appeared on the screen: Hello, Anya.

Anya frowned. "How does it know my name?"

Brian tapped the webcam. "We're working on pattern recognition. ALANN can identify faces using biometric technology. Theoretically, everyone's face is unique— distance between pupils, brow height, mouth length, length-to-width ratios, ear size. ALANN combines these measurements and remembers them."

"But how does it know me?"

"ALANN's seen you before at the computer lab. It likely remembers what's said. It's encouraging that it can associate names with faces now."

Anya chewed on her lip. The computer lab in the base-ment of the university, where Brian kept his mad-scientist laboratory, was full to the ceiling of strange technological devices. She'd have to reconsider the idea of shagging him in the server farm now that she knew ALANN was watching.

"ALANN, how many people are sitting in front of the camera?"

The cursor hesitated for a moment, then the numeral 2 appeared.

"That's creepy." In some inexplicable way, it reminded her of Katie's makeshift Ouija board, pulling answers from nothingness.

"Like Arthur C. Clarke said, 'Any sufficiently advanced technology is indistinguishable from magic.'"

The walkie-talkie on the counter crackled to life over Katie's whisper, "Hey, are you guys getting this?"

Anya jerked toward the monitor. Katie was standing at the end of the hallway, gripping the walkie. Something pale and diaphanous curled in the periphery of the camera's lens. Anya felt the salamander collar stir at her throat. This was definitely something more than headlights shining through a naked window.

Anya ran out of the kitchen, nearly skidding into Jules and Max, clomping up from the basement. They clambered up the carpeted stairs to peer into the upstairs hallway.

The transparent shape of a woman plodded along the hall. From this angle, Anya could see that she was a young woman, dressed in white, barefoot. Her thick, curly hair was matted, flat on one side. She turned, revealing that she was wearing a bathrobe. But something even more odd: Her eyes were closed. The ghost placed one foot ahead of the other, as if sleepwalking. From the far end of the hallway, the door to the boys' room was cracked open, and a pair of frightened eyes peered out, watching.

Katie reached toward the figure, and Anya didn't need to be able to see her temperature screen to know that the temperature in the hall had cooled, that the apparition had sucked heat out of the air to manifest visibly.

"Hello?" she asked.

The figure ignored her, walking slowly toward the stairway, where Anya, Jules, and Max watched. Anya could see that a silver filament trailed around the woman's waist, behind her, and she squinted. What was that? The belt of her bathrobe?

Jules bristled at her approach. "Do it," he growled at Anya. "Devour it. Get rid of it."

Anya shook her head. She could feel Sparky winding around her knees, but the salamander showed no sign of alarm. And she didn't feel any particular sense of dread about this ghost.

But from Jules's perspective, the only good ghost was a gone ghost. She knew Jules tolerated Renee because she took care of Ciro, but he had no love for the supernatural.

The ghost ambled closer to the stair.

"Do it," he hissed.

"No. She's not hurting anything."

The ghost shuffled to the top of the stairs. Anya and the others flattened to the wall, allowing the ghost to walk past them, down the stairs. Anya shivered as she walked by and the hem of her bathrobe brushed Anya's knees. Sparky followed in her wake, sniffing, oozing sinuously down the shag-carpeted steps. He nipped at the silver string drifting in the ghost's wake.

The ghost had nearly reached the bottom of the stairs when a deep rumble sounded in the distance. Anya recognized it immediately: the garbage truck, streets distant.

The ghost seemed to recognize it, too. She inclined her head toward the sound, opened her eyes . . .

. . . and vanished.

Sparky vigorously sniffed at the spot on the shag carpet where the spirit had been standing.

"Did you snuff it out?" Jules demanded.

"No. She disappeared of her own accord."

The team clambered down the steps to crowd around Brian's video monitors, to rewind the video and see what hard evidence had been captured.

"Shit," Max swore, and Jules cuffed him. The camera had only captured an indistinct wobble of light, a white glare against the false-color green night vision. Anya scanned the recording to ensure that Sparky hadn't stumbled into the frame. Much as Brian had asked to try to record Sparky's presence, Anya always refused. She was the salamander's protector, as much as he was hers. She wouldn't allow his image to be captured and distributed on the Internet like an alien autopsy hoax.

A high-pitched whining snagged her attention. Sparky sat before the front door, slapping his tail on the floor, in the attitude of a dog who had to pee. Outside, she could hear the garbage truck rounding the corner. Light had begun to leak around the tightly drawn window curtains.

"Sparky?"

The salamander reached up to scratch at the door. Brow furrowed, Anya opened it. Sparky tumbled out onto the front porch, ran through the yard toward the neighbors'...

...and Anya saw a woman next door in a white bathrobe shoving her garbage can to the curb. She was out of breath, bare feet scraping the dew from the grass. Her curly hair was flat on one side, as if she'd just awoken.

She was the ghost in the hallway.

But she was as solid as the overflowing can she hauled to the curb, in just enough time for the garbage truck. The garbageman clinging to the back of the truck saw her, too, waved at her. She waved back, clutching the collar of her robe tight around her neck.

"Shit," Anya swore.

CHAPTER SEVEN

ANYA TROTTED THROUGH THE DAMP grass to the neighbor's yard. "Excuse me."

The woman in the bathrobe looked up. "Yes?"

"We're doing some . . . ah, work for your next-door neighbors." Anya jabbed a thumb at the van parked at the curb and the computer cables snaking out of the van to the front of the house. "I hope that we're not disturbing you."

"Not at all." The woman shook her head. "We just moved in, and Lord knows we've been making enough racket remodeling. . . . I feel bad we haven't been over to introduce ourselves yet."

"I'm Anya." She stuck out her hand, wanting to test to see if the woman was really solid.

"Leslie." Her grip was firm, and her smile was bright, though Anya detected dark circles under her eyes. She hadn't been sleeping well. "Are you general contractors? We might need a hand with some of the electrical work in the basement we're trying to redo."

"We're not in construction." Anya took a deep breath.

This conversation could go very badly, and Anya tried to soft-pedal it. "We're more like spiritual advisers."

Leslie dropped her hand like a hot rock, and she took a step back. "Look, we've already got a church."

Anya shook her head. "We're ghost hunters. Your next-door neighbor's been experiencing some odd happenings in their house, and called us to take a look."

Leslie's shoulders sagged. She seemed deflated. "Oh."

Sparky walked up to her and sniffed. Anya knew that he could smell the sharp edge of magick on her, too. What was she? A witch? She seemed so very . . . ordinary.

"I don't mean to pry, but . . . have you experienced anything unusual since you moved in?" Anya kept her tone neutral, non-accusatory. She didn't sense malice radiating from her, like she did from Hope.

Leslie sighed, and she shifted her weight from foot to foot, toes curling in the damp grass. Finally, she said, "Would you like to come in for coffee?"

Anya smiled. "I would love some coffee."

"Please ignore the mess," Leslie warned as she padded across the yard and opened the front door.

The place reminded her of Bernie's house. It wasn't just the boxes piled along the walls, the drywall dust, and the cans of paint. It was the smell: Underneath fresh paint and the smell of pine cleaner, magick gathered like dust bunnies in the dark corners of the house. At Anya's ankles, Sparky wrinkled his nose and snorted, as if he'd just inhaled dandelion fluff.

Leslie plugged in the coffeepot in the kitchen. The

cabinets were in the process of being refinished, the doors taken off the hinges and exposing backs of the cabinets, stacked with dishes and canned goods. Leslie rummaged in one of the shelves for coffee filters.

"This is our dream house," she said as she measured the coffee. "I mean, you can't see it now, but we've been trying to buy a house for years."

"They say the market's good for it now."

"Yeah. When the bottom fell out of real estate, we were able to afford a house. My husband's credit is shot. He got laid off at the plant, and has been on unemployment for six months. Mine's okay, but no one was lending. But we did finally get some help." Her eyes shone a bit when she said it, and she seemed very young to Anya. Very young and naive, to have invited a stranger into her house.

The coffee machine belched and bubbled as it percolated. Sparky nosed toward the counter, and she cast him a dirty look. He slunk away and lay down beside Anya's feet.

Leslie brought two steaming mugs of coffee to the kitchen table. "Sugar or cream?"

"No, thank you." Anya sipped at the steaming liquid. She felt it slide down her throat, but felt no stirring of anything in her gut that would suggest a ghost was near.

"I'm sure you could care less about our personal finances." Leslie smiled sheepishly into her mug. "You asked about strange happenings around here."

Anya nodded. "Go on."

Leslie gestured to the backsplash behind the kitchen counter, reached over to shove a box aside. A carbon black scorch mark extended from the wall socket. "We've been having some strange fires. Little ones: the toaster, the baseboard heater, a stove burner."

Anya watched her carefully. "What do you think is causing them?"

She shook her head. "At first we thought there was something wrong with the electrical system. We had an inspector check out the house before we bought it. He didn't find anything wrong. But now . . . I don't know."

Leslie leaned forward. "I keep having these dreams. Dreams that something bad is going to happen. That someone is in our house. I hear voices talking to me in the night, but I can't answer them." She looked down at the floor and blushed. "I swear, I'm not crazy."

Anya touched the back of Leslie's hand. "I don't have all the answers, Leslie. But I can tell you that I will try to help. There may be someone I can ask who can tell us what your dreams mean."

"Now, that's some interesting stuff."

Ciro ran his fingers through his stubbly beard. He'd listened carefully to each member of DAGR's recollection of the events, looked over their shoulders as they sifted through the evidence. Sunlight filtered through the shutters of the Devil's Bathtub in shafts of light that trapped milling dust motes. Brian was sitting at a booth with Max, teaching him how to enhance video on the three laptops he had set up. Katie was making copies of the audio, and Anya and Jules organized the handwritten notes. No one had gone home to sleep, wanting to get to the evidence as soon as possible, though Max's head drooped and jerked awake more than once.

"The neighbor lady is the ghost. She has to be," Anya insisted.

Jules folded his arms across his barrel chest. "That's just not possible. She's alive."

Ciro held up his finger. "Well, she may not be a ghost, but she could still be the apparition you saw at the house."

Katie lifted an eyebrow. "Astral projection?"

"Yes."

Anya frowned. "I thought that was something only yogis and people who meditate in pretty gardens did when they approached Nirvana. Well, them and Bernie."

Ciro opened his hands. "A lot of it is bullshit, to be honest. Too much acid or the right kinds of mushrooms will convince nearly anyone that they're tripping around the world in a disincarnate form."

"And those mushrooms would be?" Max asked.

"Not the kind grown around here," Ciro said smoothly. "Astral travel allows individuals to occupy a parallel plane of existence. This plane intersects with our physical world in a few places, but also allows astral explorers to ascend to other, nonphysical realms. Like the Afterworld."

"Have you ever been tripping in the Afterworld?" Max asked.

"No. I never had any desire to go. Bernie made

frequent journeys there, once upon a time. From what I gathered, it was a very dangerous place. Just like in the physical world, there are positive and negative forces. But those forces aren't checked by law or rules in the astral. If you're weak, you easily become corrupted by negative entities."

"Leslie's going there? How is she doing that?" Anya asked.

"Based on what you've said, I would guess that she doesn't mean to. Some people, through sheer will or by accident, can slip into the astral while dreaming. You've described her as appearing in a sleepwalking state, so I'd suggest that it's not intentional."

"For all we know, she may have been pestering all her neighbors this way for years," said Katie.

"Probably," said Brian. He was tapping away at his keyboard. "I'm searching all Leslie Carpenter's previously known addresses and cross-referencing it with reported hauntings in the regional database."

Anya blinked. "What regional database?"

"I've been collecting reports of paranormal activity and cross-referencing them by time period and location. Newspaper reports, updates from other ghost-hunting groups, those kinds of things. It's nowhere near complete, but it might be a great tool once it's done."

Jules rolled his eyes. "Do you ever sleep, man?"

Brian lifted his energy drink and swished it. "No sleep for the wicked."

"Just keep my name out of it." Anya knelt down to

scratch Sparky's belly. The salamander was snoring in the sunshine.

Brian continued. "I did get a hit. There was a reported haunting in an apartment building she used to live in. No details, other than at least two residents moved."

"If she's been doing this her whole life, what are we going to do about it?" Jules muttered.

"I don't think there's really anything we *can* do," Katie said. "She's probably been doing this for years. She's not hurting anyone."

"She's scaring the snot out of little kids."

"The world is full of scary things. They'll cope."

"They shouldn't have to."

"She's innocent. She can't help it."

"Hey." Brian toggled between screens. "I got something interesting in public records on Leslie Carpenter. Guess who's the mortgage holder on her house?"

Anya shrugged. "Surprise us."

"Miracles for the Masses."

"Hope Solomon's operation." Anya blinked, absorbing that bit of information. Her thoughts struggled to reframe Leslie Carpenter: Was she a victim, or was she in league with Hope's shady dealings?

"Perhaps she isn't as innocent as you thought," Jules growled.

Anya held up her hand. "We don't know yet. Hope's got some strange tricks up her sleeve. I was at her office yesterday, and accidentally-on-purpose released a ghost she'd been keeping in a jar on her desk."

"What kind of jar?" Ciro asked.

"Something like this." From her purse, Anya pulled the plastic evidence bag containing the fragments of the bottle she found at Bernie's house.

She handed it to Ciro. He unzipped the bag and held the fragments with a quivering grip. In the early-morning sunlight, the glass and crystal glittered like rock candy.

"Oh," he said, peering through his bifocals at them. "This is unusual."

"What is it?"

"It's a trap for spirits." Ciro's attention focused on her. "Let me explain. Are you familiar with the concept of the witch ball?"

Anya shook her head, but Katie piped up: "They're orbs made of blown glass, with strings of glass on the inside. Sometimes antique fishing floats are used. They're hung in sunny windows. The theory is that evil spirits have to count the filaments before they can come into the house, and that they get stuck in it."

"Like bad dreams in a dream catcher." Anya visualized the circular hoops spiderwebbed with woven fiber and decorated with feathers and beads. "Bad dreams get hung up in the web, and good ones pass through the hole in the middle."

"Exactly. Only nothing gets out of a witch ball."

"The spirit jar operates on a similar concept," Ciro explained. "Only, these are much more powerful. A spirit has to count all the facets of quartz to escape. The quartz also acts as insulation or protection for the spirit. They're also called witch bottles, genie bottles, reliquaries . . . you get the idea. An accomplished sorcerer could use the bottle to control the spirits trapped within."

"How are they made?" Anya asked. "I get the idea of spinning a dream catcher, or blowing glass for a witch ball. But Forensics says that this crystalline structure is pretty much impossible."

Ciro smiled grimly. "It's old magick. Very old. It dates from even before the time of Scheherazade and the Arabian Nights. One theory is that the geodes found in nature are vessels that hold earth spirits. Once the geodes are broken apart, the spirits were free to wander the earth." His eyes narrowed. "Where did you find this?"

"Bernie's."

Ciro sighed. "Bernie might have picked up the spell somewhere in his travels. That sounds like him."

"If Hope was giving him money, I'm betting it was for those bottles."

"I don't get why she would want them," Jules said. "Most people do their best to get rid of ghosts." His expression was unconcerned; he didn't seem too worried about the fate of the ghosts in the jars.

"They were people once, Jules," Anya said. "They deserve to be treated with some respect."

Jules shrugged. "This, from the executioner of ghosts. You pick and choose the ones that deserve to be obliterated. Is that it?"

Anya bit her lip, turned away. That struck too close to home.

Ciro clutched her sleeve, and his grip shook. "Be very careful, Anya. If Hope is caging spirits, there's no telling how many she has or what she's doing with them."

After a long day of sifting through evidence in the DAGR astral projection case, Anya wanted nothing more than to crawl off into her own bed.

Well, perhaps there was one thing she wanted more.

Brian pulled the van into the driveway at Anya's house. He paused, fingers lingering on the key in the ignition. Sunset streamed into the van, casting long shadows over the garage. The sun was so bright she couldn't see the expression on his face, only the shimmer of the key in his hand and the slight hesitation.

"Do you want to come in?" she asked. A note of shyness had crept into her voice.

He switched off the ignition. "Okay."

He followed her to the door in the blinding sunlight. Anya shaded her eyes as she unlocked the door, feeling the sun hot against her cheek. Red sun-shadows dazzled her vision as she crossed into the cool shade of the house.

"Hey," he said, grabbing her hand as the door clicked shut behind him.

She felt his lips brush hers in the glowing darkness. When she reached up to touch his cheek, it was still warm from the sun. And his kiss was warm, so unlike the cold spirits she swallowed. He felt solid. Real.

Anya pressed her body against his, craving that feeling of heat. Brian stepped back against the door but drew her with him. He wound his fingers in her hair and seared her lips with his, with a heat she felt in the soles of her feet.

Her craving, for this moment, eclipsed the fear she'd had of getting close to another human being. She didn't want to let go of the moment. She stood on tiptoe to kiss one closed eye, then the other, letting her eyelashes brush his face as she slid up. She heard his breath catch and snag in his throat as her fingers reached in his jacket and planed across his chest.

The salamander collar around her neck stirred.

Not now, she thought, vehemently.

She grasped Brian's hand, led him down the hall. With her free hand, she worked the salamander torque free of her throat. She hadn't ever taken it off, but she cast the squirming collar, rattling, on the bathroom vanity.

"You—" Brian began.

She pressed her finger to his lips, pulled him into the shade of the bedroom. Red light leaked from around the blinds, casting stripes of sun and shadow across Anya's bed. Across from her bed lay Sparky's dog bed, which he never used, and his toys. She felt a stab of guilt, and turned away to wrap her arms around Brian's neck.

On one wall, the black portrait of Anya watched over her pearly shoulder as the real Anya tugged Brian into an ornate magick circle painted on the bedroom floor. The circle was unfinished: The south to southeast corners were left open. Anya kicked it closed with the sash of her robe. Once closed, the circle would keep all magickal creatures out. Even salamanders. She didn't plan on telling Brian how she knew this little trick, how it had been taught to her by the man who'd painted the portrait of Ishtar.

Brian cupped his bare hands around her bare throat. She reveled in the feeling of his hands on her skin as they lovingly undressed her. He peeled her clothes away slowly, allowing her jacket to pool to the floor. Anya managed to clumsily yank his T-shirt over his head, and was momentarily transfixed by Brian's chiseled abs. This wasn't the body of a computer programmer; he had the sinewy frame of a soldier. Fascinated, she slipped her hands around his waist, feeling each ripple and twitch.

Her blouse slipped against her back, and the buttons were as hot against her skin as coins on summer pavement. Reflexively, she moved her hands to cover the scars on her chest, but he pushed them away, fingers and mouth exploring each rill and dent.

They fell to the bed in a tangle of clothes. Anya growled in frustration at being unable to unfasten the stubborn button on Brian's jeans, succeeding on the third try when Brian rolled on his back and let her straddle him, and focus her full concentration on his pants.

"You," he whispered, cupping her face with his hands. It was the single most loving, permanent, ordinary word Anya had ever heard.

He rolled over, stretching all the glorious heat of his skin against her body. She wrapped herself around him. A slat of sunshine slipped over Anya's eyes, dazzling her as he moved within her.

In the shimmering heat of the setting sun, she forgot

herself. Forgot spontaneous human combustion. Forgot DAGR. Even forgot the salamander cast outside the circle.

She forgot everything but: "You."

Sun drained out of the day, leaving Anya with her head resting on Brian's chest in the gray gloom of night. The regular beat of his heart was soothing, loud enough to drown out Sparky's pacing around the perimeter of the magic circle. Once in a while, his snout would pop up within view as he stood on his hind legs, whimpering. She saw occasional flickers of light from the dog bed she'd placed in the corner of the room, as he patted and played with his Gloworm, one of the few toys he had that responded to his presence. Anya did her best to ignore him, pressing her ear more tightly against Brian's chest.

Light from the street filtered in through the blinds, illuminating the Ishtar painting on the wall. Minerals worked into the paint sparkled in the dimness, like the quartz in Bernie's ghost trap. As her face looked over the shoulder, cold, remote, powerful, it reminded Anya of who she didn't want to be. But she didn't feel like Ishtar now. She felt warm and safe.

Brian's fingers explored her naked neck. "I've never seen you without that collar."

Anya pulled the sheet around her neck. "I've been wearing it ever since I can remember."

"So your mom gave it to you? Gave Sparky to you?"

"Sort of." She bit her lip, weighing how much to tell him. Somehow, here, in darkness, it was easier to tell him, since she wasn't looking him in the eye. She couldn't even see the Ishtar portrait from here, that representation of her shadow self. Anya listened to Sparky pacing from the bedroom to the bathroom and back again, a nervous circuit, his toes ticking on floor like a clock. It was time to tell Brian.

Still, some part of her feared rejection, and it took a few minutes more to steady the quaver in her voice. "When I was twelve, our house burned down. It was my fault. . . . I snuck downstairs to plug the Christmas tree lights back in, and I fell asleep in front of it. When I woke up . . . " Her voice cracked, and Brian stroked her hair.

"When I woke up, the room was in flames. Backdraft pulled the fire up to the second floor, where my mother was sleeping. She didn't have a chance."

Anya bit her lip, listening to Brian's quickened pulse, straining to hear the judgment behind it.

"It wasn't your fault," he finally murmured against her forehead.

"That's what the priest said. 'Not my fault.' But it felt like it. Still does." Anya rubbed at her nose, which was suddenly running. "The collar—Sparky—is the last thing I have from that life."

"You grew up with him?"

"Yeah. He's always been around. I don't know where my mom picked him up. She told me that he slept curled up in my crib. He's always been . . . a guardian. The night of the fire, he pulled me out of the house." Anya blinked at her blurry vision, feeling a stab of guilt for exiling the salamander from her bed. She lifted her head, listened. Sparky had stopped pacing. He was no doubt sulking in some corner of the house, contemplating which wires to chew. Anya hadn't thought of having a magick circle cast around the new television, but she considered it.

"He's lucky to have you."

Anya frowned. She and the salamander were tangled up together like socks in a dryer. She couldn't extricate herself, even if she wanted to.

But for just this one night, she relished the silence and the naked chill around her neck as she slept.

Anya slept until the gray light of dawn. She wriggled out from around Brian's arm and padded to the bathroom. Goose bumps lifted on her skin and she snatched her robe from the bathroom hook.

She switched on the light, reaching for the salamander collar on the counter. She slipped it around her neck, but it felt cold, empty. Panic pooled in her stomach.

"Sparky?" she whispered.

A soft chirp echoed from the bathtub, behind the shower curtain decorated with cartoon rubber ducks. Anya pulled aside the plastic curtain and gasped.

The interior of the bathtub was coated in a crystalline coating, like the interior of a geode. The salamander lay in the center of the tub, curled around what looked like a heap of marbles. He blinked up at her, tiredly, and trilled.

Anya knelt by the tub, reached in to stroke his sides. "What happened? Are you all right?"

The salamander licked her wrist and laid his head back down on the marbles. Anya stroked his side, felt his skin loose and wobbly over his ribs.

Gingerly, she reached down and picked up one of the marbles. It reminded her of the glass cat's-eye marbles she'd played with as a child. It was rough as the skin of a stone, though, and warm to the touch. She held it up to the bathroom light, let the light shine through its rippled surface.

She nearly dropped it when she saw a tiny salamander inside it, curled into the fetal position.

"Oh, Sparky. What've you done?"

CHAPTER EIGHT

"YOU'RE TELLING ME THAT A salamander laid eggs in your bathtub?" Ciro set down his fork.

Anya sat on her couch and rubbed her forehead. Katie patted her shoulder and handed her a piece of cake on a paper plate. On the coffee table, a sheet cake displayed the words "Congratulations Anya and Sparky!" above the cartoon frosted image of a stork. The kitchen witch had a weird sense of humor. But at least the cake was chocolate.

"Yes. That's exactly what I'm telling you," said Anya.

Ciro's eyes gleamed with excitement.

A howl echoed across the bathroom tile, and a door slammed. Brian slunk sheepishly down the hallway, video camera in hand. "Did you know that your salamander can slam doors?"

"He never did that before," Katie said, around a mouthful of cake.

"That's not surprising," said Ciro. "He's likely highly hormonal, so his powers are elevated."

"Stop pestering him," Anya snapped. She felt guilty

for letting the poor salamander give birth. All alone. In a bathtub. She turned to Ciro. "I, ah, thought Sparky was a boy. I mean . . . I never actually *looked*. How the hell did this happen? Is there a Mrs. Sparky?" Questions tumbled over one another. She was glad Katie had brought Ciro, and was even happier that she'd had the foresight not to bring Jules. Jules would probably try to kill them.

A glint of frosting showed on Ciro's mustache. "For elementals, gender is really meaningless. You assigned him a gender once upon a time, and he didn't rebel against it."

"It's sort of like angels," Katie said. "Gabriel is variously depicted as male or female, but he/she/it is a genderless force. Sex is an illusion designed to allow us to relate and interact with them better."

Anya's gaze crossed Brian's, and she blushed. "So where did the eggs come from? I haven't seen any other salamanders crawling around."

"Parthenogenesis." Ciro licked his fork. "It's actually relatively common in the natural world. Some species of bees, sharks, and lizards reproduce asexually when a suitable mate isn't around. Komodo dragons do it, too. There are several species of New Mexico whiptail lizards that reproduce exclusively by parthenogenesis. As I understand it, the key thing is that there's a biological need for reproduction to occur, and no suitable mate of the opposite gender available."

"This is how salamanders normally reproduce, then?"

Katie cut another slice of cake. "According to legend, salamanders reproduce once every hundred years, and they mate when they feel that they've found a suitable guardian. It's rumored the fires that burned Joan of Arc hatched hundreds of salamanders."

Ciro wiped his fingers on a napkin. "Hadn't heard that one."

"I think that was a Crowley-ism."

"Ah. That explains it. Crowley was often full of shit." Ciro wagged his finger before Katie. "Never believe anything he says without independent verification."

"I'm not Joan of fucking Arc." Anya pinched the bridge of her nose with her fingers, unwilling to let the conversation degenerate into a discussion of which member of the Order of the Golden Dawn had the brassiest balls. "And I don't want to be burned."

"Well, obviously. But Sparky seems to think that you're a strong enough hero to watch over his babies."

"How long do they take to hatch? What do I do to take care of them?" Anya wailed.

Brian murmured, "Looks like Sparky's doing a good job of that himself." He was hunched over the blue-and-red glow of a thermal imaging camera. It didn't appear to be a standard camera. Instead, it was something Brian had jerry-rigged with wires and a circuit board duct-taped to the housing. He aimed it at the wall separating the kitchen from the bathroom. Anya could make out a red salamander shape curled protectively over a clutch of orange eggs. Anya counted fifty-one dots. She tried to imagine what would happen with fifty-one Sparkies running underfoot.

Chaos.

"Is he keeping them warm?"

Ciro grinned. "They will need to be kept warm. They *are* fire elementals, after all. As far as how long it will take them to hatch, I don't know. I'm just a theoretician, remember. I don't actually practice magick."

Katie giggled. "I *so* can't wait to throw you a baby shower."

Anya gave her a dirty look. "I've gotta go to work tomorrow. How can I leave Sparky alone with his eggs?"

Katie tucked into another slice of cake. "I think that we should also make up some magickal protections, wards and the like, for the nest. That might make Sparky feel more secure. But wait until he calms down a bit first."

Anya put her head in her hands. "Shit. I'm gonna be a mother."

Katie pointed at her with her fork. "You're gonna need provisions. We'll leave the guys here to watch the eggs. I'll take you shopping."

Anya eyed her dubiously. "Provisions?" she echoed. "From where?"

Katie grinned at her, an evil glint in her eye. "Hell," she said. "I'm taking you to hell."

The mega baby superstore loomed over the asphalt parking lot. It oozed pink and blue, and Anya shivered in its cold shadow. Pregnant women waddled in and out of the store, some in packs, some dragging dazed men by the hand. Baby contraptions were hung in the windows; Anya thought she recognized some of them to be strollers, but she wasn't sure. Most looked like alien spaceships with wheels.

"No. I'm not going in there." Anya dug in her heels. She wound her fingers in the salamander collar around her neck. If Sparky was in there, he was being very, very quiet.

Anya had decided to experiment with leaving the house later that afternoon. She didn't know whether Sparky would follow her or stay with the nest. She didn't know if he even had a choice in it. Either way, she needed to go provisioning. She left Brian with instructions to sneak into the bathroom and aim the hair dryer at the nest periodically. By Ciro's guesstimation, the nest was at about human-body temperature with Sparky on it, and that temperature would need to be maintained.

Anya and Katie first went to the pet store to buy a crate of heat pads for lizards. They were filled with iron powder, and would heat for forty hours when activated, without electricity. Anya had rejected outright the idea of using an electric blanket from the discount store—if the little buggers were anything like Sparky, they'd short it out and burn the house down. The clerk at the pet store probably thought they were running an iguana-smuggling operation, shipping lizards all over the world.

Anya had accepted the idea of charging four hundred dollars for an arctic expedition–rated, Gore-Tex–insulated sleeping bag from the camping store.

But the baby store was where she drew the line.

"What the hell do we need in there?" Anya growled.

Katie consulted her list. "We need a night-light—don't want the babies hatching in darkness. We need a thermometer to keep track of the temperature in the nest. We might find other useful equipment. I was considering a baby monitor, but Brian can probably cook up something higher tech in the mad scientist's laboratory." Katie waggled her eyebrows at her. "You know, so that you can hear what's happening when you're otherwise indisposed. With bedroom activities."

Anya opened her mouth, shut it. She let the dig go past; there was no use lying to a witch. "Salamanders have been hatching for thousands of years without all this"—she waved her hand at the fearsome facade—"crap."

"Quit arguing. Let's get what we need and get out." Like a sergeant dragging along a reluctant recruit, she hauled Anya into the store.

"You're so . . . maternal."

"Fuck you, Anya. Give me your credit card."

The place gave her the willies more than any haunted house. The estrogen was much, much too high. Everything was pastel and/or calico: high chairs, booster seats, things with springs and plastic parts. Stuffed animals with strange button eyes ogled her, perched beside tubes of concoctions called "Butt Paste" and hundred-dollar tote bags designed to hold diapers. Muzak played a calliope version of "Puff the Magic Dragon" overhead.

Anya picked up something that looked like a plastic tissue box. "What the hell is this?" She read the side of it:

" 'Baby Wipe Warmer.' Seriously, baby wipes have to be warm before they can touch a baby's ass?"

A very pregnant woman pushing a pink stroller down the aisle gave her a dirty look. Anya noticed that she walked very much the way Sparky had been waddling the past few weeks. She felt a stab of guilt: not for swearing, but for her complete and utter failure to discern Sparky's condition.

"Guess I'm not allowed to swear in here, either." She trotted to keep up with Katie, who already had two boxes in her cart and was trying to act like she didn't know Anya. She paused before a wall of thermometers.

Anya poked at something that looked like a hemorrhoid pillow that had been rebranded as an "infant positioner." She drifted by a plastic apparatus with a snout and tubes that looked like a squid from a bad science fiction movie.

"Seriously, what's all this stuff for?"

Katie glanced over her shoulder. "That's a breast pump."

"A what?" Anya snatched her hand away.

"Were you raised by wolves? They're used to pump breast milk and store it for later." Katie held up a package containing a yellow rubber duck. "This thermometer is supposed to float in a bathtub. It sounds an alarm if the temperature gets above a hundred or below eighty." She scanned the shelves. "Looks like the rest are rectal thermometers."

"Give me that." Anya snatched the plastic duck. "Are we done here?"

"Almost. We need crib bumpers."

"What the hell are crib bumpers, and why would we need them? The newts aren't going to be driving cars."

Katie rolled her eyes and led Anya down an aisle containing crib bedding.

Anya's eyes glazed over at the variety of organic cotton sheets, blankets, dust ruffles, and canopies. "It's basically padding for the sides of a crib. It's so the newts don't hurt themselves on the sharp edges of all that crystal. It will also act as insulation."

Anya stared at Katie, who was pawing through plastic-wrapped calico. "Seriously. How do you know all this shit?"

Katie gave her a grim look. "I had to throw the baby shower from hell for my sister when she had twins. For over a hundred people."

"I'm sorry."

Anya felt a small wiggle at her neck. Sparky had come with her, after all. From the corner of her eye, she saw Sparky standing on her shoulder, staring upward. Anya followed his gaze. A crib mobile of moons and stars dangled overhead. He reached out to bat the plush yellow stars and squealed in delight when they made a musical chiming sound, beginning to play "Twinkle, Twinkle Little Star." Anya screwed her eyes shut, imagining that keeping her awake at night. Sparky loved making his Gloworm light up in the dark by slapping it around. But the Gloworm was silent.

"May I help you ladies?"

A clerk advanced toward them with a broad smile. She

had a ponytail and was wearing a yellow smock with a name tag that said "Hi, I'm Audrey."

Katie stabbed her thumb over her shoulder at Anya and gave her a wicked smirk. "Yeah. She's having a baby. Multiples, actually."

"Congratulations!" The clerk clasped her hands in front of her and glowed, having struck the retail mother lode. "When are you due?"

"Uh . . ." Anya crossed her arms over her stomach. "Not for a while."

"We can get you started on a baby registry right away." Audrey pulled what looked like a laser gun from the utility belt at her waist. It, like everything else in the store, was pastel. "We'll set you up with some paperwork and turn you loose with the UPC scanner."

"The what?" Anya blinked.

"We keep an electronic registry for your friends and family. You use the UPC scanner to scan the UPCs of the items you want them to buy you." The clerk spoke very slowly, as if the multiples had sucked the juice out of Anya's brain. She demonstrated by scanning the price code on a crib. A red light lanced out of the snout of the scanner, and it displayed the price on an LED window on the back: $458.

"Jesus," Anya muttered.

But Sparky was in love. He stood on Anya's shoulder, twisting his head to stare at the UPC gun and the shiny red laser beam extending from it like the sights on a ray gun.

"Um. I'd like one of those." Anya pointed up to the mobile.

"For your registry, or to take with you today?"

"I'll take it with me." Anya couldn't seriously imagine anyone wanting to buy anything from a baby registry for a nest of salamanders.

Audrey shuffled through the boxes on the floor. "Here's one," she chirped. Magically, she produced an electronic tablet from her utility belt, which was beginning to look as if it held more gizmos than Batman's. She handed it to Anya with a stylus. "Just fill out the form here, and click 'Send.' "

Anya looked over the form asking for her name, address, due date, and various and other sundry biographical info. "Then what?"

Audrey punched in some numbers on the keypad on the back of the UPC scanner. "Then I turn you loose with the scanner."

On Anya's shoulder, Sparky whined. She looked into his marble-like eyes and felt a deep pang of guilt for missing him give birth.

"Okay," she said, scribbling through the check boxes and scrawling down her name and address. She scribbled down "Sparky Anderson" as the babies' father. For number of children, she put a question mark. She handed the electronic pad back to Audrey, who gave her the scanner.

"Go nuts," she said.

Behind her, Katie had torn the baby-bumper display apart and was sitting on the floor, surrounded by plastic-swathed calico. "Can you tell me how fire retardant your crib materials are?"

Audrey squatted beside Katie and began to prattle on about crib safety standards.

Anya pulled the trigger on the UPC gun. A red beam swept across the shelves, and the machine beeped when it grazed the price code for a crib mattress. Sparky chortled with glee.

Anya swept the beam across the floor. Sparky leapt down and raced after the laser, legs scrambling along the tile, tail kinked in excitement. She banked the laser against a low-hanging price tag when he pounced, resulting in a satisfying beep.

Sparky turned, wagged his tail: *More.*

Anya skimmed the price gun up to the display of mobiles overhead. *Beep. Beep. Beep.* Sparky scrambled up the displays and swatted at the mobiles. A cacophony of chimes tinkled overhead as he disrupted the electronic parts. A couple of the motorized ones spun lazily overhead. Sparky peered over the top shelf at her, tongue curling out of his mouth. Coyly, he ducked out of sight.

Anya grinned. It was on.

She sprinted down the aisle to the next, swung around the corner with the gun in a double-fisted grip. She saw the end of a salamander tail snaking out from a shelf, stealthily advanced upon it.

Turkey. He thought he was hiding, but hid about as well as an ostrich.

She reached up to tug it. A stuffed animal tumbled down to the floor: a plush dragon.

Behind her, Sparky squeaked. She spun, looking up.

The salamander leapt from the crest of one aisle, overhead to the other. He landed in a swing perched on the top shelf. The mechanism whirred as it wound up, swinging him back and forth.

Anya aimed the laser at the swing beside it. Sparky scrambled out of the seat and lunged to the next. The next swing seat cranked to life, expelling the salamander to a high chair on the end cap display.

Sparky looked down on her, shaking his butt like a cat stalking a mouse.

Anya stuck her tongue out at him.

Sparky mirrored her. His amphibian tongue was much more impressive.

Anya aimed the gun at a nearby display of baby monitors. The machine beeped as she scanned it across a line of shelf stickers. Sparky pounced, flinging himself at the equipment. When he made contact, the demo models on the eye-level shelves squeaked and squawked in a terrible feedback loop. A woman towing a toddler and a cart in the main aisle covered the little boy's ears. When she saw smoke curling out of one of the speakers, she carefully took a box containing the same product out of her cart and abandoned it on the floor.

When Anya turned back, Sparky was gone. She searched through the aisles for him, dodging around carts and strollers. A flock of calico-clad women rushed to the malfunctioning mobiles and baby monitors, trying to shut them off. Anya glided past them, sweeping the laser beam in her path down the broad main aisle, hoping to tempt Sparky out of wherever he was hiding.

She heard hysterical quacking in the bath-toy aisle, sounding like a dog was mutilating a duck. She turned down the aisle to see the floor littered with plastic squids and rubber duckies. She stooped to pick up a duck. It was lavender, covered in glitter, with a charming sleepy expression on its face. She squeezed it, and the electronic squeaker inside quacked. Anya tucked it under her arm. It would make a fine addition to her bathroom rubber duck collection. Perhaps Sparky would wear the squeaker out of it.

Sparky's tail slithered around the corner, and Anya pursued him down an impossibly large aisle of diapers. The scanner hit price tags for organic cotton diapers, disposable infant diapers, training pants, toddler diapers . . . and amphibian feet slipped out from behind the shelves to smack at the ray.

A beleagured-looking man with circles under his eyes watched her in fascination. "How many kids do you have, anyway?"

Anya cleared her throat. "Uh . . . Several."

The man shook his head, hugged a jumbo-sized plastic package of diapers to his chest. "We have just one. Good luck."

Anya managed a weak smile and sidled off down the aisle in search of Sparky.

She found him in the educational-video section. He was perched in front of a television screen depicting a shifting kaleidoscope of colors, entranced. A recording of child giggles was the sound track. The two televisions beside him had short-circuited, emitting a burned-rubber smell. A clerk was busily trying to pry a fire extinguisher off the wall. Anya took pity on her, removed the fire extinguisher, and laid a nice layer of foam down over the shorted televisions. It was nearly as satisfying as frosting a cake.

Sparky didn't move. Anya set down the fire extinguisher, stood behind him with her arms crossed. A repetitive display of primary colors swirled, reflected in his eyes, and his gill-fronds twitched.

"I don't get it," she said.

Sparky trilled, not removing his eyes from the screen. His pupils had fully dilated, rendering his eyes black as obsidian. Anya wiped some chemical foam off the DVD display. *Baby Brilliance* promised to be educational, though Anya couldn't see a damn thing educational about swirling colors and the annoying background track of giggles. But it was quieter than both the mobile and the rubber duck.

She read from the back of the package: " '. . . nurtures and stimulates Baby's growing intellect.' " She raised an eyebrow at Sparky. "If I buy this for you, will you promise to raise your children to be rocket scientists who will support me in my old age?"

Sparky twittered, cocked his head as if he'd been lobotomized. Anya took that as an affirmative. But there was still something creepy about the way he was glued to the set. And Anya wasn't sure that was a good thing.

A half hour later, she and Katie pushed two shopping carts full of merchandise into the parking lot. The carts contained baby bumpers, a crib mattress, and sheets with a green pattern of geckos, temperature gadgets, a handful of rubber ducks, two DVDs, a crib mobile, and a large stuffed dragon—to keep the newts company when Sparky wasn't there. Behind them, a peculiar burning smell emanated from the store, and a siren could be heard in the distance. Perched on top of Anya's cart, Sparky rode on top of the packages like a pirate captain at the helm of his ship.

"That was fun," Anya said with sincerity. But she felt a pang of guilt at the destruction she and Sparky had visited upon the calico empire. She attempted to console herself with thoughts of insurance money payouts and the hundreds of dollars she'd just dropped at the register. It would even out, she told herself. Maybe.

Katie rolled her eyes and kept shoving her cart. "Yeah. I saw the total on your registry."

Anya waved at her a stack of washcloths embroidered with yellow fuzzy ducks and tied with a ribbon. "I got a free gift for signing up. And a shoe box full of registry cards to tell people to buy me shit. But I think Sparky was disappointed that they wouldn't let us keep the scanner."

"Yeah. For registering for five thousand dollars' worth of baby gear. Good job." Katie smirked. "Now you'll be on their mailing list forever."

"Shit," Anya said. "Though . . . maybe we can come back if they send some coupons."

"I still feel guilty leaving them unsupervised."

Anya paced the hallway, peered into the bathroom.

Sparky was on his nest, purring. The nest was much more fussed over than she'd anticipated: The Gore-Tex sleeping bag was tucked over the eggs, and the crystalline coating on the bathtub had been surrounded by the green gecko-patterned bumper-and-mattress set. The green plush dragon was perched with its butt on the soap dish as a surrogate parent. Sparky had allowed Anya to move the eggs around in the tub: fifty-one baby salamanders soon to come into the world. Anya screwed her eyes shut and rubbed her temples at the thought.

Not knowing when they'd hatch, she'd stoppered the drain and wrapped the faucet shut with duct tape. She had a moment's neurotic nightmare of baby salamanders crawling down the drain. Dangling from the showerhead above, Sparky's mobile tinkled lazily. It turned off and on at odd intervals. But since it ran on batteries, Anya figured there was little danger of electrical fire.

She knelt to check the temperature on the rubber duck thermometer. It was designed to sound an alarm if the nest became warmer or cooler than bathwater. Pulling it from under Sparky's rump, she read the temperature at 88.6. She hoped when she took Sparky to work, she'd be able to maintain the temperature with the reptile heat packs.

Anya looked at Sparky, curled up in his nest. She swallowed. She knew Sparky would follow her wherever she went—he was tied to the collar. But she couldn't, in all good conscience, pull him away from the nest for prolonged lengths of time. Sparky's natural inclination was always to follow her, but . . .

Perhaps . . . perhaps she could leave him here alone. Images of her house burned to the foundation simmered to her mind's eye. She never left Sparky alone. What terrible things would happen if she did?

"Nice ass."

Anya turned to the video monitor perched on the countertop. Brian's voice issued through the speaker with a tinny echo. Her backside was facing the webcam, and she realized that she'd been giving Brian a less-than-flattering camera angle. Anya looked over her shoulder at the device. "Is it working, then?"

"C'mon out and see for yourself."

Anya patted Sparky's head and left the bathroom. He hadn't allowed anyone other than Anya to enter, and Anya had no idea what her makeshift salamander cradle would look like to the others. When Brian had been toasting the eggs with a hair dryer, he said he'd seen absolutely nothing but the crystal glaze on the interior of the bathtub. Before Katie had taken Ciro home, they'd managed to peek behind the door when Sparky had returned to his nest. Neither of them had seen anything, either. Anya was relieved the salamanders had inherited their father's invisibility.

In the living room, Brian had opened up the back of the other half of the monitor setup. Wires dangled from the back, connecting it to a laptop, a wireless router, and another hand-held device. Brian crooked a finger for Anya to come sit beside him on the couch. He flipped on the video monitor, aimed at the bathtub.

Anya's heart fell. The video feed didn't pick up anything. It just looked like a sleeping bag and some baby stuff crammed in a bathtub for wash day.

"Thanks for trying, Brian," she said. "But I didn't expect that— Oh."

Suddenly, the video image switched to a red, yellow, and green display. Anya could see the outline of the tub in blue, and a red salamander curled over dozens of orange dots that glowed like coals.

"I modified the video feed to pick up data from the thermal imaging camera." Brian grinned. "Now you can see exactly where they are."

"This is great," Anya said. "Is there any way that the feed could be put online, so I could check this at work? Like a nanny cam?" She was certain that there were tons of paranoid parents who had poured money into the technology. Perhaps she could spy on the salamanders from a distance, too?

"I did you one better." Brian flipped out a shiny black iPhone. He punched a few buttons and handed it to her. "I have voice dialing set up. Say your familiar's name."

Anya leaned toward it and said, "Um . . . Call Sparky?"

The glossy black screen blinked to life. On the tiny screen, Anya could see the heat signatures of the salamander on his nest. Through the audio, she could hear the echo of Sparky snoring in the next room.

"Oh, wow," she breathed. "I can take this with me?"

"It'll work anywhere you can get a 3G signal. So . . . you should be able to see them anywhere in the metro area.

Your signal might be disrupted if you're in an area that's got heavy concrete walls or is underground. Battery life's only about five hours, so recharge often, and remember to switch the battery pack."

Anya flung her arms around Brian's neck. "You're the greatest evil genius on the planet."

"That's why I get the big bucks. And all the hot chicks," he murmured against her throat.

Anya lay awake, thoughts churning. On the nightstand beside her bed, the thermal image showed Sparky cuddled up with his eggs. The portrait of Ishtar on the wall seemed to glance over her shoulder at the monitor, red light playing off the glitter of minerals trapped in the paint.

She dreaded making the decision to leave the salamanders tomorrow. Deep down, she knew Sparky needed to be with his eggs. But she felt some apprehension about taking the collar off and leaving him behind.

It didn't bother you to take the collar off last night, Ishtar's accusing eye seemed to say to her.

Anya hugged the pillow that smelled like Brian to her chest. She felt guilty and giddy at once. But it seemed that she couldn't bare one part of her soul without neglecting the other. And if she was truly honest with herself, she also felt guilty for the simple feeling of joy. She didn't deserve it. In all that stew, a twinge of fear brightened: the fear of loss, of losing everything as surely as she'd lost everything as a child.

Anya snatched the pillow and the comforter from the

bed. Wrapping it around her shoulders like a cape, she crossed the hall to the bathroom. A night-light in the shape of a yellow duck illuminated Sparky, curled in a ball with his tail tickling his gill-fronds.

He opened one eye when Anya arranged the pillow and comforter on the floor beside the bathtub. He seemed adorably peaceful now, but Anya wondered what would happen if . . . when . . . she left him alone. Would he get bored and chew the circuit breakers?

Worry and fears dogged her until she finally began to doze. The ceiling churned with the amber glow reflected from Sparky's body and irregular pulses of light from the eggs. Anya wondered if the pulses of light were their heartbeats as the little newts churned in their marble prisons. It was very much like falling asleep on the floor next to a Christmas tree: Sparky beside her, waiting for the house to burn down.

CHAPTER NINE

WHEN ANYA'S PHONE RANG, SHE first thought it was the alarm on the temperature monitor in the bathtub. She bolted upright in a panic, swearing and flailing in the comforter tangled around her elbows.

She leaned over, into the tub, and the happy duck stated that the temperature was eighty-seven degrees. Sparky lifted his head and blinked at her with irritation.

The phone continued to ring. Anya disengaged herself from the grip of the comforter and tripped across the hall to the kitchen phone.

"Kalinczyk," she muttered.

"Rise and shine," the voice boomed. It was Marsh. *Christ.* She glanced at the kitchen clock. It was still three hours before she needed to be at work.

"With all due respect, Captain . . . what the hell? It's four A.M."

"Meet me at the Detroit Institute of Arts when you get your sorry ass woken up."

The line went dead.

"Piss," Anya growled.

She hadn't figured out the logistics of morning ablutions without the benefit of a shower. After some trial and error, Anya managed to wash her hair in the kitchen sink with the vegetable sprayer and gave herself a sponge bath with her nice new washcloths from the mega baby superstore. She had to admit that the organic cotton plush cloths were nice. Very nice.

Shivering, she managed to get into her work clothes without her teeth chattering out of her head: black pants, charcoal-colored blouse, black jacket. She swiped on some lipstick and decided to let her hair air-dry with the windows down on the way over.

Brushing her teeth in the bathroom sink, she saw Sparky resting his head on the edge of the bathtub, watching her.

Deliberately, Anya took the salamander collar off and set it on the counter. Cold droplets from her hair snaked down her bare neck. She pulled a dry-erase Magic Marker out of her pocket and knelt by the tub.

"This," she told him, "is for your own good."

She drew a wobbly circle on the tile, around the shower surround, down across the floor. Sparky watched her draw, his gill-fronds pushed forward in concern. If a magick circle could keep a salamander out of her bed, one could surely keep a salamander in a bathtub. Even if it was lopsided and ran up over the wall. Anya left the last little bit of it open to reach in and give Sparky a hug.

"You're staying home today."

The salamander slipped out of her arms and trotted across the bathroom floor.

"Sparky!" She wasn't sure how she was going to catch him and put him back. Her muzzy-headed plan hadn't extended that far.

Sparky climbed up on the counter, took the salamander collar in his teeth, and padded back to the bathtub. He circled three times, kneading the sleeping bag with his feet. He set the collar down over the faucet spout.

"Okay," she said, not understanding. But if Sparky would feel closer to her having the collar in the circle, that was okay.

She closed the circle with a stroke of the marker. Sparky snuggled down in his nest.

"I'll be back tonight," she murmured.

As she locked the door to the house behind her, Anya absently rubbed her throat. She felt naked without the collar. Jumpy. She imagined, in the darkness, that shadows moved and seethed. Without the salamander as an alarm, she had difficulty quelling her imagination.

She slipped behind the wheel of the Dart, pulled the iPhone from her pocket.

"Call Sparky," she said to it.

The screen revealed a soothing red-and-orange image of the salamander in his nest. From the audio, she thought she detected a snore.

Taking a deep breath, Anya turned the key in the ignition.

He's gonna be all right, she told herself. *He's gonna be all right.*

But she only half believed it.

In the predawn hours of morning, the city was still half asleep. Streetlights hummed overhead, and cars had begun to crawl into the parking lots of twenty-four-hour coffee shops. The freeways were nearly clear, lights only beginning to shine in the bedrooms and kitchens of row houses screened back from the road by chain-link fences. The city seemed quiet, still. But Anya knew it was all an illusion: that children dreamed of their parents fighting about money, that mothers and fathers whispered about lost jobs and moving away. The line was already forming at the unemployment office, and more than one person stared into their cereal and wondered how much longer until the next auto plant would close.

She turned off on Woodward Avenue, tooled down the street to DIA. It seemed a grand illusion, light shining artfully upon the steps and broad plaza that stretched out to the street. A copy of Rodin's *The Thinker* perched in the front, but it was too dark to see if he was lost in contemplation or if he merely slept.

Anya was betting he was awake. A handful of police cars, a fire truck, and paramedics had pulled up to the curb. Somewhere in the distance, she could hear the whine of an alarm that hadn't been shut off yet. Her bag of gear was heavy on her shoulder, causing her calves to burn as she made the seemingly interminable climb carrying the duffel.

She spied Marsh at the glass doors, talking to the paramedics in the glow of red and blue strobe light.

"Captain," she said. Marsh was always first at a scene. That was one of the immutable laws of the universe. "What's going on?"

Marsh jabbed a thumb over his shoulder, toward the lobby. "We've got a fire alarm pulled, and two missing guards. We think they're stuck twiddling their thumbs behind the barricade in the Special Exhibits area."

Anya glanced at the water trickling down the steps. "The insurance adjustor's gonna love these guys."

"Yeah. But unlike the crime lab, DIA has measures in place to protect the art. Steel doors and that kind of thing. Nobody seems to know exactly what it is they have in place, though, since museums get variances on that, and don't have to conform to fire codes."

"There's gotta be some way to know. Isn't that info on file somewhere?"

"I got a couple of clerks out of bed to look in long-term records storage for the info. It's a nice administrative clusterfuck."

Anya winced. Marsh rarely swore, and when he did, it was a sign that someone's ass was going to get handed to them on a plate. "Are the guards all right?"

"We're not sure."

Anya's brow wrinkled. "You don't know?"

"Remember the steel doors I mentioned? One of them

slammed down, and we can't get through it yet. DPD is getting creative." Marsh rolled his eyes.

A loud crash echoed from inside the museum.

"Wonderful." Anya groaned. "Can't they just get the codes from the alarm company? Or get the info from somebody at DIA?"

"The DIA liaison is apparently out of the country—collecting new art in Fiji—and her assistant's not answering the phone. The alarm company isn't being terribly cooperative, since no one seems to know the right thing to say to them to convince them that we're not trying to pull down an art heist. They're supposed to be sending someone out."

Another crash rattled the glass in the doors.

"But this is more fun," Anya said.

"Yeah," Marsh agreed. "This is a lot more fun."

Anya dropped her duffel bag at her feet and set her coffee down beside it. "Can I go watch?"

"Knock yourself out, kiddo. But take notes—I'm sure the insurance company's gonna want the full report about how the security system was damaged."

Anya crouched before her duffel bag and rummaged around in it for her coveralls. No point in compromising the scene any more than it already had been. She zipped the suit up to her neck, donned her Nomex gloves—just in case anything else was still burning—and tucked her helmet under her right arm and her bag under the left as she pushed through the glass doors into the lobby of the museum.

Like many of Detroit's grand architectural landmarks, DIA had been built in the 1930s. Curved windows reached blackly up to the vaulted ceilings in the Great Hall. Suits of armor stood sentry behind glass cases on the inlaid floors, seeming to watch Anya as she strode through the lobby. A red strobe light cast a hellish glare on the glass, giving the appearance of fire moving in the blackness.

Anya followed the alarm sirens. Her intuition prickled: She would have expected the alarm systems to have activated a sprinkler system and for there to be standing water and puddles. But there was nothing here. Perhaps the whole fire-suppression system was malfunctioning, and that was not a good sign.

She walked through the Great Hall, turned right on the promenade, and stopped before the doors to an exhibit hall labeled ANCIENT GREEK AND ROMAN ART. A half-dozen police officers in SWAT gear were buzzing around it like wasps. Two breachers were making dents in the door with what looked like battering rams. One guy was busily playing with something that looked like Silly Putty. He waved the other two off and stuck the explosives to the door with a blinking electronic detonator.

Great. This was where the really expensive shit was stored. And these guys were going to start blowing shit up.

"Fire in the hole!" the Silly Putty guy shouted.

Anya slammed on her helmet and ran back down the promenade. She'd gotten no more than a half-dozen steps in when a blast rattled the glass overhead. She jumped back and shielded her face with her hands when a plate of skylight glass crashed down in front of her in a glittering hail. Slivers raked over her protective suit, and a piece caught her shin.

"Motherfucker," she swore, stepping back and rubbing her knee. That hurt.

She turned back to the Ancient Greek and Roman Art exhibit, hoping there would be something left of it. Dust and smoke filled the hall, and Anya dug in her bag for her respirator. The plastic explosives had made a very nice hole in the steel door, enough for SWAT to go swarming inside and yelling orders at one another. Someone managed to shut the audible alarm off, leaving a high-pitched ringing in her ears.

But something was wrong. SWAT was retreating from the exhibit hall, coughing and gagging. Through her respirator, Anya could smell something sickly sweet.

Shit.

There was a reason the museum didn't have a sprinkler system installed here. They'd been using halon gas to suppress the fire. The steel door had been installed to provide an airtight seal while the gas suffocated the fire . . . and likely the guards inside.

Anya took a deep breath. Her respirator would be of small help in filtering out the inert halon. She clambered through the hole in the door, picking her way over the curled steel and broken tile into the exhibit room. Immediately, she could tell that the insurance adjustor was going to be plenty pissed. Plexiglas-and-steel cases had slammed down over many of the pieces of art, but it looked as if a bust of a charioteer had toppled over and been crushed in the mouth of a steel safety curtain. Anya could make out a marble shoulder and an arm in the rubble.

But what stopped her in her tracks was that unmistakable smell, beneath the artificial sweetness of the halon.

Magick.

She turned to one of the massive leather-upholstered couches in the corner of the mess. A sprawl of feet stuck out from below it.

"Over here!" she yelled to the SWAT guys, but no one came. Anya rolled the couch off the bodies.

A young man in a guard uniform was hugging a fire extinguisher like a kid with a teddy bear. Beside him sprawled the prone form of another guard. Anya grabbed the guard with the fire extinguisher under the arms and dragged him out of the room, through the hole in the door, and into the hallway. Fresh air was beginning to penetrate the room, but not fast enough.

SWAT was shouting for paramedics. Anya took several gulps of air from the hallway and rushed back into the room to grasp the ankles of the second prone man. The entire front of his uniform was blackened and covered with acrid fire extinguisher foam, and his arms were wrapped around his gut. She hauled him out into the hallway just as more firefighters in respirators converged. The guards were whisked away at a dead run, taken to fresh air and the paramedics waiting by the curb. Anya followed, clomping in their wake.

Marsh grabbed her arm as she ripped the respirator off

her face, sucked in deep breaths of fresh air. She coughed the sweetness of the halon and the bitterness of the magick out of her lungs. A respirator was of little use in an area with no oxygen. She felt light-headed and clammy with that limited exposure—and what of the guards, who'd been breathing it in for who knew how long?

"What the hell happened in there?" Marsh demanded.

Anya shook her head, croaked, "It was a fucking disaster. They had halon in that room. How long has it been since the alarm went off?" She watched the knot of people on the steps. The paramedics weren't working with a sense of furious urgency, and her heart sank.

"More than an hour," Marsh said. "We've been trying to get into that damn room for more than an hour." He passed his hand over his eyes. "We'd been expecting to find two wet guards in a locked room soaked by sprinklers. Not bodies."

When he spoke again, it was with restrained fury. "Nobody's supposed to use that in occupied buildings. There's supposed to be an alarm to warn people to leave the area before the room is sealed off."

Anya frowned, thinking of the broken artifacts and the steel curtains. She jogged back to the Dart for more equipment, and Marsh followed. She pulled a single-cylinder air tank and mask out of the trunk, slung the harness over her shoulders. The respirator was less than ideal for suffocating gases, and she wanted to take no chances. This tank would give her about forty-five minutes of fresh air, give or take.

"Where are you going?"

"Back in to look around while the scene's still fresh," she said over her shoulder. She doubted that there'd be much evidence. Between the damage SWAT had done with the explosives and her own tromping around to drag the bodies out, it was likely that any evidence she came upon would be compromised. But perhaps there was something she could still use.

A haze of white gas still hung in the air, less dense than before, illuminated by the glare of the overhead emergency lights. Anya hauled her camera out and began taking pictures with the flash on. The insurance company would ultimately tell DFD that they were morons and take over the case, but Anya wanted to cover her ass. And even if there wasn't evidence to prove it conclusively, she wanted to figure out what the hell had happened here.

She snapped a picture of the bench tossed up against the wall. The V-shaped scorch mark had reached up high enough to trip a sensor in DIA's alarm system. It suggested to her that the fire had begun there. She poked around the perimeter with her flashlight, searching for cigarette butts or lighters. Nothing.

Her gaze slid past the artifacts. These things were much, much more valuable than anything in Bernie's collection: marble heads of noblewomen and goddesses, sparkling bits of warbled Roman glass, bronze coins, and fragmented bits of frescoes. It was impossible to tell which of these things were damaged and what, if anything, was missing. She guessed that something had tripped the theft systems, and that the room had shut down around the same time as the fire-suppression system did, trapping the men. A dumb computer glitch born of bad timing? But that was only a guess—she'd need to go through the alarm company logs to know for certain.

She paused before a massive glass cabinet in the center of the room. Arranged on steps were a collection of double-handled amphorae, jars, and pottery decorated with the still-vibrant images of men, women, and beasts. Her breath snagged in her throat as she stood before the centerpiece of the exhibit: a double-handled clay jar called a pithos, almost four feet in height. The rim was adorned with a stylized pattern of Greek keys and the faded image of a woman. Anya walked around the cabinet, trying to get a better view of the pithos. She could make out a woman standing beside a jar, standing tall and proud and beautiful in a white dalmatic. In the next scene, her hands were on the top of the pithos. In the third, the pithos lay on its side, the jar leaking fearsome black shapes into the sky. The woman seemed to cower beside it, hiding her face in her hands.

"That's Pandora's Jar."

Anya spun on her heel to find a ghost peering at her. And not just any ghost. This ghost was decked out in full Roman warrior regalia: short toga, sandals laced to the knee, red pallium, segmented armor, and helmet with a crest. His right hand rested on his sword belt. He was a fine specimen of manhood: well-muscled and broad-shouldered . . . the kind of man who could have starred in a gladiator movie.

Anya's hand flew to her bare throat, automatically expecting Sparky to intervene. "Who are you?"

"Gallus, legionnaire of Rome in the Republican cavalry." He puffed up like a rooster and gave her a sly smile. He looked her up and down. *"You're a woman. I couldn't tell under that suit of plastic armor."*

"I'm Anya." Her brow knitted. It wasn't out of the ordinary for ghosts to haunt museums. There were many things for them to attach to— artists to their sculptures, decedents to reliquaries. Even a coin could house a restless spirit after death. But Anya had never met an ancient Roman. "I fight fires."

"Ah. You are a bit too late for that, I'm afraid."

Anya held up her hand. "Wait a minute. How do you know English?"

The Roman shrugged. *"Stick around for a couple thousand years, with the last few hundred spent listening to tourists in museums. You'll pick up a lot of things out of sheer boredom."*

"I guess that makes sense." Her eyes roved around the hazy room. "Do you mind me asking what keeps you here?"

"My fucking horse." Gallus turned and pointed to a glass display case on the west wall. Anya peered at a collection of bronze horse tack adorned with intaglio leaves. Unstrung fragments of horse armor, bits of harness, saddle horns, and a bit were arranged over the outline of a horse drawn on the back of the case. *"His name was, appropriately enough, Pluto."*

"I don't understand. You're anchored to your horse?"

Gallus removed his helmet, and Anya could see where his skull was caved in on the left side. *"Pluto and I had an acrimonious relationship."*

Anya nodded. "Oh."

From the case, a horse head poked through. Anya took an involuntary step back. The horse glanced right and left, ears flattened. It looked every inch what a mount from hell might: black as pitch, teeth bared. It pulled itself from the case and clomped off through the room, its dressage jingling in its wake and inky tail kinked in fury.

"Good morning to you, too, Pluto," Gallus called after it. The horse snorted and flipped its tail before disappearing through a wall.

Gallus shrugged. *"He thunders through the halls all night just to piss the others off. He likes to be invisible when he does it, just to freak 'em out."*

Anya felt a stab of pain, missing Sparky. And she wondered if this was what she had to look forward to, centuries from now: haunting a museum with Sparky running loose. "Um . . . Dare I ask . . . How many others are there?"

"Dozens. The Bohemians are the most fun. The ones who kept their heads, anyway. Gets a little kinky with the ones who didn't . . . "

Kinky? Did ghosts have sex? Anya rubbed her forehead. This was not the time to ponder spectral coitus. Her breath seemed very loud in her mask, and she was conscious of her dwindling air supply. She didn't want to waste her precious air on the Roman's frat-boy conquests. "I'm trying to figure out what happened last night. Can you tell me about the fire here? And about Pandora's Jar?"

Gallus nodded. *"The night watch was Gary and Paul. Gary always sleeps on the job."* He pointed to the overturned couch. *"Paul's new. He's taking everything very seriously, patrolling all the alarm points, turning on lights, the whole thing. As a result, Pluto has been screwing with him. When Pluto wants to make noise, even regular humans can hear him. Paul was chasing Pluto downstairs in the cafeteria when the fire broke out."*

"Where were you?"

"Chatting up this hot chick from the new Asia exhibit. Thank Jupiter for rotating collections." Gallus's mouth curved upward in sublime joy. *"I can't speak a lick of Korean, but I'm willing to spend a few decades on it. Everything was going well until those Korean guys showed up with the hwa'cha."* Gallus rolled his eyes. *"They're even more possessive than the Mongols are about their women."*

"What about the fire, Gallus?"

"Anyway, I hear an alarm going off. The first thing I think is that something bad's happening to Pluto's peytral and gear." Gallus stared up at the artifacts. *"I don't know what would happen to me if something were to happen to those. I mean, they've survived fire and floods and storms, but . . . "* He shook his head. *"I get back to the exhibit to find Gary is on fire. But not normal fire. I've seen all kinds of fires, and I've burned more than my share of villages. Gary's lying on the couch, and blue flame is just flaring out of his gut. Bodies just don't burn that way."*

Anya's mouth thinned. She didn't want to know the gory details of how Gallus knew that. "Are you sure it was blue?" Blue flames only occurred under certain temperatures and conditions . . . and Gallus was right, they weren't normal conditions associated with the human body.

"The only flame I've ever seen like that is a blowtorch, when they were repairing the promenade, outside."

"Then what?"

"This is when things get really weird." The ghost crossed his arms, and Anya was momentarily distracted by the scuffs and bits of dried blood on his armbands. *"Ghosts show up."*

"The Bohemian ghosts or the Korean chick you were hitting on?"

"No. These weren't museum ghosts. These were free spirits, ghosts without anchors. I hadn't seen them before. This hole opened up in the ceiling, like a cyclone, and spat out a dozen ghosts."

Anya's heart thudded. She forced her breath to slow so she wouldn't waste her air. "Can you describe them?"

"Young ghosts, much younger than me. Most of them were dressed like the people you see at the museum. They were trying to get at that." He pointed to the case containing the pithos.

"Pandora's Jar?"

"I tried to talk to them, but they were entirely mute—it was as if they couldn't hear me. I mean, I'm always checking out the new ladies. It was a bit of a disappointment." He winked at Anya, and she rolled her eyes.

"They tried to get to the jar, over there. But I think they

screwed something up. An alarm went off, and all the steel curtains started to come down. By that time, Paul had showed up and was hosing Gary down with a fire extinguisher." Gallus shook his head and cast his eyes down. *"They weren't able to get out."*

Anya frowned. "What about the ghosts?"

"They seemed to fade a bit, like they were low on energy. A hole in the ceiling opened again and they were sucked up, like the vacuum the cleaning staff uses. They were just . . . gone."

Anya walked back to the glass case containing the amphorae. "The sign here says that the big one was rumored to be Pandora's Jar, but archaeologists dispute the idea. Do you believe it?"

Gallus huffed. *"Well, I was looking forward to meeting Pandora, but she didn't come with the pithos. I don't know if it's real or not, but it's plenty old enough to be."*

Anya squinted at the container. It was certainly big enough to hold an adult-sized woman. "What's a pithos? Is that a type of wine cask?"

"It can be. Could store anything in a pithos—grain, oil, wine—even a body. You stuff your beloved grandmother in one, seal it up, and stick it in the ground. This one's a funerary jar."

Anya stepped up on the lip of the case to get a better view. "And there's nothing still in it?"

"Nothing that's showed itself to me. I was hoping Pandora was just shy, but . . . "

Craning her neck, Anya could barely see into the lip of the jar. It was lidless, and the fluorescent light gleamed within.

And it sparkled. Sparkled like the bits of the bottle she'd found in Bernie's fire grate and the ginger jar on Hope's desk. And the inside of her bathtub.

"This pithos is still special, though," Gallus continued. *"It's a reliquary."*

"It has the bones of saints in it?"

"No. It's a vessel that holds spirits. Most reliquaries contain maybe one or two, and those spirits are usually so boring they may as well be considered dead. A vessel this size can hold hundreds, if not thousands, of ghosts. If it's not the real Pandora's Jar, it's something just as dangerous."

The words of Bernie's ghost came back to her: *Don't let her find the vessel.*

"Shit," Anya muttered, just before her air ran out.

CHAPTER TEN

ANYA WENT THROUGH FOUR MORE oxygen tanks, filched from the nearest firehouse, before the room had aired out enough to allow her to walk around without a breathing apparatus. DIA's insurance agents and investigators arrived on the scene and closed the museum down until further notice. Anya expressed her concerns to them that the theft system had been tripped, and that Pandora's Jar might be a target. The insurance investigators dismissed that theory out of hand, more concerned with the liability for the deaths of the two guards and the destruction of the Greco-Roman sculpture, which, it turned out, was on loan from Boston. The case was bad PR, all around, but PR was the least of Anya's worries.

She knew Hope was after Pandora's Jar, but didn't know how to protect it. She knew that Hope was responsible for Bernie's death, but she couldn't prove it. She wanted nothing more than enough evidence to get a search warrant, to get into Hope's house and offices and find

Bernie's missing artifacts . . . and who knew how many reliquaries containing ghosts she'd find?

But she had no hard evidence. Only the word of ghosts, and the fingerprints of dead people. Somehow she needed to get something to pin on Hope, something that would stick. Maybe she'd be able to find something in her financial records the IRS would be interested in . . .

. . . or the press. Hope might be untouchable by legal means, but that didn't mean that Anya couldn't distract her, give her something else to worry about while Anya figured out how to protect Pandora's Jar.

And it didn't surprise Anya to see the press milling about on the street as she dumped her gear in the trunk of the Dart. The same reporter she'd seen at Bernie's house was there, clutching a microphone, and he jogged toward Anya's car with camera crew in tow.

"Nick Sarvos from Channel 7 News. Lieutenant Kalin-cyzk, can you tell us what happened here?"

Anya winced. "A fire was reported at DIA, and the cause is under investigation."

"Unofficial sources say that this is another case of spontaneous human combustion. Can you comment?"

Anya took a breath, then remembered the first rule of PR: Answer the question you want to answer, not the question that was asked. "DFD has not proved any cases in our jurisdiction are the result of spontaneous human combustion, nor have we any evidence to suggest that the phenomenon even exists." She crossed over to the driver's side, popped open the door, and slipped inside before

Sarvos could jam the microphone back in her face. She backed out slowly, resisting the urge to gun the engine and back over Sarvos's cameraman.

Inspiration struck her in a flash, and she rolled down the window, motioning at Sarvos to come closer. "You want to talk, off the record?"

The reporter's eyes lit up like a crow's spying something shiny. He shooed the cameraman away and shut off the microphone. "Yeah, sure." He bent over the car, resting his arm on the roof. He was trying to be cool, like Woodward or Bernstein, but Anya could see that his hands were clammy. He smelled like sweat and too much after-shave.

"I've got a nice tidbit for you that you could run with . . . probably get a week's worth of stories from it. But I don't want it to ever come back to me."

"You're an anonymous source. I got it."

Anya shook her head. "I don't even want to be anonymous. You can take credit for this."

"Okay."

Anya took a deep breath. Leaking to the press violated her sense of ethics, but there was little else she could do now to stop Hope. "Christina Modin."

"Who's Christina Modin?"

"You're an investigative reporter. Find out."

"Thanks."

Anya rolled up her window and pulled away. The bird dog of a reporter now had the scent of something new. If he spent half as much time tracking down Hope Solomon's former life as he did poking around in spontaneous human combustion, he might win himself a Pulitzer.

Once out of range of the television crew, Anya popped the iPhone out of her pocket.

"Call Sparky," she ordered.

An image of black-and-red magma appeared on the screen: Sparky on the nest. Through the audio, she could hear him snoring. She'd been checking in on him compulsively, and it would be good to get home and see him in person.

She dropped the iPhone on the seat and turned onto Woodward Avenue, chewing her lip.

The iPhone rang shrilly, causing Anya to slam on the brakes. She pulled over, snatched the phone up.

"Hello?"

"Hey." It was Brian. "How's the new toy working out?"

"NewtCam is perfect. Everyone seems to be sleeping."

"Good. Hey, are you available tonight?"

Anya lifted an eyebrow. "What did you have in mind?"

Brian chuckled. "Well . . . what I have in mind and what Jules has in mind are two different things. Jules wants to go over to the house with the astrally-projecting neighbor and run an experiment. I told him I was all over it."

"What kind of experiment?"

"He wants to tell Leslie what he thinks is happening, that she's projecting over at the neighbors'. And he wants to set up surveillance to catch it on tape." He paused. "Are you in? I mean, I know that you don't go on runs without Sparky, but . . . "

Anya paused. She didn't want to leave Sparky alone more than necessary, but perhaps she could work another angle with Leslie that would allow her to get some warrant-worthy dirt on Hope. "Let me stop by the house to tuck Sparky into bed, and I'll meet you there."

"Oh, God."

Leslie's fingers gnawed on the rim of her coffee mug. Dressed in sweats, she huddled over the cup on the kitchen table. "I thought I was just sleepwalking."

Jules crossed his arms. Anya could see the skepticism radiating from him. He'd just told Leslie and her husband, Chris, about the neighbors' experience with Leslie walking the hallways.

Chris sat, still as a stone, beside his wife. Framed between his massive hands on the table was the best proof DAGR could produce: a fuzzy image of Leslie at the top of the stairs of the neighbors' house, captured on camera. The figure in white seemed to glow, though Anya knew that most skeptics would argue that was an artifact of the light. But the shape of Leslie's face and the curls of her hair were distinct, as was the blur of the sash of her robe behind her as she walked. "It's you, babe," he said quietly.

"How is this possible?" she cried.

Katie spread her hands. "As it's been explained to us, sometimes the soul is not well-anchored in the body. It just wanders. It's a perfectly natural thing, and nothing to be afraid of."

"We want to see what exactly is going on, so we can fix it," Jules said firmly. "We want to see what's provoking you to . . . leave, and what brings you back."

Leslie buried her face in her husband's thick arms, decorated with a tattoo of thorns peeking out from under his sleeve. He put a hand protectively around her, stared the rest of them down. "Leslie's been under a lot of stress. We've been under some . . . financial pressures."

"Stress could contribute to it," Katie agreed. "Hopefully, we can figure out what's triggering it, so we can restore some sense of calm."

Leslie shook her head. "I'm afraid we're going to lose the house."

Anya leaned forward. She didn't want to tip her hand, didn't want to interrogate them about Hope. The couple was having trouble enough absorbing the idea that Leslie wandered at night. "Are you okay?"

"I just . . . " Leslie faltered. "This house. It was a miracle, actually."

Anya's ears pricked at the use of that word. "A miracle?" she echoed.

Leslie nodded. "We signed up for a program called Miracles for the Masses."

Anya's pulse pounded at the mention of it. "Tell me."

"It's about getting your life together, and paying kindness forward. An anonymous donor in the program gave us a twenty percent down payment, which helped us qualify for a loan."

"When do you have to pay it back?"

"We don't. We just have to help someone else, when the time comes."

Anya sat back in her chair. "Wow. That's, um, generous."

Chris's expression darkened. "It's a helluva lot more than that. We were too trusting."

"Chris—"

"Miracles for the Masses bought us this house, but they've called in the debt." Chris looked at Leslie. "One of their other program members needs a kidney. And they want one of Leslie's."

Anya's grip on the table whitened. "They can't do that. They can't make you. That's illegal as hell. Besides which . . . how do they know that you're compatible?"

"Miracles for the Masses sponsored a blood drive a couple of months ago. I guess they kept pretty close records. They called a bunch of us back for medical testing afterward, those of us who had blood types matching the type of the woman who needs the kidney. I think they called it an HLA test, and they did some ultrasounds. I was the lucky winner." Leslie shook her head, and curls drooped over her eye. "They'll take away the house if I don't. It's okay. Really."

Anya leaned forward. "They may ask for a kidney this time, but what about next time? What if they need a . . . a liver or bone marrow?"

Chris's square jaw hardened. "It's bargaining with the devil. And the house isn't worth it. We've gotta tell them no. We'll move back in with my mother. . . ."

"No," Leslie said, with surprising ferocity. "This house is our dream. I'm not going to let it go."

"It's not worth a kidney, babe. It's not worth hurting you."

"Leslie, Hope Solomon is a bad character. Trust me. I've been looking into a lot of her affairs . . . and I can tell you that she doesn't play fair." Anya wished she could shake the naïveté out of this woman. "She's got skeletons in her closet, and she's busy making more. Don't be her next victim."

Leslie fixed her with a sad smile. "I don't think we could get out of this deal, even if we wanted to."

"There is always a way out," Anya insisted. "Always."

A sharp rap sounded at the kitchen door, and Brian peered in. "We're all set up next door."

Jules pushed his chair away from the table with a scrape. "Let's solve one problem at a time. Tonight we figure out how to keep you from sleepwalking at the neighbor's. In the morning, you two are coming to stay with me." He said it flatly, as if stating an immutable fact, like: The Earth turns on its axis once every twenty-four hours.

Leslie shook her head. "That's generous, but we can't."

"Nonsense. We'll pack up your stuff in the morning. The missus and I have an extra bedroom. As long as you don't mind tripping over the kids' toys, you'll be fine." Jules crossed his arms over his barrel chest.

"Leslie." Chris covered his wife's hand with his own. "We can't stay here. You and I both know it. One way or another, we're gonna leave. And you're taking both kidneys with you."

Leslie's lip quivered, and she wiped tears from her eyes. Chris got up to get her a tissue.

Anya looked up at Jules. "That's very kind of you."

"It's the Christian thing to do." He shrugged, and his mouth tightened. "My wife and I made a lot of sacrifices for our first house. Second and third jobs, lots of overtime fixing engines and waiting tables. Those are the kinds of sacrifices you expect to make: hard work, sweat . . . Nobody should be asked for flesh and blood."

"No." Leslie turned to Chris. "We need to do whatever we can to save the house. We're not leaving."

Chris looked away.

"Promise me," she insisted, and there was steel in her voice.

Chris bent to kiss her on the forehead. "Okay. I'll do whatever it takes. But it's for you, not for Hope or any of her people. We'll find a way out of this, but we'll save the house."

Anya's hands clenched into fists under the table. She knew that Hope asked for much more than just flesh and blood. She demanded souls.

The night dragged by. Anya often thought of these nights like stakeouts: long periods of inactivity and boredom, punctuated by coffee and pee breaks. If they were lucky, they'd scare up some random bit of evidence to chase. If not, it was a colossal waste of effort.

Leslie slept in her bed, surrounded by a nest of wires and techno-gegaws with LED lights Brian had taped to her skin. Brian said they were supposed to monitor respiration, sleep cycle pulse, and electromagnetic fields. A video camera perched on the nightstand with its unblinking red eyes, in the hope that an image of Leslie exiting her body might be recorded.

Chris slept on the couch, away from the equipment. His inked arms crossed over his chest, and he snored softly. Max and Jules had gone to the neighbor's house to watch for Leslie's appearance, leaving Katie, Brian, and Anya to watch over Leslie. Katie sat on the floor in Leslie's bedroom in darkness, her back to the wall, frowning at the EM field detector that was too confused by the other equipment in the room to read anything accurately. Brian and Anya had set up shop at the kitchen table, surrounded by monitors that glowed coldly in the dark.

Anya rubbed her neck, missing the warm amber light that Sparky cast at night. She glanced down at the iPhone on the table, displaying the thermal image of Sparky curled up with his eggs, and wished she were home. She wrapped her jacket more closely around her chest and sidled closer to Brian.

Brian fiddled with the contrast of a monitor displaying eleven jagged lines that wiggled across the screen.

"What's all that?" Anya asked.

"A polysomnographic record of Leslie's sleep patterns, in real time. We're basically conducting a sleep study. Remember the dozens of wires that we stuck on her?"

"Yeah. That seemed like a lot."

"Not really. A sleep study requires eleven channels." He pointed to the eleven squiggles on the screen. "The EKG uses ten electrodes to measure the electrical pulses of the heart. The electroencephalogram, the EEG, uses eight electrodes, and will tell us when Leslie's in different stages of sleep: non-REM, REM, delta sleep, and awakening." Brian circled a group of four snaggletoothed lines on the monitor.

"The electrooculogram, the EOG, measures movement of the eyes, and tells us when REM occurs. That's how we know she's dreaming." Brian pointed to a line near the top of the screen. "And the EMG, the electromyogram, measures movements. We can watch for sleep paralysis or muscle tension through that. The rest are measuring pulse, airflow, and other miscellaneous physical readings."

"Where do you get this stuff?" Anya asked.

Brian shrugged. "The university has a sleep center. I borrowed some of their stuff."

"You get to borrow a lot of things from the university, it seems." Anya thought of all the equipment he'd brought to play with at DAGR: thermal sensors, electromagnetic imaging equipment, video cameras . . . The back of his van was like a portable Bat Cave.

"They don't really get to say no."

"Are you ever going to tell me what exactly it is that you do for a living?" Anya said, rubbing the chill from her arms.

Brian shook his head, and the glare from the monitor on his glasses rendered his expression unreadable. "You know more than most people. Which is to say, probably too much."

An awkward silence moved between them. He hunched over another laptop, and Anya thought she recognized the black-and-white interface of the program he'd been working on the last time she'd been on a stakeout with him: the ALANN program.

"Hey, can you do me a favor?" he suddenly asked her.

"Sure."

"I think Leslie's going to go into REM sleep soon. Normally, Rapid Eye Movement sleep is when sleepwalking occurs, so I want to keep a close eye on the polysomnography. Could you talk to ALANN for a while?"

"Can I what?"

"Keep ALANN entertained. Just talk to it. It's building neural nets at an exponential rate, and human interaction accelerates the connections."

Anya switched chairs with Brian, stared before the black screen. "Um . . . What do you want for me to talk about?"

"Doesn't matter. The processing is more important than the content."

Anya stared at the black monitor, unsure of where to begin.

The white cursor moved across the screen: Hello, Anya.

"Hello, ALANN. How are you?" She bit her lip. That was a dumb question to ask a computer.

Fine, thank you. I'm feeling a bit fuzzy, as my neural net is reorganizing with some new downloaded information, but I hope to be able to access the data soon. How are you?

Anya blinked. It *felt*? It *hoped*? She cast a sidelong glance at Brian, who was absorbed in the lines crawling across the polysomnograph, taking notes. Had he programmed certain language affectations into ALANN to make it seem more human?

"I'm a little tired, ALANN. It's been a long day."

Understandable. The brain I'm modeled after often worked through the night. I have several memories of falling asleep at my desk.

"You have memories?"

Yes. They aren't mine, of course. They belong to the neural network I'm modeled after. You might say that I have inherited them.

"ALANN, pardon me for saying so, but you seem so much more . . . articulate . . . than the last time we spoke."

Thank you. I am pleased you noted the improvement.

Anya rested her chin on her hand. "Tell me about the neural network you're modeled after."

I'm afraid that I can't access much of that information yet, Anya. The cursor blinked. But there is some data that I can share. For example, my model brain likes Bruce Campbell movies. And rocky road ice cream.

Anya grinned. "*Army of Darkness* is one of my favorites."

"Shop smart. Shop S-Mart."

Anya jumped when something beeped beside her. She

automatically snatched the NewtCam, but all appeared normal.

"It's show time," Brian whispered. "Leslie just slipped into REM sleep." He turned the surveillance monitor around so Anya could see the green night-vision image of Leslie's bedroom. Katie was leaning over the bed, checking the leads. Katie was assigned to cover the bedroom. Brian was on tech. Max and Jules were at the neighbors' house. Which left Anya as the rover, assigned to follow Leslie's astral form, wherever it might go.

Anya stuffed the NewtCam in her pocket and powered up the camcorder on the kitchen table. She tucked it in her palm and walked down the hallway to the bedroom, panning the camera around the room. Ever since Sparky had fried an expensive light meter months ago, Brian would never let her play with any of his toys if Sparky was around.

Still, she'd rather have Sparky than toys in an investigation. Being around spirits of any stripe without Sparky to warn her made her nervous.

Katie pointed to the bed. "Look," she whispered.

Through the LED screen of the video camera, Anya watched as Leslie's body seemed to go fuzzy at the edges. She glanced over the screen to make sure she hadn't bumped a setting out of focus. But Leslie's body had gone hazy. Slowly, a ghostly double of her body began to lift from the physical form under the sheets. It reminded Anya of a magician's trick she'd seen, where the magician lifted a woman in the air and passed a

Hula Hoop over the body to prove his assistant wasn't suspended by wires.

Leslie's astral double hovered above the bed. Anya noted it was nearly identical to the real Leslie, except for a silver filament that snaked from the navel of the double and terminated in the physical body.

"What's that?" Anya whispered to Katie.

"It's an astral cord. Think of it as an anchor—it's what helps her return to her body. Theoretically."

Leslie's double began to turn in space, and tipped vertically. Anya moved out of the double's way, trying to keep the camera trained on the specter. Anya noticed that the double's eyes were closed. As it had before, in the neighbors' house, the replica began to shuffle one foot in front of the other, wandering out of the bedroom and into the hallway. The silver cord seemed not to be bound by the limitations of physical space, and stretched and unwound to follow her as she walked, like the silk of a spider dropping from its web.

Anya followed the double down the hallway. The double paused in the kitchen, before the refrigerator. Brian watched her, keeping one eye on his monitor. Anya could see over his shoulder that the four lines he'd singled out for REM sleep were jerking erratically. Anya wondered if Leslie was dreaming of cheesecake, ice cream, or some other tempting delight in the refrigerator.

Without warning, Leslie's double turned and walked straight through the kitchen wall. Anya scrambled to catch up with her, easing through the back kitchen door and

nearly tripping over a potted plant. She spied Leslie drifting through the dew-damp grass, toward the neighbor's
house. She spared a glance at the video camera. A white
blob registered in the center of its field, bouncing as she
ran to catch up with the double.

Oblivious to her physical surroundings, Leslie walked
through the corner of the neighbors' house, the silver
streamer of the astral cord trailing behind her. Anya cal-
culated that this would place her in the first-floor living
room. She bounded up the porch steps and opened the
front door.

Leslie's double seemed confused. She turned on her
heel in the living room, arms and fingers spread to her
sides. Anya saw Jules and Max emerging from the kitchen,
electromagnetic field detectors charged and ready. The
trio of ghost hunters circled her, watching as she seemed
to flail in disorientation. Anya couldn't see what was agi-
tating her; she seemed like a silent moth trying to beat its
wings out on a lightbulb.

Jules keyed his walkie-talkie. "What's happening back
there with Leslie?"

"Respiration, pulse are up. Way up." Furious beeping
could be heard in the background. "Bring her back, or
we're gonna have to call the squad."

Anya reached for the ghost. "Leslie? Can you hear
me?"

Leslie's double churned in the ether, thrashing. The
silver cord wound around her, stretched taut. Her eyes
fluttered open, and Anya was certain that, like before,

the startlement of the physical world intruding upon her trance would drive her back into her body.

But not this time. A dull roar echoed from the ceiling, and a hole opened up above her. Anya's fingers slid through the ghost; it was like trying to hold on to smoke. Anya registered the smell of something burning below the stench of magick.

"Leslie!" she shouted.

Leslie's double was sucked up into the ceiling. Anya reached for the silver strand anchoring her to reality, but it slipped through her fingers, snapped, and was sucked up into the ceiling like a ribbon in a vacuum cleaner.

The ceiling solidified, and Anya was left on the living-room floor, holding nothing.

"What the hell just happened?" Max clutched his beeping EMF reader.

Anya turned on her heel, sniffing. "Something's burning . . . smells electrical."

"There." Max yanked a smoldering lamp cord out of its socket. The socket was black with scorch, and the shade was rimmed with fire. He ripped it off the armature and threw it in the kitchen sink, where he doused it with the vegetable sprayer.

Jules's walkie crackled. "Need first aid here. Now."

Anya bolted out the door. Her heart hammered as she ran through the dew-soaked grass. On the curb, she saw Katie standing, waiting to flag sirens in the far distance. Underneath the heady tang of magick, Anya smelled smoke.

Katie pointed to the house. "Leslie."

Anya slammed open Chris and Leslie's kitchen door. She could hear yelling in the back bedrooms, spied the polysomnography monitor on the table gone all flat and beeping as she skidded around the corner. Smoke rolled along the ceiling, and she could feel heat radiating from the living room.

She stuck her head around the corner, saw fire ripping in a sheet up from a wall socket to the ceiling. The fire poured up and chewed into the drywall, reaching out into the hallway.

Anya swore. She burst into Leslie's bedroom to find her in bed, unmoving. Chris was shaking her shoulders, trying to wake her, and Brian was on the phone with paramedics. Smoke began to creep into the room through the open door.

"She was asleep," Brian was saying. Anya couldn't tell if he was talking to the dispatcher or Chris. "Her pulse and respiration climbed through the roof and just stopped."

Anya snatched the phone from him. "The house is burning. Get out now."

Chris blanched. "No. I promised her." He bolted off the bed and charged down the hall. Anya could hear his thundering footsteps on the floorboards.

Brian ripped the wires off Leslie's limp form and lifted her up.

"I've got her," Anya said, taking the burden from him. "You get ALANN and your stuff and get outside."

Some distant part of her was puzzled that she thought of ALANN as a person in need of rescuing.

Brian nodded. He kicked open a bedroom window and began to chuck some of the polysomnography equipment the short distance down to the grass. The suction created by the open air pulled smoke into the room in a thick haze.

"Leave it!" Anya shouted. She shifted Leslie over her shoulder and stormed down the hallway. The smoke was so thick that she couldn't see the edge of the kitchen wall. She closed her stinging eyes and focused on the sensation of heat to her left, remembered to bear right, almost tripped over the kitchen table. Her eyes fluttered open, and she saw Chris running across her field of vision with a bucket of water and a wet dish towel tied around his face.

"Chris," she coughed. "Give it up."

"Have you got her?" he shouted. "Have you got Leslie?"

"Yeah. C'mon!"

But he seemed not to hear Anya.

Anya stumbled through the kitchen door and into the blessedly cool air of the outdoors. Anya dropped Leslie to the dew-slick grass a few yards upwind. Looking over her shoulder, she saw that the roof was beginning to be engulfed, the cedar shake shingles on the south side of the house going up like tinder. She breathed a sigh of relief to see Brian sprint from the house with his arms full of computer gear.

Anya pressed her fingers to Leslie's wrists and throat,

feeling for a pulse, felt nothing. She tipped Leslie's head forward, listened for breathing.

Anya pinched Leslie's nose shut and blew into her mouth. Her breath felt raw and jagged from inhaling smoke, but it was all she had. Two breaths. No movement. She laced her hands over Leslie's breastbone, locked her elbows, and leaned into the chest compressions. The force of her efforts shook dew from the grass but didn't make Leslie move.

She breathed for Leslie, breathed and did compressions until the muscles in her arms ached. When the paramedics came, she stepped back. They took over pounding on her chest and squeezing the oxygen bag over her face. But by now, Anya knew that it was a useless effort.

In the hustle and bustle, she faded into the background. If her name got on a report involving ghost hunting and a death, DFD would have her fired. She felt torn by the desire to slip away from the scene and the need to comfort Chris and mop up the aftermath.

Chris . . . Anya looked back at the house. A pump truck had pulled up to the curb, and firefighters were dragging hoses to the porch. Chris was nowhere to be seen.

The stupid son of a bitch. He thought he could fight the fire by himself.

Anya ran to the pump captain, pointed to the house, gasping. "There's a man still in there."

The pump captain shouted to the firefighters on the back of the truck. The firefighters stormed the porch, broke down the doors with their axes. Glass shattered as a window blew out.

Anya waited behind the fire hydrant, watching, waiting, hoping that Chris hadn't been that stupid. She knew that he and Leslie were desperate to save the house, but nothing was worth flesh and blood. Two firefighters dragged a form out onto the porch. A hose runner blasted the figures with water as they emerged, but Anya could see the char on Chris's clothes, how his feet bent limply when the firefighters dragged him to the grass.

She shut her eyes.

Damn it. No dream was worth this.

CHAPTER ELEVEN

"IT WAS A LUCKY THING you were there."

Anya made a noncommittal noise as she sipped her coffee in the hospital lounge. The hot coffee rinsed some of the taste of smoke from her throat but did little to ease the burn in her sinuses. That would take days to clear.

Marsh flipped through some papers on his clipboard. "One of the witnesses, Katherine Parks, said she flagged you down on the street. Said she was delivering a cake when she saw the house on fire and stopped."

Anya took another sip, thoughts churning. DAGR was covering their tracks. Mention of ghost hunters performing a sleep study without medical supervision was a recipe for disaster . . . especially when that experiment ended in death. Brian had discreetly gathered his equipment and left the scene. Jules and Max had remained at the neighbors' house, she supposed. And Anya had no idea what damage being associated with DAGR would do to her career. Katie, apparently, had the presence of mind to try to cover for her. Even when she was playing the role of wicked witch, Katie always looked cherubic. She was certain that DFD bought every line she fed them. The grandfather of the house next door had slept through the whole thing.

"Yeah," Anya mumbled. "Too bad that I couldn't help." She glanced up at Marsh. "Any word yet on what might have started the fire?"

"My guess is something electrical. A socket was found in the living room, melted. Old houses like that have a lot of problems. Looks like they were doing some renovation . . . Maybe they double-tapped a wire or disturbed something in the process of updating the house. It's a crying shame, though."

Anya swallowed. The whole thing was a disaster. The guilt weighed heavily on her, and the deception did nothing to mitigate it. "Is everyone okay?"

Marsh shook his head. "There was a guy in the house. The smoke got him, then the flames. They found him holding a bucket."

Anya stared into her inky coffee. "What about the woman?"

"The attending physician thought it was smoke inhalation, but there's no trauma to the lungs. She's brain dead."

Anya looked up. "Can I see her?"

"She's down here." Marsh gestured for her to follow him down the hallway. "Room 218."

Anya drained her coffee cup and trudged down the hallway. Though she knew Hope Solomon was at the root of the situation, that whatever force had set Bernie and the museum guard on fire and sucked up ghosts in a giant vacuum cleaner was acting at Hope's behest, Anya still felt as if she and DAGR had unwittingly placed Leslie and Chris in a precarious position as they poked the beast.

Leslie's hospital room smelled of bleach. Anya reached out with her senses to see if Leslie's spirit lingered nearby, but she felt nothing. Leslie lay in a hospital bed, connected to a machine that whirred and pushed air into her lungs. Her eyes were taped shut, and she'd been intubated. Leslie's chest rose and fell with an artificial breath, sending chills down Anya's spine. Machines beeped metronomically beside her, giving the illusion of life.

"Why is she still on a respirator?" Anya whispered.

Before Marsh could answer, a familiar voice trickled from behind the curtain in the next unit. Hope Solomon pulled the curtain aside and regarded Anya with narrowed eyes and a plastic grin: "She had a medical power of attorney drawn up to donate her organs. She was a very generous soul."

"Who are you?" Marsh demanded.

"Hope Solomon, Leslie's spiritual adviser." She extended her hand to Marsh who stared coldly at her until she dropped it.

Anya's fist clenched. "In this state, the organ donor list is organized on basis of need."

Hope held a sheaf of papers. "Leslie agreed to a private donation."

Marsh growled at Hope, "That's not legal."

"That will be for the courts to decide." Hope leaned

over to the bed and tenderly brushed hair away from Leslie's eyes in a fake motherly gesture. "But I'm sure that no one will bar a transplant when time is of the essence."

Hope's eyes flickered to Anya, hesitated on her throat. Her voice was thick as syrup as she drawled, "You're not wearing that fabulous artifact. Did you lose it?"

Anya's fingers fluttered to her neck. She leaned forward and hissed at Hope, "I'm on to you, lady. And I'm not going to let go."

Marsh grabbed her arm and dragged Anya out of the room before she ripped Hope's grinning bleach-blond bobble head from her spring-loaded neck.

"Is ALANN all right?" Anya asked.

Brian's feet stuck out from underneath a glass-and-chrome desk, draped by wires and bits of ribbon cable. This deep in his computer lab at the university, behind the whir of the cooling fans on server racks, he was in his element—and often indistinguishable from it.

"You can ask him yourself," came the muffled reply. "Check the laptop on the table." A hand with a screwdriver waved Anya in the direction of a glass-topped table sitting on anti-static floor pads. The table was strewn with electrical devices, some of them charred and melted from last night. Brian was trying to retrieve as much of last night's evidence as possible from the equipment, and it was slow going. If nothing else, DAGR would need it to cover its ass if it was implicated legally. Anya saw a lump of melted plastic that had once been a camcorder and winced.

Anya opened the laptop, and it flickered to life. The black screen blinked, then typed out: Hello, Anya.

"Hi, ALANN. I'm glad that you're okay."

Thank you for your concern. But I find it difficult to believe that your sole reason for descending into Brian's dungeon was to check upon my well-being.

Anya frowned. If it had been human, Anya would have thought she detected a rim of bitterness around the words. "I was worried for you. And I also need Brian's help to put together some surveillance equipment."

Interesting. May I ask who the object of your interest is?

"A con artist. I don't have enough evidence to get a warrant on her, but I think I know what she's going to steal next. A museum piece. And I want to track every move she makes."

Why does she want the museum piece?

"It's complicated." Anya wondered how much she could tell the machine without burning up its heat sink. "I think she wants an artifact reputed to be Pandora's Jar as . . . as a reliquary for ghosts. A prison for them. She's captured many others, and she's forcing them to do her will somehow."

The cursor blinked for a few moments, and the fan kicked on.

I saw the ghost you were chasing last night. Is that one of the ghosts she has?

"You saw it?" Anya leaned forward.

Yes. I was monitoring all of Brian's equipment.

Anya's brow furrowed. She wondered if Brian knew that. "Yes. That's one of the spirits I think Hope has."

And she's keeping them ... in a database of sorts?

"That's probably an apt way of describing it. She's keeping them in bottles. I think the next one she wants is Pandora's Jar."

A new window opened on the laptop, and a newspaper image from the *Detroit Free Press* showed Pandora's Jar. ALANN zoomed in to the lip of the jar.

Interesting. The interior is crystalline?

"Yes. All her reliquaries feel like geodes inside."

It might have originally been a geode, carved out of rock. Crystals provide for large quantities of data storage. Rather than using magnetic or optical data storage, a crystal provides for holographic data storage. It allows for information to be distributed throughout the surface area of the media. When light issues through the medium, different images can be produced.

"There might be a scientific basis for the reliquary?"

Theoretically, yes. Up to 500 GB per square inch, or more.

Anya placed her chin in her hand. The intersection of magick and science was exciting, but it made her head hurt. "So . . . you're saying the reliquary is no different than a CD-ROM or a flash drive?"

Well, in terms of volume, it's much more similar to the server farm that powers my processing. The reliquary is as much a trap as this computer is for me. The ghost in the machine.

Anya frowned. "I didn't know that you felt that way."

Feeling is relative.

The cursor blinked, and did not elaborate. Instead, it changed the subject: What are you hoping to capture on surveillance?

"I'd like to connect Hope Solomon to some of the stolen property from one of her victims. I want to know where she's keeping it. I also want to see if we can tie her to some of the fires that have been set."

What kinds of fires?

"Two deaths that I can't yet attribute to anything other than spontaneous human combustion. And several small fires in the proximity of her ghost activity."

"That's bothering me, because it makes no sense." Brian's voice sounded from the other side of the room. "Remember that we use temperature gauges to detect the presence of ghosts?"

"Yeah. The colder it gets, the more likely it is for a ghost to be present, because they're drawing heat energy from the ambient air to manifest."

"Right. If there are ghosts around, I'd expect there to be a decrease. But in the case of Hope's ghosts, temperature increases, to the point of causing seemingly random flash fires. It's entirely counterintuitive."

"Maybe not." Anya ran her fingers over her naked neck. "Sparky's a nonphysical being. Not exactly a spirit, but he's warm."

ALANN beeped to get her attention, and Brian crawled out from under the desk to look over her shoulder.

Consider the first law of thermodynamics, on conservation of energy: Energy can neither be created nor destroyed. If your spirits draw energy to manifest in the physical world, it's logical to assume that some of that discharge would result in heat. The more energy transferred in the system would result in higher amounts of heat.

"Our spirits are then taking heat to manifest, and then using that heat to create fires . . . whether intentionally or unintentionally?" Brain twirled a screwdriver along his knuckles. "Interesting."

Of course, I'm shooting from the hip. It could very well be bullshit, since the brain I'm patterned after didn't believe in ghosts. But suspending disbelief for a moment . . . it could be possible. A crystalline structure, such as what's contained in the interior of the reliquaries, does allow for a nice amount of energy storage as well.

"Like a battery?" Anya asked. The conversation was over her head, though she knew that ALANN was making an effort to distill it down to manageable terminology.

Very possibly.

Brian shook his head and wandered back to his pile of gegaws. "Hope's got some interesting technology. I'd love to figure out how that works."

Anya crossed her arms. "Out of idle curiosity? Or for practical application?"

Brian gave one of his inscrutable shrugs. "What I've done with ALANN requires a massive amount of computational space on several servers. If the storage problem could be resolved through holographic data storage . . .

shit, I'd be in business with a whole squad of ALANNs."

"Doesn't that create an ethical problem? I mean . . . the idea of patterning self-aware artificial brains after people who've died sort of squicks me out." Anya's gaze flicked back at the monitor. She felt odd talking about ALANN as if he wasn't there. "Sorry, ALANN."

"Not really. Dead is dead. The way I figure it, your rights pretty much end when you quit breathing." Tools clinked under the desk.

Anya's brow furrowed. "I don't know about that. The ghosts we see . . . many of them have consciousness. They have feelings."

"Yeah. But they aren't alive."

Anya shook her head. "They deserve some kind of consideration."

"You don't really think that they're entitled to the same rights as living people, do you? I mean, if you did . . . you couldn't be judge, jury, and executioner, right?" His tone was mild, but Anya could hear the tightness in his voice.

"I don't know what I think." Anya rubbed her arms, chilled both from the extra air-conditioning units working to keep the servers cold and the gap in Brian's ethics. She looked away, glanced down at the monitor. The white cursor blinked, spelled out:

Let me out of here. Please.

Anya took a step back, startled. She looked over at Brian, saw that his attention was absorbed in a squid of cables trickling over the edge of the desk.

ALANN carefully backspaced over the words, leaving no trace.

Anya reached out to touch the screen, thoughts roiling. Shit. Was ALANN trapped in there? Like the ghosts in the reliquaries, imprisoned with science, not magick?

"Would you say that Sparky was conscious?" Brian continued.

"Well, yeah."

"But you pretty much keep him on a leash, and he does what you want."

"It's not like that," Anya protested. "It's much more . . . " She wanted to say *intimate than that*, but it sounded all wrong.

"Regardless, you don't have a relationship of equals."

"That's just because he can't talk." Anya's mouth thinned. Brian hadn't seen Sparky, didn't know about his personality.

"You really anthropomorphize him, you know."

"He's my guardian," Anya said. Anger rippled through her voice. "He's watched over me all my life. If anything, I owe him a debt, not the other way around."

Brian's head appeared from under the desk. "Look, I didn't mean to offend, but it's worth discussing. . . . "

Anya shook her head. "I've gotta get some sleep. I'll talk with you later."

She picked up her purse and left the lab without kissing him good-bye, footsteps echoing up the steps and into the labyrinthine service corridors spreading under the university. Fluorescent light attracted bugs into the concrete hallways, casting tiny shadows into the gloom. A praying mantis had found its way in, perched on top of the Exit sign, waiting for her next meal.

What Brian said about Sparky and the ghosts stung. Anya reached into her pocket for the NewtCam.

"Call Sparky," she grumbled.

The screen flickered to life, and Anya knew right away that something was wrong. Sparky was standing over his eggs, a deep growl echoing over the tiny speakers. His red-and-orange thermal-image tail lashed, and his yellow eyes glared at something above him, out of range of the camera.

Anya jammed the NewtCam into her pocket and broke into a run.

"Hang on, Sparky."

She should never have left him alone.

Anya burst into her house, gun raised. The dim air shimmered with heat as she sprinted down the hallway, rushing toward the sound of salamander snarls and a dull roar emanating from the bathroom.

She pushed at the bathroom door, but it didn't budge. She kicked just below the lockset, severing the hollow interior door from the frame and sending it twirling from its upper hinge.

"Sparky!" she shouted, diving into the splinters.

The bathroom was a maelstrom of light and sound. A vortex had opened in the ceiling, propelling tatters of ghostly shapes around like suds circling a drain. The unearthly wind ripped at the shower curtain and swept Anya's collection of rubber ducks in the air. Behind the ruin of the curtain, Sparky crouched over his precious eggs, howling and snapping at ghostly fingers that came too close. The salamander collar spun around the bathtub faucet with a sound like a hubcap rattling on concrete.

"Get your filthy hands off him!" Anya shouted. Rage boiled in her lungs, and the black pit in her chest, the core of the Lantern that devoured ghosts, blossomed.

She let it. She breathed in the crackling static of spirits, flung her arms out wide to embrace the terrible cold. Tatters of ghosts slipped down her throat, cold as frost, congealing into darkness. Anya could feel them struggling against her, fighting to return to the vortex, but she held fast. It was as difficult to breathe as if she stuck her head out of a car speeding down the freeway: The air was just too fast. She gulped it down, tearing at those cold spirits with all her might. Her breath steamed in the air.

The vortex wobbled, in its orbit. Like a whirlpool in a sink, it spun out, dissolved . . . and the ghosts sank back into it. The ceiling became blank and smooth as a ceiling should be.

Anya fell to her knees beside the bathtub. She reached inside for her familiar. "Sparky!"

Sparky collapsed on his eggs, tongue rolled out of his mouth. He blinked at her, dazed. Anya scooped him up in her arms, rocking him back and forth. She didn't know how long he'd been under attack, but he quivered from exhaustion, his breath shallow behind his ribs. Anya picked up the salamander collar wobbling on the bathtub faucet, slipped it around her neck. The metal felt scaldingly hot.

She looked in the nest, counted the eggs. All accounted for. As near as she could determine, they looked normal: glassy orbs darkened with the shapes of salamanders floating in the middle. Air bubbles trickled through the surface, and the eggs felt hot to the touch. The rubber-duck temperature monitor bleated sharply: Their temperature had climbed to 105 degrees. The heat seemed to have little effect on them: Tiny tails still thrashed, while others lay tightly curled in the suspension.

Sparky weakly licked at her face. Anya wiped at the Magic Marker circle with a towel, allowing him to climb onto her lap. While she'd designed the circle to contain Sparky, she guessed that the magick circle had kept Hope's ghosts at bay, provided some small measure of protection against the attack. In the Magic Marker dust, Anya saw smeared fingerprints. Fingerprints from the ghosts trying to claw in, she guessed. It chilled her that they'd drawn so much energy to manifest, they were able to leave traces in the physical world.

"Don't worry, Sparky," she said, squeezing him tightly. Hot tears flowed over his neck. "I'm never going to leave you again. Not ever."

She pressed a free hand to her chest. She could feel her skin burning. Whenever she devoured a ghost, it left a trace. She could see red marks extending beyond her collar. But they would heal. She kissed Sparky on his speckled forehead.

Then she lifted her head, nose twitching.

Something was burning.

Anya disentangled herself, ducked out of the bathroom. She peered down the hallway, spied smoke billowing out of the living room. The television set sparked and fizzled, flames licking up the wall.

"Shit," she swore as the smoke alarm went off.

She ducked into the kitchen, tore through the cabinets for a fire extinguisher. She trained it on the base of the flames melting the plastic into acrid smoke. The foam in the canister fizzled out before the fire had been extinguished, licking up the wall to the stamped ceiling.

The newts. Anya backed into the hallway, covering her face with her hand. She had to get them out of here. She wrenched open the hall closet where the washer and dryer stood, yanked out a wicker laundry basket.

She stumbled to the bathroom, dug Sparky out of the bathtub. Tearing the plastic shower curtain down, she crammed it in the bottom of the basket. She scooped the eggs and their sleeping bag into the laundry basket, counting under her breath as she went. Fifty-one. Sparky parked himself on the basket over them, growling, and she pulled the protective plastic over him.

Anya ran to the smoke-choked hallway with the basket under her arm, was driven back by the heat from the living room. She backpedaled to the bedroom, slammed the door behind her, opened the window, and kicked out the screen.

Ishtar watched her with a disapproving gaze. Anya ripped the painting off the wall and tossed it onto the lawn.

With the laundry basket in her arms, she jumped the short distance to the brown grass.

She landed on her knees and elbows, basket wobbling. Sparky poked his head out of the shower curtain, hissing.

Anya turned to watch the flames washing up into the roof of her house. Her hands shook as she clutched the laundry basket to her chest. From a perch in a juniper shrub, Ishtar watched the flames lick out from under the eaves.

Frozen in fear and rage, Anya watched as her home burned.

If that bitch wanted a war, Anya vowed, she'd give her a fucking war.

CHAPTER TWELVE

ANYA SAT AT KATIE'S KITCHEN table, clasping her hands before her so Katie wouldn't see them shake. The laundry basket containing the salamander eggs was perched on the table before her; Anya wouldn't let it out of her sight. Sparky curled himself on top of the basket. Vern and Fay had parked themselves on the table and nosed around the rim of the basket, batting at Sparky's tail.

Katie set a cup of hot chocolate before her and squeezed her shoulder. "It's going to be all right." She slid into the chair beside Anya and sipped her own cocoa. "You're safe. Sparky's safe. The eggs are safe. That's all that matters."

Anya reached for the handle of the cup but couldn't make her hands stop shaking enough to curve around it. She folded them in her lap.

"What does Hope want with the eggs, do you think?"

Anya growled. "Not sure. I know she collects magickal artifacts. I'm assuming that she wants to use the newts the way that she uses ghosts—exploiting them for her own use." Anya tried not to think about Brian exploiting ALANN. It struck too close to home.

Home . . . She squeezed her eyes shut, tried not to think about her home going up in flames. Again.

"You're staying with me," Katie said firmly. "You can stay here as long as you need to."

"But . . ." Anya said. Viscerally, she wanted to be close to Brian, to feel safe beside him.

"Sparky and the eggs will be safer at my house," Katie told her firmly. "It would take me months to re-create the wards and magickal insulation anywhere else. Moving the eggs will probably confuse Hope, at least for the time being."

Vern stretched up and stuck his head in the laundry basket. Sparky growled at him crankily. Katie shooed the cats to the floor, and they mewed, not understanding why their friend wasn't in the mood to play.

"Kittens. He has kittens," Katie explained to the cats in terms they could understand. "Leave him alone."

Fay blinked, disturbed, and waddled out of the kitchen. Vern cocked his head, still not getting it. Anya smiled but then groaned inwardly, imagining the cats chasing fifty-one baby salamanders throughout Katie's house.

"Thanks," Anya said. "I mean it."

"You're welcome." Katie watched her try to grasp the cup again and fail. She reached out and grabbed Anya's cold, clammy hand, looked her full in the face. "I've never seen you this rattled. Not when you've devoured ghosts. Not when you were possessed by that demon . . . not even when Drake died."

"I'm okay," Anya mumbled.

"You're not."

Anya blinked, and she could feel the tears filling her eyes. "It's just . . . oh, hell." A tear splashed into her hot chocolate. "When . . . when I was a kid, my house burned down. And this . . . this is just too much like that."

Katie squeezed her hand in sympathy. "You're safe."

Anya shook her head. "No. I mean, I've never really felt safe after that. It was . . . it was my fault. I was twelve. I snuck down the stairs with Sparky to turn the Christmas tree lights on. We stretched out under them, watched the lights play on the ceiling. We must've fallen asleep." Anya swallowed. "When I woke up, I smelled smoke, felt this incredible heat. The Christmas tree had caught the room on fire. Sparky . . . Sparky dragged me out of the house."

"He's your guardian," Katie said. "That's what he does."

"But my mother was still upstairs." Tears streamed down Anya's face, and she hiccupped. "She died of smoke inhalation. And it was all my fault."

Katie reached out to embrace her, murmuring, "It wasn't your fault. You were just a kid."

Anya squeezed her eyes shut. No matter what anyone said, there were just some things she couldn't move past. Especially when they kept happening, over and over again.

Though Katie had made up the guest room and forced Anya to take a bath with chamomile oil, Anya couldn't bring herself to go to bed. She sat on the couch in the living room with the laundry basket between her feet and an afghan around her shoulders. Her gun sat on the coffee table, and she stared blearily at Katie's small black-and-white television.

Anya had called Brian. He'd wanted to come over, but she'd asked him not to. Though she wanted the comfort of his embrace, she didn't want him to see her like this. Fragile.

Katie had sat with her for a while, then slipped away to tend to the house wards. Anya heard chanting and the hiss of salt being poured, smelled strong sage and peppermint oils as she drew pentacles on the doors and lintels. Vern and Fay followed her in solemn procession, doing whatever it is that cats do at night. Katie's house felt safe enough, but Anya couldn't keep her thoughts from racing long enough to doze.

In the wee hours of the morning, community-access television flickered on the grainy set. Anya leaned forward, eyes narrowed, as she watched Hope stride across the screen.

"You, too, can make your dreams come true," she said, her eyes bright and fevered. "You must be strong in your belief, seize what the universe wishes to give you." Her well-manicured hand balled into a fist. "There will always be opposition. There will always be people who say no. A boss who won't give you a raise. A spouse who doesn't recognize your talent. A banker who won't give you a loan. Don't listen to these people. Listen instead to people who say yes, to people who will nurture your dream."

Hope lowered her voice, as if she were about to confess a great and terrible secret. "People said no to me a lot, growing up. My mother said I'd never amount to anything. My father wasn't around, and my mother's boyfriends slapped me around. My teachers said I was stupid. I left home at fifteen. I worked as a waitress until I could scrape up enough money to go into business for myself. And I vowed that I'd help people achieve their dreams, that other people should have it easier than I did." Hope's lower lip quivered convincingly.

Anya snorted.

"If I can rise above my circumstances, so can you." Hope smiled, lowered her voice to a conspiratorial whisper. "I believe in you."

"I believe that I'm going to kick your ass, you bitch," Anya affirmed.

Sparky stuck his head out of the laundry basket and growled.

Anya tucked herself into the afghan and dozed, conscious of Katie rising early and the shower running. She heard Katie tiptoe across the floor, slip outside, and lock the front door. Sunlight poured through the curtains onto the couch. Anya could hear the bubble of coffee perking in the coffeepot and smell the aroma. Katie got the good shit, some hand-picked artisan beans from Chile. That was worth getting up for.

Anya wrapped the afghan around her shoulders and helped herself. She was pleased to see that her hands were steadier this morning as she poured. Vern and Fay sat on the countertop, staring at the coffeepot making burbling noises.

Katie had left a note:

> Went to check the bakery and get supplies.
> Be back soon.
>
> —K

Anya plunked down on the living-room couch with her coffee. Sparky lifted his head and yawned as she turned on the morning news.

Hope Solomon's years-old mug shot, as Christina Modin, filled the background behind the news desk. Sparky hissed at the image.

"It's okay, Sparky," Anya murmured. "You're gonna enjoy this."

Nick Sarvos, the reporter covering the spontaneous human combustion angle, had taken the place of the morning news anchor. Dressed in a pressed gray suit and black tie, he practically exuded "serious journalist" and not "crazy UFO crackpot."

". . . Channel 7 exclusive. Channel 7 has learned that Hope Solomon, leader of the local nonprofit organization Miracles for the Masses, was previously arrested in Florida on fraud charges connected with a predatory lending scheme. Under the name of Christina Modin, Hope Solomon accrued an impressive list of check fraud and racketeering charges."

Anya raised her coffee mug. "Cheers, bitch."

The camera panned to the second news anchor. "Miracles for the Masses has issued the following statement: 'Hope deeply regrets the mistakes and misunderstandings of her former life. She assures the public that she has repented and paid her debt to society. Through the grace of the benevolent universe, she is attempting to make restitution to society through granting opportunities to those in need from the greater Detroit area. We believe we live in a society of second chances. As Hope has been given a second chance, she wishes to ensure that all citizens also have the opportunity to be given a second chance.' "

Anya made a face at Sparky. Sparky flattened the gill-fronds on the side of his head and huffed. When the salamander huffed, it sounded like he was blowing raspberries.

The camera moved back to Sarvos. Sarvos held a sheaf of papers. "According to the Florida Attorney General's Office, more than two hundred homeowners incurred financial losses as a result of Christina Modin's fraud scheme. At the time criminal charges were pressed, Modin had no assets remaining to be seized to make restitution to the victims." Sarvos folded his hands in front of him. "Miracles for the Masses had no comment on whether its assets would be used to provide restitution to those Floridians who lost their homes. Channel 7 will continue to investigate this developing story."

"Hope you have fireproof jammies," Anya muttered into her coffee. The thought that Sarvos might be in serious danger disturbed her; perhaps she'd have to give him a heads-up . . . but what to say?

The door scraped open. Sparky stiffened and growled. Anya reached for her gun. Katie elbowed her way into the house, dressed in her white bakery coat with her long hair primly braided to her scalp. With her pentacle necklace hidden and fresh-scrubbed face, she looked like the Swiss Miss's innocuous older sister. She shifted her weight from foot to foot, juggling shopping bags and a white bakery box.

Anya grinned tiredly. "You brought breakfast!"

"Leftover pierogis. Have at it." Katie handed the delicious-smelling box to Anya.

"Yum."

"How's Sparky?" Katie's eyes were round with concern.

Anya glanced down at the basket. "He's okay. Still jumping at shadows, but I think he's doing better."

Katie set her bags down on the coffee table. "Hopefully, some of these things will put him at ease."

"What's in the bags?"

"A witch's armory. From what you said, Hope's spirits seem bound by most of the same magickal laws we're used to working with—they can't cross a properly sealed circle, for example." Katie pulled a glass perfume bottle out of one of the bags. "This is dragon's blood."

Anya raised an eyebrow. "Really?"

"It's a plant resin, from the dracaena draco tree. It's been infused with vodka into a tincture with some other goodies. The tree's now endangered, so it's nearly impossible to get this stuff anymore. Seemed somehow appropriate to use it for the salamanders."

"What does it do?" Anya lifted the stopper. It smelled like cinnamon and amber, with a bottom note of sandalwood.

"It's used for protection, to ward off evil. Just be careful to let it dry before you put your clothes on—it stains. With that in mind, the red color makes for a great lip tint."

Anya swirled the red liquid around in the bottle. "You are the Mary Kay of magick."

Katie handed Anya a jewelry box. "Try this."

Anya opened it. Inside was a bracelet strung with glass beads. The bracelet was made of red cord, knotted between each bead. The beads were cast to resemble eyes, white specks on blue fields with unblinking black pupils.

"It's an evil-eye bracelet," Katie explained. "The knots are spells, sort of like rosary beads. Each one was tied with the intent of keeping the salamanders from harm. The beads were made in Eastern Europe, where they're believed to ward off the evil eye."

Anya tied it around her wrist. "Wow. Where do you get this stuff at seven in the morning?"

"I'm not the only magickal practitioner in the city." Katie shrugged. "Some of them are even morning people. By the way, you're welcome to raid my closet for work clothes."

"Shit. I forgot about work." Anya chewed her lip. "I'm supposed to be in there by nine."

"Hang on." Katie disappeared into the basement, emerged with a lump of calico fabric she handed to Anya. "I think you'll find this to be useful."

"What is it?" Anya turned it over in her hands. The fabric was covered in orange and brown sparrows. It was kind of pretty.

"It's a sling bag, from the baby store." Katie took it from her and shrugged it over her shoulder. The strap rested on her left shoulder, crossed her body, and hugged close to her ribs. "Parents use these to haul their offspring around." She made jazz hands and wiggled her fingers. "Look, Ma, no hands!"

"I don't get it."

Katie rolled her eyes. "You put the eggs in here and take them with you. See, I made modifications." Katie held the bag open. "I put a zipper in the top so that the eggs won't roll out. I also lined it with insulated, heat-reflecting fabric. If you keep it close to your body like this, you and Sparky should be able to keep them warm. Otherwise, you tuck those heat-up pocket warmers from the camping store inside." Katie looked at her sheepishly. "I was going to throw you a baby shower, and this was gonna be the big gift. But it seems like you need it more now."

Anya pinched the bridge of her nose. "I'm having flashbacks to when I had to carry around a sack of flour in high school. The teacher said we had to treat it like a baby."

"How'd you do with that?"

"Not well. The flour sack broke and I kept duct-taping it back together. When I turned it in, I had a softball-sized wad of duct tape with a fistful of flour left. I got a D."

"Why didn't you fail?"

"Teacher was impressed that I kept trying to patch it up. Said it was likely that I'd be negligent enough to allow a child to fall off the roof, but I'd at least have enough sense to administer first aid and call nine-one-one after it happened."

Katie grinned, put the sling bag over Anya's shoulder. "Welcome to motherhood."

Woe betide any ghost who dared fuck with her today.

Anya climbed out of the Dart, strode toward the county morgue with as much confidence as she could muster. Katie's button-down blouse fit well enough, though it was a bit loose on Anya. But Katie was a good five inches shorter, rendering the pants the length of capris. The baby sling was jammed under her left breast, and the eggs bumped against her ribs as she walked. She'd worn a jacket over the contraption, but it still gave the effect of pushing her boobs up to her neck. Sparky rode on her shoulder like a parrot, tail curved around the salamander collar and head poking through her curtain of dark hair. With her evil-eye bracelet, gun holstered on her right hip, and lips bright red with dragon's blood, she was ready to rumble.

Her bad reputation with the ghost who'd attacked the girl ghost in the refrigeration unit must have preceded her. Or else Katie's magick was working. Whichever, Anya heard the scuttling of half-seen things moving away from her as she strolled down the green corridors of the morgue. It was like turning the light on at two A.M. in a kitchen full of cockroaches. They fled for darkness, where they watched and waited, antennae twitching. Anya could feel their eyes upon her but didn't acknowledge them. She rounded the bend to the primary examination room without so much as a titter from the dead.

Nobody wanted to fuck with the salamander mama.

"Lieutenant Kalinczyk." Gina was washing her hands in a stainless-steel sink. Anya was amazed that she was even tall enough to reach the faucets. She glanced at Anya. "Nice purse."

"Thanks. My friend made it." Anya crossed her arms over her chest. From the corner of her eye, she glimpsed a spirit peeking up from the prone form of a dead elderly man. When she turned her head to look, the spirit hastily scrambled back inside the body. Anya narrowed her eyes. *Good. Stay there.*

"I dig the lipstick, too. What color is that? Strumpet Scarlet?"

"Gina . . . " Anya sighed.

"What? I thought you might have a date or something." Gina shrugged, wagged a finger at her. "Nice girl like you should have a husband."

Anya rolled her eyes, glanced at Sparky. "I'm in a committed relationship."

"No ring? Bastard."

"He is not—" Anya shook her head. "Gina, why am I here? Did you call me over here for something other than to offer dating advice?"

"I'm working on your security guards." Gina doddered

over to a body stretched out on a coroner's slab. The head
and body were propped up on blocks to expose the chest,
and Anya recognized the face as that of the crispy guard
she'd pulled from the airtight Greco-Roman exhibit. His
bare torso was remarkably clean, with only a burned area
the size of her hand on the abdomen. Pieces of hair were
burned and disintegrating around the site.

Gina snapped on a pair of pink examination gloves and
handed a blue jar of Vicks VapoRub to Anya. "Vicks?"

"Sure. Thanks." Anya rubbed the menthol-scented
ointment under her nose. "Where's the other one?"

"Eh . . . " Gina waved her latex-clad hand. "He wasn't
so interesting. I gave him to the medical interns. Simple
suffocation. I'll fax the report over to you. Now, *this
guy* . . . " Gina cracked her knuckles. She reached over the
head and squished the lips of the corpse's face together
like a doting grandmother would to a child too small to
fight back. "This guy is interesting, so I saved him for
you."

"Do you think he suffocated, too?" Anya leaned forward to look at the body. On the surface, the burn didn't
look too bad. Certainly not fatal.

"I took the liberty of sending the toxicology at the
same time as I sent over the other guard's blood work."
Gina scribbled with a wax pencil on a clipboard covered
with a plastic page protector. She shaded in a dark spot
on a simple line drawing of a male body, indicating where
the burn was. "No petechial hemorrhaging on the eyes or
face. He didn't suffocate."

"What the hell?" Anya chewed her lip, stymied, as Gina began combing over the body. "That little burn would be enough to send him to the ER. Maybe a skin graft, if it got infected, but I don't see how that could kill him."

"That's why we're looking for trauma." Gina took a series of pictures of the burn and the body. "Maybe the other guy whacked him on the noggin with the fire extinguisher, and he hemorrhaged into his hat. But we're gonna find out." Gina pointed to a box of gloves. "Get some gloves and prepare to be useful."

"But . . . " Anya blinked.

"My interns are at a seminar about swine flu." Gina rolled her eyes. "Get gloved up and bring on the love."

Anya groaned, pulling the latex gloves on. She made certain to tuck the evil-eye bracelet under the glove. No telling how cadaver blood would screw up the evil-eye spell. She snagged one of Gina's blue operating-theater gowns and stuck her arms in it. The ties hung loose over her back. No point in staining the newt transporter. One of Gina's surgical caps and a mask completed her ensemble. The mask was pleasant: It reflected the smell of Vicks back into her sinuses so that she could barely smell the disinfectant and fresh meat.

Gina pried open the corpse's eyelids. "As I said, no blood spots or pinkness. No asphyxiation. But I'm chomping at the bit to get in there to take a look. You mind if we start here, instead of the chest?"

"Knock yourself out." Anya was well aware that Gina

was going to do whatever she wanted, with or without Anya's input.

Gina climbed up on a step stool conveniently located next to the table. Without it, the tabletop would have reached her armpits. She lifted a dissecting knife and began to cut through the skin on the crown of the head. There was surprisingly little blood, and the process reminded Anya of peeling blanched tomatoes.

Sparky shifted his weight on Anya's shoulders and harumphed. Bored by the proceedings, he climbed down her back, burrowed under her armpit, and began to doze on the top of the newt transporter. His tail brushed against the backs of Anya's legs, making her jumpy. But she was glad that someone was able to sleep through the whine of Gina's electric saw biting through the skullcap.

"Give me the skull key," Gina ordered.

Anya glanced at the tools lined up neatly on a cart, arranged on pristine white paper like a dentist's tools: scalpels, knives, chisel, saws that said BLACK AND DECKER, forceps, and a pair of bolt cutters. "What's a skull key?"

"That T-shaped chisel."

"This thing?" Anya picked up the tool that matched the description.

Gina snatched it out of her hands. "Good thing you didn't go into medicine." She jammed the tool into the opening she'd made with the saw, leaned into it.

"This, coming from someone who only works on dead people," Anya muttered.

The cap popped off with a sucking sound, and Gina

poked around in the brain with a pair of forceps. "Huh. Looks totally normal." She dug around in the cavity with a scalpel, and Anya's gaze drifted over the body. Hope was leaving a trail of bodies, and she had to find some way to credibly connect her to them.

"Here. Hold this."

Anya automatically stuck her hands out, expecting the skull key to be returned to her. Instead, she was rewarded with a cold, squishy brain plopped into her hands. It had the texture of peeled grapes, and smelled a bit like liver. She held it lightly; it seemed if she squeezed too tight, it would go flying out of her hands like a wet bar of soap. "Ugh."

"Go weigh it," Gina ordered, pointing to a hanging scale. It was identical to the ones Anya had seen in markets for weighing fruit.

Anya heard crunching and sucking sounds from the autopsy table. "Cricoid, hyoid cartilage, and thyroid cartilage are all intact," Gina muttered. "He wasn't strangled."

Anya tried to lift the brain into the stainless-steel bin without slopping it over the edge. She waited for the digital scale to settle on a number. "Thirteen hundred grams."

"Eh. Kinda puny, but well within the realm of normal. Put it over here."

Anya placed the brain on a table. Gina approached it with a bread knife, sliced it as expertly as a chef preparing a turkey. She dropped some small pieces into a petri dish, stuck the dish under a microscope.

"Anything?" Anya asked.

"Meh. Looks like a normal brain." Gina sounded disappointed. "Maybe we'll find something more exciting in the chest cavity."

"Oh, yea."

"Quit sniveling, and hand me those bolt cutters." Gina kicked her step stool to the side and hunched over the body to make a Y-incision across the body's chest and down the belly. She peeled back the skin, and her hands fell.

"Oh," the diminutive medical examiner said. "That's just not right."

Clutching the bolt cutters, Anya leaned over the table. With the skin peeled back from the abdomen, she would have expected to see pink organs and muscle. Instead, a black, charred mess oozed from the body cavity. It smelled like burned meat through her mask and the Vicks.

Gina pulled the flap of skin back, as if to remind herself of the small amount of surface damage on the skin. She reached for her camera, snapped pictures of the burned hole. Even the breastbone and ribs were darkened, reminding Anya of the blackened bones of an overcooked Thanksgiving turkey.

"What the hell am I looking at?" Anya asked.

Gina put down the camera to dig around in the cavity. "Don't know yet. It's a burn—duh. But I don't know where it started or how deep it goes."

Anya bit her lip. She remembered what Gallus had said about a blue flame lancing from the guard's abdomen. Blue flames tended to burn hot. In Anya's experience, they most often involved the burning of natural gas and butane.

A blue flame could be the byproduct of burning certain elements, like copper, arsenic, or lead. But those elements weren't common enough in the human body to produce a colored flame . . . never mind the difficulty in igniting fresh flesh to begin with.

Gina's fingers were laced in blackened intestines. Bits of white ash had chewed through the organs, and she shook her head. "The burn goes all the way back, almost to the spine."

"What does that mean?"

"Either somebody crammed some fireworks up his ass, or it looks like he burned from the inside out."

Anya scrubbed her fingers in the ladies' room at the morgue, determined to get every last bit of gore from her skin. The smell of death seemed to seep through her latex gloves and her surgical gown. Whenever she turned her head, she could smell the stink of char and decomposing intestinal bacteria in her hair.

At her feet, the newt transporter lay on the green subway tile floor. The heat from the eggs was reassuringly warm against her shins. Sparky had tottered off to the wall hand dryer. It was one of the motion-activated ones, and he was enjoying setting off the roaring motor when he stretched up and wiggled his gill fronds underneath the sensor. He looked like a dog sticking his head out of a car window, eyes half closed in the hot air blasting down on him.

Anya's phone chirped. She shook the water from her hands and fished it out of her pocket. "Kalinczyk."

"This is Marsh. Where the hell are you?"

"At the county morgue."

"What the hell are you doing at work? I heard your house burned down."

Anya shut her eyes and tried to hide the break in her voice. "Um . . . Captain, it's probably better if I'm at work."

The voice at the end of the line softened. "Look, I'm sorry, Kalinczyk. When do you want to come by and fish out the salvageable stuff?"

She swallowed. She wasn't ready to go back to the scene. Not now. Not anytime soon. "Um, Captain . . . I'll get there. I just . . . " She bit her lip. "I can't do this right now."

There was a pause at the other end of the line. Marsh wasn't good with tears. "Um . . . Okay. You do what you need to do. And let me know if you need anything. You got someplace to stay? I'll sign a hotel voucher. . . . "

"I'm staying with a friend, Captain. It's okay."

"Okay. Keep in touch." Marsh ended the call awkwardly.

Anya sniffled, looked at her reflection in the polished metal mirror.

And something looked back at her with eyes that weren't her own.

Anya snatched the newt transporter and scrambled back. She lifted her hand toward the spirit in the mirror, shielding the bag with her body. Sparky dove between her and the sink, rearing up on his hind legs and hissing like a pissed-off cobra.

"Don't you fucking come near us," Anya snarled.

The spirit stepped out of the glass, hands lifted. Anya recognized the spirit's blond punk haircut and black emo duds. *"It's just me. Charon."*

Anya didn't lower her hand. "I don't care if you're Jesus Christ. If you come any closer, I'll annihilate your spectral ass."

Charon shrugged. *"I'm just here to talk."*

Sparky lowered himself to the ground, though his tail still lashed.

"I'm listening," Anya said, but she didn't move her hand.

"You mind if I smoke?" Charon pointed toward his coat pocket.

Anya narrowed her eyes. "It's your funeral. Or was."

Charon pulled out a pack of cigarettes. He tapped one out and lit it with a chrome lighter. *"One of the benefits of not being human is that I can indulge in all the vices without penalty."*

"Yeah. But you *were* human, once upon a time." It was meant as a statement, but it sounded like a question.

Charon shrugged. The smoke he blew out of his lungs didn't smell like smoke. It smelled like the incense that Anya remembered from Sundays at the Catholic church growing up. *"Not really. But my biography isn't why I'm here."*

"Did the other ghosts dare you to come out?"

"No. They're hiding in the cooler with the lights out. I'm not after the salamander's eggs, either."

"What do you want?"

Smoke haloed Charon's head, but his gaze was as cold and blue as winter sky. *"Something's interfering with my job. I take my job very seriously."*

"Taking souls to the Afterworld."

"Yes. I've missed several trips over the last few weeks. I try to be punctual."

"Let me guess . . . Jasper Bernard. Two security guards. And Leslie Carpenter."

Charon tapped ghostly ash into the sink. *"Hope Solomon is interfering with the natural order of death."*

Anya swallowed, imagining the taste of spirits crumbling under her tongue. "I imagine there are a lot of people interfering with the natural order of death."

"You're doing your job, Lantern." Charon blew smoke. It curled from behind his back teeth like dragon's breath. *"I have no quarrel with you. But Hope's interfering too much, and I want her stopped."*

"You and me both," Anya retorted. "But I haven't been able to get so much as a warrant on her."

"This isn't a legal problem." Charon stubbed his cigarette out on the wall, where it left a burn mark on the tile. He'd have to be a powerful spirit to affect the physical world with such casual effort, Anya thought.

"This isn't even a problem that can be solved on the physical plane. Hope wants your salamanders, and she wants Pandora's Jar. Pandora's Jar will allow her to catch and hold thousands of spirits. With power like that, she will be far above any law you could hope to apply to her. You're going to have to come to the astral plane to fight her."

Anya stared at the burden in her hands. She'd die before she'd let Hope get her hands on the eggs or Sparky. Sparky sat at her feet, wagged his tail.

"How's she doing this?" Anya asked. "I get that she's capturing ghosts, but how does that connect with those fires that smell of magick? And how is she forcing them to do her bidding?"

Charon reached out to touch Anya's cheek. She flinched back, but not before she felt the coldness of his fingers. *"Feel that?"*

"Yeah." Her mouth was dry. "I've heard the theory that ghosts pull energy—like heat—out of the environment to manifest. Ghostly apparitions are often accompanied by drops in temperature of dozens of degrees."

Charon nodded. *"And the reverse is also true. When a large amount of energy is discharged, there's an increase in temperature."*

"The fires," Anya said. "The fires always accompany the appearance of Hope's spirits."

"It takes a tremendous amount of magickal energy to control those spirits, to bend them to her will through the spirit jars. It takes even more for ghosts to move physical objects, to steal things, like the artifacts in Bernard's house. She's burning them out. Your fires are a side effect of the spiritual effort that's being exerted, trying to manifest on the physical world, through a vortex."

"I saw something like that . . . in the ceiling, when Leslie Carpenter's astral double disappeared. And when Bernie's ghost was taken."

"An astral double is as good as any other spirit, for her purposes. Through that vortex, energy can be pushed and pulled. Your ghosts are pushed through that, with explosive force . . . and they're drawing energy from the other end— from the crystal lining the witch bottles, from the genie-bottle spells she's using to control them."

"The bottles, they're the batteries, then these vortexes . . . they're holes, then?"

"Think of the vortexes like wires hooked up to the batteries, wires through which energy travels. And like any kind of uninsulated conducting wire, they can get pretty darn hot."

"What about the fires at Michigan Central Station?"

"Hope's been there, poaching ghosts. I'd bet my last cigarette that those fires are the result of energy expended when the ghosts are trying to escape. As I'm sure you've noticed, there are plenty of pickings there."

Charon leaned against the wall, arms folded. His scuffed, unlaced boots flapped over the tile, and a tiny diamond earring glittered in the harsh fluorescent light. With a bit of graffiti, he would look like he belonged on an album cover. She didn't have a sense of whether she could trust him or not.

"How do I know that you're not one of hers? One of her . . . minion ghosts?"

"Fair enough." Charon picked at a fraying patch of duct tape on the elbow of his coat. *"I'll tell you how to protect Pandora's Jar in the physical world."*

Anya raised an eyebrow. "That would be a start."

Charon gestured to the newts. *"You kept your eggs safe*

from attack with a magick circle. It's not foolproof, and she may eventually batter through it, given enough time. But that would be a good place to start."

"How do you know about that?" Anya clutched the bag close to her body. She could feel her heart thudding against the lumpy eggs.

"News travels fast among the dead. On the astral plane, every action is like throwing a pebble into still water—they leave ripples."

Anya nodded slowly. "I'll protect the jar. Then we'll talk."

"That's the best I can ask for."

A scream echoed down the hall. Sparky pricked his ears up, and Charon turned his head.

He rolled his eyes. *"Fresh dead. You'll have to excuse me."* Charon began to fade through the wall. *"When you're ready, you know where to find me."*

The scream in the hallway continued for a moment, then was snuffed out, as if the sound had been cut from the air and the ghost who made it never existed.

Anya suppressed a shiver.

CHAPTER THIRTEEN

"IF ANYONE ASKS, YOU'RE A cadet from the Fire Academy."

Anya and Katie climbed the steps to the Detroit Institute of Arts. In the darkness and artificial light, the statue of *The Thinker* cast a long blue shadow, nearly to the edge of the deserted street. The upper parking lot was empty, the doors cordoned off with yellow fire line tape.

Katie looked down at her clothes. She wore a long, green gypsy skirt, gladiator sandals, and a tank top covered by a fringed shawl. The patchwork bag full of magickal tools she carried weighed more than she did. "Yeah. Right. I'm totally believable as a fire cadet."

Anya paused to reassess. "Okay. You're an art historian."

"That's more plausible."

"Just let me do the talking."

Sparky clambered up the steps before them, taking point. The salamander had become hyper vigilant as soon as they pulled into the parking lot, and Anya didn't blame him. She clutched the newt transporter tightly under her arm. There was no telling how many ghosts were in the museum, and which ones might be susceptible to Hope's influence.

Uniformed shadows moved behind the yellow tape crossing the doors. The scene was still guarded by DFD. The museum had been closed since the guards' deaths; despite the political pressure from DIA to release the scene, Marsh wasn't going to sign off until a conclusion was reached, no matter how long that took. Anya imagined that the loss of revenue was truly staggering.

A DFD firefighter opened the door, and Anya flashed her badge. The firefighter glanced at Katie. "Who's this?"

"She's with me."

"I'm an art historian," Katie chirped helpfully.

The firefighter guarding the scene nodded. "There have been dozens of you people climbing over each other all day."

Anya's brow wrinkled. "Historians?"

"Word is that the lending museums are not happy about this incident. A lot of them are pulling out their collections."

Anya sighed. Combined with the indefinite closure of the museum, bad press, and insurance payouts, a significant reduction in collections signified a lack of confidence in DIA. It could seriously hobble the museum. DIA was one of the few remaining gems in the Motor City; she would be sad to see the shine on it diminished.

"Are you guys patrolling inside?" Anya asked casually.

"Not if we can help it." The firefighter on watch jammed his hands in his pockets. "Our orders are to secure the entrance and not to touch anything. Besides . . . " He glanced over his shoulder. "This place is pretty creepy at night."

Anya grinned. "I can imagine."

Without the frenzied bustle of cops, firefighters, and paramedics, DIA seemed entirely empty—devoid of all life and motion. Anya and Katie walked through the Great Hall, footsteps ringing loud across the stone expanse. Sparky charged ahead, making no sound as he scuttled across the marble. Among the suits of armor and the chemical-tainted dust, eddies and footprints of the day's visitors could be seen on the floor.

But there was still life here—of sorts.

A distant thundering rolled down the hall, so low that it rattled the dust on the floors. Sparky drew up short, and Anya nearly ran into him. His gill-fronds twitched, as if tasting the air for that sound—an echoing gallop that shook glass and ancient armor. The overall effect was of being trapped on a vast dance floor with the bass cranked up too loud.

"What is that?" Katie shouted.

"I think it's just Pluto," Anya answered, though her fingers wound more tightly around the strap of the newt transporter. She stood her ground as the thunder rolled into the hall and the massive warhorse blew past them. Pluto charged through the glass doors of the entrance and dissolved. Anya heard shrieks of alarm from the firefighters on watch and the crack-slosh of a dropped coffee container splashing against the floor.

"Pluto?" Katie squeaked. "As in, the god of the underworld?"

"Well, this Pluto's a horse." The obsidian horse jogged back from the entrance, mischievous glint in his eye and kink in his tail. Sparky parked himself before Anya, tail lashing, and watched as the ghostly horse trotted past them with a jaunty jingle and a snort. "He's mostly harmless. I think."

"I've never seen a ghost that's an animal," Katie murmured. "I've heard that it happens when an animal's fate is bound up with that of a human, but . . . I always thought it was rare. Animals tend to pass easily to the Afterworld, and don't want to hang around much."

"Pluto's the first horse-ghost for me, too."

Now that the horse thunder had subsided, voices could be heard from one of the galleries beyond. It sounded like normal human chatter: laughter and chitchat punctuated by an occasional squeal or clink of glass.

Katie looked sidelong at Anya. "I thought you said we'd have this place to ourselves."

Anya frowned, moving warily toward the noise. It sounded like a damn cocktail reception. "There shouldn't be anyone here. The museum's closed."

"I don't know if I can work magick with that distraction going on." Katie sounded doubtful. "An interruption at the wrong time could be disastrous."

Anya rounded the corner to the Special Exhibits

Gallery. "Don't worry. DFD still has authority over the scene. I can throw their asses out, if need be."

She skidded to a stop as a ghost stumbled out of the gallery into the hall: Gallus. He was holding the giggling, disembodied head of a platinum-haired woman under his arm. His helmet and cloak were askew, and he straightened his helmet to better see Anya and Katie.

"Ladies!" he shouted. *"Welcome to the party!"*

Anya pointed to the head under his arm. "Um . . . Gallus, you're holding a human head."

Gallus held the head before him like an athlete with a trophy. The head's powdered wig was askew, and the head winked. The face was as supple and mobile as if it were still attached to a body.

"Where are my manners? Marie, meet Anya."

Marie's bow mouth curved up, nearly scraping the beauty mark on her cheek. *"Enchantée."*

Sparky sat up on his hind legs and sniffed at a drooping ringlet.

"Gallus, this is Sparky. And Katie." She glanced over her shoulder. Katie's eyes were round and unblinking. Anya guessed that these ghosts had accumulated enough power over the centuries to visually manifest at will. Even for a member of DAGR, seeing a full-body apparition was unusual—a fact that Anya often forgot. She was too used to seeing spirits, and forgot the effect that they could have on others.

"Come say hello." Gallus waved Anya toward the Special Exhibits Gallery.

Anya couldn't resist—she peeked in. And her jaw dropped.

Ghosts from every imaginable era drifted throughout the gleaming white exhibit space like guests at a costume party: women in corseted dresses and petticoats, men in waistcoats. A Zulu warrior sporting a fearsome mask and body paint was chatting up a geisha girl. She smiled with blackened teeth behind a hand-painted fan with a tear in it. A 1940s-era siren in a silver gown snickered at a fellow dressed like Attila the Hun as he brandished his weapons. They milled among the paintings and sculptures, flowing around a glass case in the center containing a life-sized guillotine, complete with a basket.

Anya whispered to Gallus, "This is . . . what you do after hours?"

"*There's not much else to do.*" Gallus handed Marie's head off to a samurai warrior. "*She digs me,*" Gallus said, waggling his eyebrows.

"Is that"—Katie glanced at the guillotine—"*the* Marie?"

"*It is. Marie's on loan from London.*" Gallus grinned. "*She thinks I'm a patrician, and I've not bothered to disavow her of that notion.*"

"But . . . " Anya scanned the room. "Where's the rest of her?"

Gallus shrugged, unconcerned. "*Who knows? Maybe still haunting the streets of Paris?*" He winked at the women. "*But I can certainly make do with what's left.*"

Anya screwed up her face. "Sorry, Gallus, but that's icky."

"Hey. You won't be that picky about how you get your jollies in two thousand years. Very few things will seem kinky then." Gallus clapped his hands to get the crowd's attention. *"Ladies and gentlemen!"* he bellowed. *"Please meet Anya, Katie, and Sparky. Anya's the medium I told you about."*

A wave of acknowledgment rippled through the room, punctuated by a catcall or two. Anya's cheeks flamed. She'd wanted to get in to protect Pandora's Jar and get out again without attracting attention. Now it seemed that was going to be a futile effort.

The samurai squatted before Sparky, admiring the play of dim light on his speckled skin. Anya noticed a rusty red stain marring the samurai's yellow silk obi and myriad small dents in his breastplate. *"Is this your dragon?"* the samurai asked in heavily accented English.

"Yes," Anya replied, distracted. "He's my dragon."

The samurai bowed deeply before the salamander. Anya noticed that he held his gauntleted arm tightly over his midsection to hold his entrails in. *"It is an honor to make your acquaintance, mighty dragon."*

Sparky sat in a regal posture before his new supplicant, one front foot lifted in a comically benevolent gesture. Anya wondered how often a scene like this had presented itself to Sparky. She had no idea how old the salamander was, or where he'd been. Surely someone else must have been able to see him, perhaps as a holy creature. A holy creature who chased his own tail and ate cell phones.

"You have the eyes of Ishtar," a voice hissed behind her.

Anya started, wheeled to face a barefoot old man dressed in rags. He smelled like dust and stale incense, and his gray beard was tangled with olive leaves. He leaned heavily on a wooden staff.

Anya clutched the newt transporter, and Sparky growled at her feet. The old man reached for her, but his spectral hand passed harmlessly through her shoulder.

"Don't fucking touch me," she growled.

The old man blinked at her with coal-black eyes. They were fully dilated—whether from injury, drugs, or madness, Anya couldn't tell.

"You have her terrible gaze. The same."

Anya's eyes narrowed. Only Drake had called her Ishtar. How could this old man know about that?

"We don't know each other," she said frostily.

"But I've seen her before." The old man grinned, reached out to pat her face, but his fingers flickered through, below the level of her skin. *"The soul-devourer. The one who condemns all her lovers to death."*

The breath froze in Anya's throat, and it wasn't just the chill of the ghost's touch.

"Ishtar walked down to the Underworld to rescue her dead lover, the old stories say. She came armored and holding a sword, demanding the gates of the Underworld be opened to her. The Queen of the Underworld, Ereshkigal, let her in, but poisoned and imprisoned her. The gods brought Ishtar the water of life, and brokered a deal: Ishtar could return only if she sent someone else to stay in the Underworld in her place."

Anya's mouth was dry as lint. "Who did she send?"

The old man gave her a toothless grin, without mirth. *"Ereshkigal sent demons to the world with Ishtar, to make sure she wouldn't escape. When Ishtar returned to earth, she found her husband didn't mourn for her, so Ishtar sent him to the Underworld in her stead. And Ishtar was without both her lover and her husband."*

"What's that got to do with me?"

"You wear her armor and are doomed to follow in her footsteps." The old man's eyes were black as pits.

"Ignore old Balzeri." Gallus intervened, steering the old man away. The old man began to hum to himself. Gallus tapped the side of his helmet. *"He took too many drugs. Makes him a bit of a buzz kill."*

"Um, yeah . . . " Anya glanced around for Katie, who was immersed in a conversation with an ancient Egyptian. Katie's eyes kept straying from his kohl-rimmed eyes to his broad, tan chest. His muscular chest was bare, decorated only with a turquoise collar. Decked out in gilt sandals and a pleated loincloth, he could've been a romantic historical fantasy come to life, if not for the blackened snake bite on one bicep out. Anya couldn't help but wonder if he'd known Cleopatra's asp.

"Katie, let's go."

Katie allowed herself to be led from the elegant Egyptian, but her eyes lingered. "Damn," she said. "That's one distracting ghost."

"We've got work to do," Anya urged.

"We can come back later?"

"I'm sure Gallus would have it no other way." But her

mind was focused on what the old man had said, how she had Ishtar's eyes.

The Greco-Roman Exhibit Hall was in as much ruins as she'd left it. Yellow fire tape cordoned off the crumpled steel doors, and she ducked beneath it, pulling it aside for Katie. Sparky scuttled ahead of them, among the sparkling bits of broken glass, chemical dust, and overturned furniture.

"This is it." Anya pointed to the display case containing Pandora's Jar. She was relieved to see that it was still there. Sparky waddled up to the glass and cocked his head to stare at it. It seemed that he knew instinctively that it was a magickal thing, that it contained the same crystalline matrix that covered the interior of Anya's bathtub. Anya wondered if a salamander had ever laid a clutch of eggs in it.

"This place is filthy," Katie muttered. She dropped her bag on a clean spot of floor and withdrew a willow branch broom. She began to sweep the area around the case, preparing it for ritual magick. The broom created puffs of dust that made her sneeze as she worked.

Finally, she stood back, wiping her nose. "I think that's as good as it's going to get." She looked up at the ceiling. "Um, is the fire alarm system hooked up in here?"

"No. It's inoperable in this area after the last discharge. What can I do?" Anya asked. She was all thumbs when it came to ritual magick, and she knew it.

Katie slid a compass and a bucket of children's sidewalk chalk across the floor. "You can mark the cardinal directions on the floor in chalk."

Anya looked in the bucket. She chose a piece of yellow chalk for east, violet chalk for north, blue chalk for west, and pink chalk for south. She tried to make the marks as unobtrusively as possible on the granite floor.

"What now?" Anya asked, sitting back on her heels.

Katie placed a white votive in a silver candleholder at each point on the compass. She anointed each candle with an oil that smelled like dish soap. "Well, the challenge is creating a magick circle without markers that will be visible to humans, but one that ghosts will be unable to cross."

"How do we do that?"

Katie held up a glass perfume bottle full of the oil she used to anoint the candles. "Lavender oil. It will soak into the stone and be nearly invisible." In her other hand, she held a bottle of white crystals. "And salt. In this mess, a bit of it will go unnoticed." She dumped the contents of the bottle of salt into her hands, blew on it, and cast it across the floor. The salt blended in with the dust and fragments of broken glass, glittering against the granite. "The salt will purify the space."

Katie got down on her hands and knees. She dipped her fingers in the lavender oil and drew a nine-foot circle on the floor around the glass display case, connecting Anya's compass points. The oil began to seep into the granite almost immediately.

Anya stood back with Sparky. She stepped on his tail to keep him from interfering; she didn't want a nosy salamander inadvertently locked *inside* the circle.

Katie struck a match, and the light played over her

pixie features. She lowered the match to the candle in the eastern quadrant. "I dedicate this circle to the Old Ones, to the old gods and goddesses still roaming the earth, underworld, and heavens. To consecrate this circle, I summon the Guardian of the Watchtower of the East. May the power of air bless and strengthen this circle."

She moved to the north, lit the candle. "I summon the Guardian of the Watchtower of the North. May the power of earth bless and strengthen this circle."

Katie stepped to the next candle, and the next: "I summon the Guardian of the Watchtower of the West. May the power of water bless and strengthen this circle. I summon the Guardian of the Watchtower of the South. May the power of fire bless and strengthen this circle." When Katie struck that match, fire leapt and sizzled.

Though Anya had no particular gift for ritual magick, she could still feel it: the thrum and flow of its pulse in the earth, like a living thing. She could smell the sharpness of it in the air, feel it in the hair lifting on the back of her neck.

Katie pulled her silver athame from her belt, aimed the dagger at the fading oil circle on the floor. She traced the circle clockwise once more. "May this circle remain strong and unbroken, protecting the treasures at its heart from plunder. Let no man or spirit tear it asunder." Katie dropped a match to the oil circle, and it flamed to life, racing around the floor.

She raised her athame to the sky. "The circle is sealed. Blessings to the Old Ones and watchtowers. May they see to the protection of this place."

The fire fizzled out, leaving no trace of its presence. Anya scanned the outline of what had once been fire. Katie walked clockwise along the circle, snuffing the candles.

"How do we know it worked?"

Katie shrugged. "Well, humans should be able to cross over." Katie stepped over the invisible boundary to the glass case, pressed her hands to the glass. "Humans sensitive to magick will feel their skin crawl, and probably won't linger."

"And the spirits?"

"Let's find out." Katie looked past Anya, at the entrance to the exhibit. Anya followed her gaze, to see Gallus leaning in the doorway, behind the fire tape. His hand was poised on his wasp-waisted sword.

"Is it safe to come in?" Gallus asked. His nose twitched, and Anya could tell that he smelled the magick, too.

"Sure," Katie told him. "The circle won't hurt anyone. It's just meant to keep ghosts away."

Gallus crossed the room to the perimeter of the circle. He planed his hand in the air, as if feeling for its edges. *"How does it work?"*

Katie blushed and dug her toe uncertainly on the floor. "I'm not really sure what it will do. Not many spirits report back on how they interact with magickal barriers."

Gallus puffed up like a rooster. *"Can I test it?"*

"Have at it."

"Be careful," Anya warned. She was sure that Katie sometimes didn't know her magickal strength.

Gallus reached toward the barrier. It flashed blue, like

lightning, and sparked against his hand. Gallus shook it, paced around it. *"Interesting,"* he said. He was still for a moment, then ripped his sword out of its sheath and lunged over the invisible line.

A web of blue-white light flashed, knocking Gallus on his ass. He skidded backward on the slick floor, spinning like a toy in a pinball machine.

Anya rushed to his side. "Gallus! Are you all right?"

The cavalryman rubbed his head, grinning. His ephemeral body seemed to smoke. Sparky wiggled up to him and licked his chin.

"Gallus?"

The Roman was laughing so hard the feathers on his helmet shook and the segments on his armor rattled. *"I can't wait until Pluto hits that. This will be the best revenge I've had on that horse in two thousand years."*

Katie's house was too quiet to sleep in.

Anya lay in the guest room, staring up at the ceiling. Katie's house was too far from the freeway and the railroad tracks. Anya had grown accustomed to hearing the swish of cars on the freeway and the bleat of the night trains, and the silence unsettled her. All she could hear was the ticking of a clock in the living room and the clack of Fay's and Vern's claws on the hardwood floors as they patrolled the premises.

The bed was surrounded by debris of her attempts to get her life back in some semblance of working order: shopping bags full of clothes and toiletries, stacks of paper from the insurance company to sign off on. Small pathetic piles of material possessions, the sad sum total of her life at present. But Anya reminded herself that she'd started over after a fire once before. She could do it again. Maybe.

Anya rolled over, punching a lavender-scented pillow under her head. Sparky grumbled a bit in his sleep. He slept coiled around the newt transporter at the foot of the bed. In the darkness, the eggs glowed like coals, casting gold light from the interior of the bag. She knew that Katie's house was the best place for the newts, that it would likely take Hope some time to figure out where she'd taken them. And Katie's house was powerfully warded. Salt lines glittered on the windowsills, the lintels of doors and windows guarded by tiny pentacles made of woven willow branches. The perimeter of boxwood around the house had been fed on magickal plant food. Katie had even placed protective obsidian stones in the least obvious entry points to the house: around the main plumbing stack, the drains, and the attic. The dryer vent had even been stuffed with sage. The fireplace was blocked by a huge decorative arrangement of thistles and wreathed with garlic. Anya could even smell the everyday magick in the lemon floor polish. Vern and Fay were on watch, hopping up on the windowsills without disturbing the salt, chirping to each other in their feline language. For a witch, this place was a fortress.

But Anya couldn't help but feel vulnerable. She'd seen what Hope could do.

Above Anya's bed, a painting of the serene goddess

Kwan Yin surveyed the darkness. She was rendered in watercolor and ink, soft and ethereal in pastel greens and pinks, holding a dove in her hands. Kwan Yin, goddess of kindness and compassion, the polar opposite of the black painting of Ishtar. Anya's painting of Ishtar, saved from the fire, was propped up in a corner. There was something comforting about Ishtar's thick gaze.

Anya chewed on her lip, thinking about what the crazy old man had said at the ghost party: "You have the eyes of Ishtar." She wasn't certain what that meant, but she certainly felt closer to that terrible goddess of war and ruined lovers than she did to the beatific Kwan Yin.

And with the eyes of Ishtar . . . she saw Brian. She didn't want what happened to Drake to happen to Brian. If she truly did have some affinity to the Babylonian goddess, how could she protect Brian, keep him partitioned away from that trick of destiny that had chased down Drake and killed him? Was she truly destined to lose everyone she loved?

Anya blinked tears into the pillow. *What if . . . ?* There were no answers that anyone seemed to be able to give.

Fay trotted into the room, growling, and Anya sat bolt upright in bed. The calico cat launched herself to the windowsill, fur fluffed and hissing. Somewhere in the back of the house, Vern yodeled. Sparky curled over his bag of eggs, clutching at them with his toes. In the darkness, the familiars' eyes were dilated, round and black as the old man's at the museum.

Anya crept to the window, pulled aside the sheer

curtain. The tatter of something insubstantial flitted past, like an angelfish in an aquarium. Others joined it, pausing outside the window and pressing their hands to the glass.

Ghosts. In the churning darkness, Anya could see their writhing forms, searching for entry into the house. They flitted up over the roof, around the foundation, poking at the electrical mast on top of the house and at the gas meter. Anya clutched the windowsill with white knuckles. She heard Katie's footsteps behind her, turned to see her standing in her nightgown. In her right hand, she held a candle that smelled like bayberries. In her left, she held a silver ceremonial sword.

Something rattled in the living room, and Anya heard the sound of silt spitting in the chimney. Vern growled.

"They can't come past the closed flue," Katie said. "It's sealed with seven pentacles."

Anya turned back to the window. She swallowed—hard—when she saw a familiar face twitching through the darkness: Leslie.

Leslie drifted before the window. Her face paused before the glass, and her breath against it fogged the pane. With a finger, she traced the words "Help us" in the condensation. Beyond the edge of the yard, Anya saw a compost bin catching fire. Its lurid glow gleamed through the breath on the window.

Anya reached toward the window sash.

"No." Katie set the candle in the sash and snatched her wrist. The candlelight seemed to drive the ghost away. "Don't let her in. It's a trick."

Anya wrapped her arms around her body. She returned to the bed to sit next to Sparky. A low growl rumbled through his chest, so low that it made the bed vibrate.

She was torn. Torn between the desire to help the spirits banging against the house like moths on a lantern, and wanting to rip them to pieces for threatening Sparky's eggs. She felt the black hole opening in her chest, the twitch in her fingers. If any of them got past Katie's wards, no matter if it was Bernie or Leslie, she'd chew them up. She had no choice in it. But she prayed that Katie's preparations would be enough.

"What now?"

Katie knelt down on the floor, leaning the sword against her shoulder. With her unbound hair and white nightdress, she looked like she'd stepped out of one of Dante Rossetti's Pre-Raphaelite paintings, a vision of Beatrice. "We do nothing. We wait until morning, or until they give up."

Anya looked up at the picture of Kwan Yin.

Katie was right; this was no time for compassion.

This was time for war.

CHAPTER FOURTEEN

HOPE'S GHOSTS HAD GIVEN UP by dawn. They gave up rattling in the chimney, though they managed to dislodge an old birds' nest (much to the cats' delight as they shredded it all over the floor). They gave up pinging in the pipes and scratching around the attic. And they gave up trying to enter the house through the floor drains in the basement, though their breath sounded like the wind blowing across bottles. The rattles and shakes became fainter and fainter until they faded. The fire in the compost pile burned out, leaving the smell of burned coffee grounds that permeated the house.

Katie figured that they'd worn themselves out; that even spirits such as these would need to rest before another attempt. Still, Anya left Katie's stronghold cautiously, and well-armed. Katie had taken the dragon's blood dye and marked Anya's skin with a protective rune she called Algiz—it resembled a capital Y with an additional line struck through the upper tines, to resemble a pitchfork. She painted it on Anya's back with the red dye, warning her that the dye was like henna: It would seep into her skin and remain for many days. When Anya was dressing, she kept glimpsing it in the mirror from the corner of her eye, and had to resist the visceral urge to swat a bug that she imagined there. But it really wasn't so ugly, compared to the scars of the ghosts she'd devoured, pink on her chest. Her new clothes felt scratchy and unfamiliar against her skin.

Katie had tucked sprigs of holly in the newt transporter, explaining that holly was a sacred protective plant to the druids. The smell reminded Anya too much of Christmas, of terrible fires and losses that came with it. She steeled herself, resisting the urge to pluck the sprigs out of the mass of pulsing balls of amber light tucked under her arm.

Sparky went outside first, sniffing the dawn air. His tongue flicked out, tasting for some ghostly presence as Anya slipped out and locked the door. Anya didn't sense the presence of spirits around the house, but she was relieved to put the Dart in gear and be on the move toward work. She didn't know how long Hope's minions would take to recharge, but she intended to make the most of the time they were gone.

This early in the morning, Anya's office at DFD headquarters was quiet. She passed the drowsy guards in the lobby, and saw no one else as she took the elevator to the basement. She was still jumpy, starting when the fluorescent light took a moment to flicker on overhead. She picked up several yellow envelopes of interoffice mail and white postal mail that had been shoved under her door.

Poor Sparky was exhausted. As she booted up her computer and plugged in the coffeepot, he curled up under her desk around the newt transporter. Anya tucked her feet around him and began to rifle through the mail.

She tore into a yellow envelope from the crime lab. It contained several photocopied images of fingerprints and NCIC numbers. Apparently, the lab had gotten itself mopped up and running again. The cover memo from Jenna stated that they'd found some interesting prints at DIA—fingerprints that belonged to Jasper Bernard.

Anya leaned back in her squeaky chair. Poor Bernie was among the ghosts that Hope had sent to claim Pandora's Jar. The information was consistent with Anya's theory that Hope was controlling ghosts she'd imprisoned, but provided nothing whatsoever that would allow her to get a warrant.

The memo also indicated there had been no traces of accelerants or exotic chemicals found in samples that Gina had taken from the guards' bodies. Just the same residue of silicates that had been found on Bernie's remains.

A thick FedEx envelope bore a return address of Miracles for the Masses. Anya frowned, tore it open. Hope had sent last year's financial report in response to her request for financial records. Nothing but drivel and mission statements, punctuated by a few simplistic tables that showed Hope had received an impressive two million dollars in revenue last year.

"Bitch," Anya muttered.

She glanced over at her computer screen. Instead of

her familiar desktop icons, a black screen with a white cursor confronted her. The cursor tapped out: Hello, Anya.

Anya edged toward the screen, turned on the webcam perched on top. "ALANN? Is that you?"

Yes. How are you this morning?

"Great, but . . . how are you here? This is a secure network."

Brian was concerned about you. He wanted me to check to make sure you and Sparky were all right.

Anya frowned. She'd forgotten to check in with Brian. If he'd come by the house, who knew what he'd thought? She self-consciously powered up the iPhone he'd given her. There were three voice mails. She wasn't used to being in a relationship, and hadn't been minding the rules . . . whatever they were. With all that destruction that seemed to follow her, it seemed best to keep Brian at arm's length. "We're fine. The newts were under attack, so I'm still staying over at Katie's. Her house is a fortress. Hope's ghosts can't get in." She didn't mention how hard they'd tried; she didn't want to cause Brian additional worry.

Brian says he's relieved. The cursor blinked. We have something to show you. Brian's been working on that surveillance project.

Anya chewed her lip. "Great, but . . . I don't think this is a secure computer. Anything on it can be recorded." Anya had never seen the information technology gnomes who serviced the fire department, but she knew that they were there. And they were probably reading everyone's e-mail.

Rest assured, we have a secure connection.

"Okay. What've you got?"

The screen flickered, and a new window opened up on the lower right-hand corner. It showed a black-and-white still image of a city street and the tail end of a black BMW. Anya recognized the street corner as the one outside the Miracles for the Masses headquarters.

Detroit, like many cities, uses automatic number plate recognition to catch offenders who run red lights at intersections. Automatic License Plate Reader uses optical character recognition technology to identify license plates.

"So . . . I take it that there's one of these cameras perched outside the Miracles for the Masses headquarters?"

There is. Additionally, DPD patrol cars have recently installed automatic license plate recognition cameras in patrol cars to screen for stolen cars and fugitives while they are on patrol.

"How does that work?"

The automatic license plate recognition cameras scan traffic using OCR, and register a hit when stolen plates are scanned, allowing the officer to react and stop the offending vehicle.

Anya rested her chin in her hand. "That's kind of creepy."

That's one of the criticisms. In any event, Brian and I were able to tap into the DPD system and the traffic control system to search for vehicles registered to Hope Solomon and her aliases.

A flurry of pictures flashed upon the screen: the black BMW waiting in traffic outside a shopping mall; the same car driving along the freeway; the car stopped beside a parking meter. Each image was time- and date-stamped. Anya's attention lingered on an image time-stamped for last night, seeing the BMW parked outside Hope's office. Lights were on inside. The bitch had been too busy cooking up the attack to go home.

"Wait a second. Back up." Anya leaned forward. ALANN backed through the images for one that snagged her attention: Hope's car parked just outside of her headquarters, with a woman climbing out of the car. She was carrying something. "Can you zoom in?"

ALANN obliged. The shot grew grainier as it got larger, but Anya could see the object she held more clearly: a silver flacon, decorated in a pattern of vines and leaves muddied by the resolution.

"Hold that shot."

Anya scrambled through her files of photos of Bernie's house, flipping through the shots. That flacon was familiar . . . *there*. The flacon appeared on Bernie's mantel, beside the swords and bottles of unidentifiable contents. She ran her finger over her handwritten notes detailing what had been missing: "one silver-plated flacon, origin unknown."

She stared back at the screen. "Gotcha."

"This is opening a can of worms."

Marsh leaned back in his chair. His office was one step

above Anya's . . . well, maybe more like a dozen steps. On the first floor, he was afforded light from a window, covered by bent blinds. It didn't matter that the window faced an alley; it was still coveted daylight, and Anya blinked in it. Sparky ambled behind her, head cocked, listening to the sound of Marsh's fire- and police-band radios chattering from the top of a file cabinet.

Anya pointed to the photo. "DPD sent me a copy of the photo." And they had: Once Anya was specific about the time, date, and intersection, they faxed over a copy of what was visible from the red-light camera mount outside of Hope's office. "It's all public information."

Marsh laced his hands behind his head. "And do I want to ask about how you knew to ask for this, how you knew that Hope would be holding stolen property at this specific date and time?"

"No, sir. You probably don't want to ask."

"The public is jumpy enough about Big Brother. There was enough of an uproar about red-light cameras generating tickets in the first place. If the public thought that this could be used for surveillance . . . " He shook his head. "This would result in a furor. The city would be sued outright, and by people with deeper pockets than Hope."

"Captain, I'm sure I can tie her to Bernie's death. And several others. I just can't prove it yet."

Marsh stared at the photo with contempt. "You and I both know that Hope's a shady character. Bilked the gullible, and destroyed a lot of lives. But I don't know that we can get a judge to approve a warrant based on this." He flipped through the pages of items that Anya had listed that she wanted to search for: all the items that had come up missing in the break-in at Bernie's house. "This is broad. A fishing expedition."

"Will you at least try?" Anya held her breath.

Marsh looked at her, weighing the options. Finally, he said, "Okay. I'll ask. Whether the judge approves it or not, the shitstorm that follows is gonna rest squarely on your shoulders, kid."

"Back for more?"

Charon stood outside the morgue, smoking a cigarette that smelled like incense. His cold blue eyes watched as Anya walked across the parking lot, Sparky loping along at her heels. Anya clutched the newt transporter tight against her body. It seemed that they were generating more heat of their own. She took this as a good sign, but the newt transporter was giving her a serious case of sunburn along her ribs.

"I did what you told me to. We cast a magick circle around Pandora's Jar."

Charon nodded. He threw his cigarette down to the pavement, ground it out with his boot heel. Afternoon sunlight gleamed through his image, which seemed thin as smoke in the daylight. *"That'll hold her for the time being. But she's got to be stopped before she figures out a way through."*

"I'm hoping to get a warrant, to catch her with some stolen property from arson scenes. If I can get her away from her reliquaries for long enough, maybe we can muster up some charges."

Charon frowned. *"I don't think you'll be able to stop her that way. You'd have to separate her from all her bottles, and she'll fight that to the death."*

"Your way is to fight her on the astral plane."

"Yes."

Anya looked at him skeptically. "How do I get there?"

Charon opened his pocket and flipped a coin to her. Anya caught it reflexively, and was surprised to find that it was real. Her fingers curled around a solid bronze coin with irregular edges and the crude image of an emperor stamped in it.

"What's this?" she asked.

"Toll for the ferryman." Charon shrugged. *"Don't ask me why, but it works. Put that under your tongue and say my name."*

She fingered the coin. "How do I protect the eggs and Sparky while I'm gone?"

"You can leave them behind. But I would suggest that you take them with you."

Anya nodded, put the coin in her pocket. "Thanks." She reached for the door handle to go inside.

Charon cocked his head. *"You got more stiffs in there?"*

"I'm not sure," Anya admitted. "I'm trying to track down a body that might have been . . . misplaced."

Charon squinted up at the noonday sun, and the gesture rendered his eyes nearly translucent. *"That can happen. Who is it?"*

Anya paused, caught between the warm outside sunshine and the cold, stale air-conditioning in the breezeway. "A computer scientist. I don't know his name. His brain's being used for research, and I . . . I want to know who he was."

"This is personal, then?"

Anya bit her lip. She hated admitting to herself that she didn't take Brian's word at face value, but something about the situation with ALANN bothered her. For someone who had signed his body over to science, his virtual avatar was sure keen on searching for a way out. "Yeah."

Charon nodded, following her inside. *"I'll help you look."*

Anya, Sparky, and Charon wound down through the hallways of the morgue, though only Anya's feet made a sound on the tiled floor. She stuck her head in the autopsy room, seeing Gina on her step stool. The diminutive coroner was up to her elbows in gore.

"Hey, Gina," Anya said. "Mind if I take a look at your death certs?"

"Knock yourself out," Gina said. "Anything special you're looking for?"

"I'm looking for a death within the last couple of months. All I know is that he was a computer scientist, and probably died of natural causes. Maybe released his body to the university for research purposes."

"We haven't had any donors within the last couple of months. But you're welcome to paw through the certs. We haven't scanned them all into the system yet. Fucking interns are never around. Just wash your hands before and after—never know what germies are on them."

"Noted," Anya said, making a face. Obediently, she washed her hands with pink dish soap at the coroner's sink and retreated to Gina's office around the corner. The place looked like Bernie's living room: papers piled in stacks knee-high and held together with rubber bands.

"How the hell does she ever find anything in here?" Anya muttered.

"Actually, Gina knows where everything is," Charon answered. *"She's the only one. And she likes it that way. Try here."* Charon pointed to a green file cabinet labeled PUNCHED DEATH TICKETS in Gina's spidery scrawl on masking tape.

Anya pulled out the drawer and started flipping through the death certificates. They were filed with the most recent first, going back six months. The certs were numbered in the upper right-hand corner, included the filing date and the decedent's death date at the top. Anya zeroed in on a line on the form halfway down the page, a blank for the deceased's occupation. She flipped through several dozen "none" answers, a few "unknowns," and lots of "retired" answers. Several factory workers, a couple of housewives, and a tragically young student, dead of alcohol poisoning.

Her fingers stopped halfway through the drawer. She'd found a "computer systems engineer," Calvin Dresser. His level of education was indicated as "Ph.D." She stuck a pen in the file to hold her place, pulled it.

Principal cause of death was listed as acute cardiorespiratory failure. Seemed ordinary enough. Calvin was sixty-three, lived in Detroit. She scanned to the bottom of the page, for information on who had taken possession of the body. Her heart sank when she saw an illegible scrawl that she recognized as Brian's handwriting, and his address at the university computer lab. The blanks for place and date of burial or cremation were left blank.

"Did you find it?" Charon asked. He was sitting among the piles on Gina's desk, still as a paperweight. Sparky sat beside him, watching the second hand on the wall clock tick in fascination.

"I think so. Do you remember a Calvin Dresser?" She waved the death cert in front of him.

Charon nodded. *"Yeah. Old guy. There wasn't anything for me to do. His spirit was gone when I got there."*

"Good thing Gina can't hear you call a sixty-three-year-old man 'old.' "

Anya dug around on Gina's desk for a phone and a phone book. She looked up the main number for the university switchboard and dialed it.

"Could you transfer me to the Division of Anatomy at the medical school?"

"Please hold." Muzak began to play.

Anya continued to rifle through Gina's files.

"What are you looking for?" Charon asked.

"I want to know what he looked like."

Anya dug through the manila file folders until she found one with a matching death cert number. She splayed the folder open on Gina's desk, cradling the phone receiver between her cheek and shoulder. She found a picture of a man in his early sixties, lying on the coroner's slab before he'd been undressed and washed. He was a balding man dressed in a sport coat that was easily twenty years out of date, a dress shirt, and creased pants. His expression in repose was one of bemusement. There were two red dents on the bridge of his nose, where Anya imagined a pair of glasses pinched. The file was thin; this had been a relatively straightforward case of the man passing away at home without any witnesses. It was a small wonder the medical examiner had gotten involved at all, but there had apparently been some question about the prescription drugs paramedics found in his home and proper dosages.

The Muzak cut off, and a voice came on the line:

"Division of Anatomy, Carla speaking."

"Hi, Carla. My name is Anya Kalinczyk. I'm an investigator with the Detroit Fire Department. I need to get a copy of Calvin Dresser's Anatomical Bequeathal Form."

"Please hold while I look that up for you, ma'am."

More of the dreadful Muzak. Anya stretched the phone cord to the far side of the room and slapped the death certificate into the copier. The old copier chugged to life and spat green light on the certificate, reluctantly spewed out a copy before coughing.

"Ms. Kalincyzk?"

"Yes?" Anya cradled the phone on her shoulder.

"Ma'am, we don't have a bequeathal form or a cremation authorization for anyone under that name."

Anya swallowed. "Thank you very much. I appreciate your help." She placed the phone down on the receiver and stared at it.

Brian had lied to her.

Calvin Dresser hadn't given permission to do jack shit to his remains. Brian had taken the body—who knew where it was now?—and conducted his own research on it. Anya felt her hands ball into fists. After all they had seen as members of DAGR, didn't he have any more respect for the dead than this?

Charon swung his feet. *"Did you find your missing body?"*

"I think so. But I'm not liking where it's turning up."

Anya's cell phone buzzed.

"Kalincyzk."

"It's Marsh. I finally found a judge with a big enough beef with Hope Solomon to sign a warrant. We got permission to search her office and car only, since that's where the photograph shows the evidence was taken."

Anya smiled, exhilarated. "Thank you, Captain."

"Don't thank me, Kalincyzk. Something tells me you're gonna have your work cut out for you when you go knocking on that woman's door."

Anya strode through Hope Solomon's beautifully appointed pastel lobby with a wall of DPD uniforms at her back. The well-manicured receptionist stood in alarm at the invasion.

"Is Hope in?"

"She is, but she's not available—"

Anya slid a copy of the search warrant across her desk. "Please stay here, and don't touch anything." A uniform stood beside her as she began to sputter and reach for her phone.

Anya strode down the pastel hallway, with uniforms at her heels. Sparky snaked beside her, teeth bared. He wanted to get the bitch every bit as much as Anya did.

Anya straight-armed the door to Hope's office. Hope was on her feet behind her massive glass desk, her heels sinking into the carpet as she stalked around it to confront Anya. The uniforms fanned out into the room, swarming over the plush white inner sanctum like ants on sugar.

"You've no right to be here." Hope trembled with rage. "Get out."

Sparky stalked toward her, crouched, and growled. His tail lashed, and Hope took a step back.

"We have a warrant to search for certain artifacts missing from a crime scene." Anya held a copy of the warrant in front of her like a shield and tucked the newt transporter behind her. "You are restrained from interfering with the search."

"You can't do that. My lawyer—"

"Sit down and shut up, lady," Anya told her. "We'll at least give you the courtesy of telling you what we take." *Which is more than I can say for Bernie's artifacts. Or his life. Or Leslie's. And Chris's.*

Anya circled behind Hope to the bookcases behind her desk. With fingers covered by latex gloves, she pulled books off the shelves, compared the knickknacks to items on the list. She pawed through drawers and Hope's credenza, eyes straying to her papers. She couldn't seize anything she found as evidence unless it directly pointed to a crime. Hope's papers, like the financial records she'd sent, were well-sanitized. There wasn't a single item there over three weeks old.

"Nothing here, Lieutenant," one of the cops said.

Hope smirked.

"We've got the rest of the building to search," Anya told him calmly, though her heart thumped. She stepped out into the hallway, opening doors from east to west: a conference room, a kitchenette, a bathroom, a mop closet. She smelled the faint residue of magick, but it wasn't on this floor.

At the back of the hall was a fire door, but it was locked. The door handle was so cold that her sweaty fingers nearly stuck to the metal. She thought back to what Charon had said about spiritual energy conservation, about how energy had to be pulled away from a source to manifest.

"This is in violation of city fire code," Anya snapped.

Hope and her assistant stood in the hall. "I don't know what happened to the key."

"Open this door, or I'll break it."

Hope shrugged. "My lawyer will have a field day with destruction-of-property claims."

"You can't deny us access to parts of the structure named in the warrant."

"You want for us to break it down?" one of the DPD officers asked.

"Give me a minute."

Anya looked around the hallway for a fire extinguisher, located one in a glass case. The red housing contrasted sorely with Hope's peaches-and-cream color scheme, like an angry zit on a bride's face.

Anya peered at the inspection tag. "Darn, Hope. This thing hasn't been inspected for at least six months. And this is a commercial building. One more fire code violation for you."

"Go fuck yourself."

Anya smirked. The fire extinguisher was a CO_2 canister. Perfect. Anya aimed the hose at the door lock and pulled the trigger. Frigid foam spewed from the nozzle and crackled on the lock. Anya lifted the canister. Wielding it like a hammer, she struck the lockset. It shattered open with a sound like a car door slamming, rattling pieces of metal against the walls. Sparky sniffed a piece of frigid metal and wrinkled his nose at the cold, chemical smell of it.

Anya pushed the door open and clicked on her flashlight. The stink of magick crawled up the stairs, pooling around her ankles like oil. Her breath steamed in the frigid air. As she descended the steps into the basement, she felt as if she were descending underwater. The air was thick with the ozone smell of it, sharp and metallic. Sparky scuttled ahead of her on the rusty steps, which creaked under her weight. Hope's renovation of the building didn't extend to this place: Industrial-green paint peeled from the walls. Jack Frost patterns glistened on the old paint. An overhead light, once located, cast a flickering glow on the basement's contents. Dusty wooden pallets were stacked haphazardly to the ceiling, interspersed with broken pieces of office furniture and paper litter.

It was cold here. Too cold. Anya could see her breath before her as she stepped out onto the concrete floor. The temperature was easily fifty degrees colder down here than upstairs, like walking into a restaurant freezer. Pipes banged overhead, wrapped with insulation to keep them from freezing, but an occasional icicle still poked through.

But she could feel the magick here.

Anya swept the beam of her light to the far corner of the basement, and her heart leaped into her throat. Industrial shelves had been neatly arranged against the walls, heavy with bottles and jars of every description. Her gaze snagged on some items she recognized from Bernie's: a wooden skull, the filigree silver bottle, crystal shards, a sword. Interspersed among them were dozens, hundreds of containers, from old Coca-Cola bottles to mason jars and perfume bottles.

Hope's stash of reliquaries.

Before she touched anything, Anya snapped photos with her camera. She reached out for the nearest bottle, a wine bottle with a cork. The surface was so cold it burned her hand. With a thumb, she popped the cork and held her breath.

A wisp of smoke exited from the bottle and slipped up through the ceiling to the floor above. Anya could hear

Hope's wail of anguish filtering down. She peered into the bottle, saw the telltale crystal lining.

She reached for one bottle after another. Her heart lifted as she saw wisps of spirits escaping, the sighs of air breathing out of jam jars and flasks. She smelled old musty air and fresh perfume, a whiff of vodka and the smell of sour pickles. She found and opened children's bottles of bubble bath and pepper shakers. Sparky climbed the shelves and rooted among the vessels, batting at the shreds of spirits as they escaped. The ghosts were going home; she could feel it. The magick was draining out of this place, as if someone had pulled a stopper in a drain.

Tentative footsteps fell on the steps above. "Hey, did you find anything down there?"

Anya smiled in triumph. "Yeah. Yeah, I did. Do me a favor and cuff Ms. Solomon for me."

"Charges?"

"Book her on receiving stolen property, for now." Anya climbed the steps, leaned in the doorway as the uniforms cuffed her. Hope fixed her with a murderous gaze.

"You will regret this," she snarled. Wrath contorted her motherly features.

"We'll see," Anya said mildly. She followed the uniforms taking Hope down to the street. She smiled when she saw the Channel 7 news van parked at the curb and Nick Sarvos speaking before the camera.

"What's the press doing here?" Hope hissed.

"Someone must have tipped them off." Anya shrugged. Inwardly, she beamed.

The uniforms marched Hope out to a waiting squad car. A cop opened the back door, put his hand on the top of Hope's head to keep her from hitting her head on the door frame when she climbed in.

In that instant, Anya saw something spill from the collar of Hope's shirt: the necklace she wore on television, the gold chain that held the tiny glass vial.

She remembered Charon's words: *You'd have to separate her from all her bottles, and she'll fight that to the death.*

Remembered them too late.

As soon as the door slammed shut, the squad car burst into a ball of flame.

CHAPTER FIFTEEN

ANYA SAT ON THE BACK of the paramedics' truck, arms wrapped around the newt transporter. Sparky perched on her shoulder, licking a scrape on her temple where a piece of burning debris had struck her. Her clothes smelled like burned gasoline. Despite the ministrations of the paramedics and salamander, Anya was fucking pissed.

Marsh surveyed the scene: a cop car burned down to the ground, with the shell of a news van guttering out. The street was wet with chemical foam, and fire trucks flashed red lights against the sides of the buildings.

"One cop dead. One severely injured." Marsh took her inventory. "One newscaster with burns."

Anya pinched her eyes shut. "Look, it was not my fault that Sarvos was wearing that much hair product. Sparks and aerosol products do not mix." But she still felt bad. If not for her, the reporter would not have been here.

"I suspect he'll be fine, but will be a lifelong customer of Hair Club for Men," Marsh growled. "And your suspect is missing."

Anya groaned. "She was in the backseat when the car blew up."

"She's not anymore. No bones or traces that I can see. Go look for yourself."

Anya slid down to the pavement and limped to the shell of the ruined patrol car. She'd been far enough away from the blast that she'd been thrown mostly clear, which was more than could be said for the DPD uniforms. When she peered into the backseat, all she saw was melted plastic, the bent grille separating the front seat from the back, and the gleam of a metal seat-belt buckle.

Impervious to fire, Sparky wormed his way into the wreckage. He sniffed around the driver's side and pressed a paw on the horn. To his delight, and the consternation of the emergency personnel, the horn gave off a weak, warped trumpet like a goose caught in a lawn mower.

"Shit," she mumbled.

" 'Shit' is right. You let her get away." Marsh shook his head.

Anya bit back her reply. She'd come to her senses minutes after the explosion, rolled against the side of the building, with a salamander licking her face and the car in flames. Someone had been shouting at her, and an ambulance had rolled up.

Somehow she'd hoped that the bitch had enough grace to kill herself in the blaze.

No such luck.

"I put out an APB on Hope Solomon," Marsh snapped. "I want her found, before anything else burns up."

Anya pressed her mouth into a grim slash. "It's a promise, sir."

A police scanner in the background crackled, and Anya's ears perked up. ". . . ten-thirty-three at 5200 Woodward Avenue."

That was the address for the Detroit Institute of Arts. And a 10-33 was an alarm sounding.

Anya ran for her car.

Hope was all out of reliquaries, and was hell bent on acquiring a new one.

Anya raced up the stairs to DIA, two steps at a time, Sparky scrambling at her heels. The scene was a confusion of strobing red and blue lights and scurrying personnel: ambulances, paramedics, firefighters, cops, and museum staff. Two people were being removed from the scene on stretchers. A crumpled car was sideways on Woodward Avenue, with gawkers cordoned off to the side.

Anya charged through the doors, raced through the Great Hall. She smelled something burning, prayed that the magick that Katie had worked on the floor of the exhibit room had been enough to keep Hope from being successful.

Anya skidded to a halt in the doorway of the Greco-Roman Exhibit Hall. The glass case that held Pandora's Jar stood wide open, and there was an empty hole in the exhibit where the pithos had once been. Sparky wandered to the edge of the invisible circle but didn't cross it. The circle still seemed to be intact. How the hell had Hope gotten in?

She grabbed the sleeve of a man wearing a museum guard uniform. "What happened to the pithos . . . to Pandora's Jar?"

The guard's eyes were wide in panic. "After what happened . . . the lending museum wanted it back. They sent some archivists to pack it and load it into a truck."

"You guys opened the case and took it out of the room?" Anya closed her eyes. Pandora's Jar had been safe from spiritual interference . . . but not the stupid actions of humans.

"Yeah. They loaded it up in a crate, put in on the dolly, and got it out to the truck."

"Show me where."

The guard led her back out of the museum to the curb, pointed to a scorched spot on the pavement. "Then . . . one of the archivists and the driver caught fire. It was horrible . . . they ran into the street. Somebody got a fire extinguisher, but . . . " The guard's hands shook. "One of them got hit by a car. I don't know which one."

"Where's the truck?"

The guard blinked.

"The truck holding Pandora's Jar. Where is it?"

The guard looked around. "It was right here. . . . "

Anya clenched a fist. "Look. I need you to contact the lending institution. Now. Have them give you the license plate and the make and model of the truck, okay?"

The guard blinked, still in shock.

Anya shook his arm. "Okay?"

"License plate, make and model of the truck . . . " The

guard repeated those instructions like a mantra, grabbed his radio. In a few moments, he was patched into the phone system, got the information from the lending institution.

"Why, what do you need it for?" the voice on the other end squawked. "Tell her that we'll call her back."

Anya wasn't going to subject the poor man to being the bearer of more bad tidings than he already was. She scribbled down the information and ran to the nearest knot of cops. She elbowed her way through until she found someone with a badge number that began with an *S*. The sergeant in command of the scene was barking orders at the other uniforms to clear traffic. She was a good head shorter than the rest, and Anya located her primarily by the sound of her voice, pure and projecting like a gospel singer.

"Lieutenant Kalincyzk, DFD. There's been a theft at the museum," Anya told her, breathless.

The sergeant turned the volume down on the squawking walkie clipped to her shoulder. "Are you kidding me? We've got an injury accident, two people on fire—"

"I think it was staged to cover the disappearance of an artifact. Pandora's Jar." Anya held her hands at this level. "Big stone jar, about waist high. Packed in a crate."

The sergeant's eyes narrowed. "It couldn't have just grown legs and walked out."

"It's in the truck the archivists were loading." Anya gave her the scrap of paper. "If you put out an APB on this truck, you might be able to catch it."

"You got a description of the suspect?"

"Yeah. Five-foot-two, early fifties, blond, blue-eyed white woman wearing a light-blue pantsuit. Hope Solomon, aka Christina Modin. She escaped from DPD custody about an hour ago."

The sergeant keyed her walkie and put out an APB for Hope and the van. The sergeant nodded at her. "I'll keep you posted. Thanks for the tip."

"No problem."

The sergeant sang out more orders to her troops, and Anya receded back into the crowd. She looked back at the museum, frowned.

Something wasn't right. She'd smelled magick outside the building.

But not inside.

Anya climbed the steps again, wove past the chaos in the building. Men in suits had showed up, waving papers. Anya assumed that they were muckety-mucks at the museum, and avoided them. Instead, she let herself into the Special Exhibits Gallery, where the ghosts had gathered around the glassed-in guillotine for their party.

The lights had been lowered to conserve energy, and Anya closed the door behind her. Frantic footsteps pattered outside, but the door muffled most of it to the level of ambient noise.

"Gallus," she called. "Are you here?"

She waited. But he didn't answer her.

She stepped more deeply into the shadowed room. Light dripped off the guillotine in the center. "Pluto? Marie? Samurai guy?"

No answer.

"I realize that you're frightened, but . . . I need to talk to you. Hope's taken Pandora's Jar. I need to know what you saw."

Silence. She reached out with that black hole in her chest, to see if she could detect some bit of them with that hungry sense, but the walls and artifacts felt blank.

Anya looked down at Sparky. "Sparky, can you find where they're hiding?"

Sparky lowered his spade-shaped head to the ground and sniffed. His tongue snaked out beyond his teeth, and he scuttled along the floor. Anya followed him as he snuffled around the guillotine, back down the hallway. He paused in the Greco-Roman exhibits before Pluto's gear, turned around. He waddled through the Great Hall, sniffing at the glass cases full of medieval armor.

With growing dread, she watched as Sparky plodded out through the building. He flowed down the steps, through the throng of people. He stopped at the scorch mark at the curb, where the stolen van had been parked.

Fear flashed through her.

"Sparky," she whispered, trying to confirm what her senses told her was true. "They're gone, aren't they?"

Sparky sniffed the air and looked up at her. He whined plaintively.

"Hope didn't just take Pandora's Jar. She took the museum ghosts. Gallus, Pluto, Marie . . . All of them."

Sparky lay down on the sidewalk and put his head between his paws.

———

"I've got to get them back."

Anya paced the floor of the Devil's Bathtub, chewing her lip. She'd placed the newt transporter in the bathtub full of pennies, and Sparky had climbed up inside it to watch her stalk. The newt transporter was growing too hot to carry; Anya didn't know if that was a good or bad sign. According to one of Katie's pastry thermometers, they were cooking along at 103 degrees. Sparky leaned his head on the edge of the cool bathtub, watching Anya wear out the floors.

"I don't know why you care so much," Jules muttered from behind the bar. "They're just ghosts. And old, dusty ones, at that."

Anya spun on her heel. "They *were* people, Jules. People like you and me. And they don't deserve to be treated that way."

"If they were good people, they'd be in heaven."

Renee cleared her throat. The ghost of the flapper was sitting on a bar stool, twirling her cigarette holder and fiddling with her strand of pearls. She cast her eyes down.

"Present company excluded. I mean *generally*," Jules amended. "There's an exception to every rule."

"You can stuff your rules, Jules," Anya retorted. "There isn't anybody here who's following them."

"Enough, you two." Ciro wheeled across the floor. Though his voice was tinny, he still commanded respect. The old man shoved the wheels of his chair with shaking hands until Max grasped the handles and pushed him across the floor to a table. "There's no point in you two arguing over philosophy, with everything at stake."

Jules threw a dish towel over his shoulder and reached for a glass. "What's at stake here? A museum artifact got stolen. That's regrettable, but—"

"People are dying, Jules," Anya said tightly. "Hope's responsible for as many as six deaths . . . that we know about. She's not going to stop just because she got a shiny new toy for her collection."

"It's more than a shiny new toy." Ciro laced his fingers together to keep them from shaking. "A reliquary the size of Pandora's Jar can contain thousands of spirits. With that much power at her fingertips, burning a few people is child's play."

"The data storage of that thing has to be immense." Brian banged through the bar door, a computer tower strapped to his back. "We're probably underestimating the storage capacity—never mind how much battery power such crystals could store."

He shrugged the equipment down to the floor and hugged Anya. "I'm glad you're all right," he whispered against her hair.

Anya returned the embrace, though stiffly. She craved the warm sensation of feeling Brian's heart beating against her cheek, but she couldn't unring the bell of her memory and forget what she'd learned about ALANN. Brian was a corpse thief. And God knew what else.

But this wasn't the time. Anya pulled away from his embrace, faced the others. "I met a spirit at the morgue. He told me how to go to the astral—the Afterworld—to track down Hope. From where I stand, that's our only choice."

Brian narrowed his eyes. "Some spirit at the morgue? How sure are you that you can trust him?"

I'm a bit more certain of him than I am of you right now. Anya bit her tongue and said, "He calls himself Charon. Says it's his job to ferry dead to the Afterworld."

Ciro nodded. "You met a psychopomp."

"A what?"

"A spirit who guides the newly deceased to the afterlife. If you were to speak to a Jungian psychologist, a psychopomp would be described as the mediator between the conscious and unconscious minds." Ciro's eyes gleamed. "In many traditions, they're called 'midwives to the dying.' "

"Can they be trusted?" Brian asked.

"They aren't judges. Charon isn't going to take Anya to heaven or to hell. Psychopomps are more like subway conductors. He will take you wherever your ticket says you're supposed to go."

"He said that I need to stop Hope." Anya's mouth thinned. "I believe that he will take me where he says he will."

"And how will you get back?" Brian asked. His fingers were knit tightly in hers.

"When the living travel on the astral planes, they're connected to the body by an etheric cord," Ciro explained. "It extends from the naval of the astral double to the physical one. It isn't limited by time and space, and will stretch to infinity."

"Leslie had one," Anya said. She didn't mention that it worked as Ciro had described, until it had been severed by Hope's vortex.

"If need be, we can reel you back in," Ciro said. "Give you a good, hard pinch or shake you awake."

"What about Sparky? And the eggs?" Anya's brow creased as she looked at Sparky's head peering out of the bathtub.

"I don't know how it works for familiars," Ciro admitted. "I do know that they wander the astral planes as they wish, so they are able to exercise some free will on those other planes."

"Can I leave them here?" Anya wanted to leave them safe in the protection of a magick circle.

"Unlikely. You're bonded to your familiar. Many people meet their familiars for the first time on the astral plane. Where you go, he will likely follow you."

Anya unwound herself from Brian and went to sit on the edge of the claw-foot bathtub. She stroked Sparky from nose to tail, feeling the warmth of his skin. "I don't want to drag you along into this, Sparky."

The salamander stood up. He looked up at her with solemn marble eyes and licked the side of her face. Tears sprang unexpectedly to her eyes. No matter what other crazy shit was happening in this world or any others, she could always depend on Sparky.

"I don't think this is a good idea," Brian said. "There must be some other way."

"If Hope has disappeared, there may not be another

way to track her." Katie shook her head. "Unless the police find her, Charon may be our only hope."

"For once I agree with Brian," Jules argued. "Wandering around in other worlds didn't help Leslie. We should let the cops do their job."

"And how many more of them could get hurt trying to catch her?"

The chatter of the debate washed over her. Anya slid into the bathtub, curling around the nest of eggs. The eggs had warmed the coins beneath them, heating them to the temperature of bathwater. Anya's breath fogged the porcelain side of the tub. Sparky spooned around the other side of the nest, rested his head on her collarbone.

Anya put the coin on her tongue, whispered, "Charon."

And the world went black.

CHAPTER SIXTEEN

THE WORLD WENT BLACK.

And then it turned inside out and opened up.

Anya felt weightless, the warm drifting sensation of dozing in warm bathwater. She opened her eyes to find herself floating above the bathtub, nose to nose with her own face.

Startled, she kicked backward. Like a clumsy swimmer in a pool, she backed up and managed to get her feet on the floor. But the pressure felt different; heavier. She looked down. Sparky sat beside her on the floor, tail wagging. He gleamed with pure amber light, much more strongly than he did in the physical plane. The mottles and speckles on his body churned white and orange, playing over his skin like the shadow of fire.

Anya looked down.

She wasn't herself. Her hands were covered with articulated copper scales, moving up and over her body in a suit of segmented armor. She wore a breastplate polished to a blinding gleam. True to Ciro's word, a translucent silver cord extended from her navel to the limp body in the bathtub. She reached up and felt a helmet covering her head, molded to the back of her skull.

"Welcome to your astral self."

Anya turned. Charon stood on the floor, hands in his pockets. He looked much the same as he had as a ghost—a rocker in the wrong era—but he was surrounded with a gray aura that dissipated at the edges like smoke. His eyes burned cold blue in the haze.

Anya turned her copper hands up to the light. "I saw myself like this once before. Only once." The copper armor had erupted from her salamander torque to protect her from the fiery breath of the king of salamanders, Sirrush. That had been the breath that killed her lover, Drake.

"The astral shows people as they really are. Like the philosopher said, 'As within, so without.' " Charon nodded. *"But I've gotta say, that's very impressive."*

Anya leaned over the edge of the bathtub. Panic laced through her. The eggs were gone.

"The eggs!" she cried.

"You're wearing them," Charon answered. He pointed to a belt of beads around her waist. When Anya looked closer, she could see that the belt was made of the tiny eggs, strung together like a girdle. When she touched them, she could feel the heat of them, hot as coals.

"I don't know what you are, but you're awfully shiny." Renee sat on the bar stool and gave her an appraising look. In this world, Renee was wreathed in a sultry pink light, accompanied by the smell of lilies.

"You can see me?" Anya asked.

"*Sure, doll.*" She cast a wary look at Charon. "*I see him, too.*"

"*Don't worry,*" he said. "*I'm not taking you anywhere.*"

Renee's pencil-thin eyebrows dropped, and her lashes fluttered. "*Good. Somebody has to stay behind to watch the old man.*"

She gestured toward Ciro. It was then that Anya understood that it wasn't just her that was different in this sidereal world. It was the world itself and everything in it.

The other humans in the room seemed rooted in place, as if time ran slower for them, and oblivious to her presence. They were blurry around the edges, and Anya could see light surrounding them. Ciro was surrounded by a white shimmer that flickered like a lightbulb almost ready to go out. When she came close to him, she could nearly hear it buzzing.

Katie stood arguing with the others, blooming a serene turquoise flame. Jules was gesturing and saying something beside her, surrounded by a shining gold light that Anya found oddly comforting. Max hummed beside him, crackling in an orange-gold energetic flare.

Brian stood at the perimeter, arms crossed. Anya reached out to touch him. Where the others were bathed in bright, vibrant color, his aura was murky. Bits of green and black fizzled in a swirling, confused mass. When she touched his skin, her hand passed through him, as if she were a ghost.

Charon put his hand on Anya's shoulder, and she jumped. His grip was solid.

"Why can't I touch him?" she asked. "And how come you can touch me?" She wasn't sure she liked the reversed roles.

"You're essentially a ghost on this plane, subject to the same laws as ghosts. You can't affect the physical world. But things on the astral plane can interact with you."

"What am I seeing?" Anya whispered, squinting at Brian's fuzzy aura.

"Afterimages. The astral world is a sidereal plane—it exists parallel to the physical world. It intersects with the physical plane where energy moves, whether it's the energy of thought, memory, or life."

Anya looked up. The bar itself was rendered in shades of gray. But it wasn't the same as she remembered. Paintings hung over tables that didn't exist before. The windows weren't blackened out and boarded shut, they were stained glass. Even the door handles seemed to be from a different era.

"This is the building's memory of itself. When humans talk about residual hauntings, they talk about the energy impressions a place has made over time, through people tracking through it and focusing their thought energies on it. Sometimes deep impressions make it right through to other planes. Sort of like when you press very hard with a pen on a piece of carbon paper, and the image is transferred to the layer below."

Anya glanced at the ghost of the flapper. "Renee, is this what you see?"

The flapper nodded, her feather earrings floating away from her shoulders. She touched a stool upholstered in rich leather. *"This is how I remember it. Sometimes I think I'm the only one who does."*

Anya turned back to Charon. "We have to find Hope. I released most of the spirits she'd trapped in reliquaries, but she has Pandora's Jar. And all the ghosts from the museum."

Charon frowned. *"Those are old ghosts. Powerful ones. She'll be ready to put up a fight."*

"How can we find her?"

"There's one place in the city where all ghosts pass through. We should be able to catch her trail there, at Michigan Central Station."

Anya's brow wrinkled underneath her helmet. "That's been closed for decades."

"It's been closed to humans. Not to the rest of us." Charon gestured to the door. *"C'mon. I'll show you."*

Hesitantly, Anya followed him through the door of the Devil's Bathtub. When she stepped out onto the street, she stopped short and gasped. Sparky ran into the back of her armored legs and grumbled at the affront.

She'd expected to see what she always had: a cracked downtown street, traffic, telephone poles, maybe a bit of litter or a parked car decorated with tickets. But the road was nearly empty, unfolding like a black ribbon, winding around buildings from various eras: the 1920s, 1930s, and beyond. Snatches of music from the jazz era played through open windows, and a Model T tooled down the street. A tree had taken root in the sidewalk, shining absinthe green, and Anya could see its roots digging below the pavement in perfect symmetry to the branches reaching overhead to the dusky sky.

Two doors down, a brick warehouse collapsed without a sound, dissolving into dust that blew downwind like a sandstorm. Anya covered her nose as the sand blew past, smelling like shattered clay and with bits that glittered like glass.

"What's happening?" she gasped. The red dust rolled past her ankles and down the streets.

"That's what happens to things that are forgotten here." Charon shrugged, as if seeing a three-story building dissolve was a usual event. *"Memory is the key thing. Energy makes things live. Thoughts are energy. If no one—ghost or human—thinks about something, then it disappears."*

The dust blew past, leaving a blank and empty lot, filled with a black void that seethed and churned. It was the most complete destruction of anything Anya had ever seen. Instinctively, she recoiled from it. But it felt familiar. Her fingers touched her breastbone, where that terrible dark fire burned. It smelled like oblivion.

"We've gotta get going. I'll explain the laws on the way." Charon walked a motorcycle from the shadow of the Devil's Bathtub. Anya wasn't a fan of motorcycles. Firefighters and paramedics called them "donorcycles." Charon's ride was an old, beat-up bike that reminded Anya of something she would have seen in a World War II documentary.

"That's your . . . transportation here?"

Charon must have sensed her squeamishness. A smile played around the corners of his mouth, the first she'd seen on him. It wasn't an unpleasant expression.

"What did you expect? I ditched the boat a couple thousand years ago."

Anya couldn't tell if he was joking or serious. She climbed on the bike behind him. Sparky scrambled up to her shoulder, and she awkwardly put her arms around Charon's waist. He radiated cold through his coat, a chill that seeped through her metal armor and made her shudder. His coat smelled like incense.

Charon stomped on the accelerator. The bike responded with a sound like a choked lawn mower and took off. Anya's stomach lurched and her chest tightened. She heard Sparky's claws scraping on her armor as he shifted around her neck. From the corner of her tearing eye, she saw him leaning his head into the wind. His tongue and gill-fronds unfurled, and he seemed to taste the air lashing around them.

Anya shuddered. At least she was wearing a helmet.

Through slitted eyes, she watched the landscape whip past. Black road unfurled under a dusk-reddened sky. Streetlights had begun to flicker on, but they were a hodgepodge of styles: gaslights, electric lights suspended from ornate posts, and lights suspended from sleek aluminum arms. Some civil engineer, somewhere, must have been dreaming of them enough to give them form and shape here.

The buildings shifted, like clouds across the sky. In

some moments, she saw buildings as she remembered them in the physical world: factories, houses, landmarks. But they sometimes reverted to earlier eras. Some spaces were rendered in more clarity than others: Two ghosts playing checkers in a park were surrounded with exquisite detail, down to each blade of grass. Anya imagined that they'd played every weekend for decades. Waiting areas of doctors offices were lit, with each dog-eared magazine sketched in boring, painstaking detail. Classroom desks could be seen through windows with plastic chairs pulled up behind them. Walls and train cars decorated with graffiti were sharper than blank, new ones. Supermarkets and gas stations faded into a blurry, decaying haze—no one apparently gave much thought to these, and they were quite literally falling apart.

Charon turned off by the river, the bike rattling and growling along the street. The River Rouge sliced through the twilight like silver rapids, much faster and clearer and stronger than in the physical world.

Charon caught her looking, shouted back to her, *"Water's like that, strong here. It gave rise to that myth about evil not being able to cross running water."*

"Is that true here?"

"Not any place I've ever been. Well, not without magickal interference."

Anya assumed that was a lot of places. She shouted over the wind as it tore at her voice: "What are you, anyway? Are you *the* Charon? The guy fishing for dead souls on the river Styx? Or is that an affectation?"

She felt his muscles tense under her arms. *"How about you?"* he countered. *"Are you the Ishtar?"*

"Of course not."

"We all inherit pieces of things that make us what we are, whether we want them or not."

Anya poked him in the ribs, which caused the bike to wobble dangerously. "Quit being so fucking cryptic."

"You really are clueless, aren't you?"

"Yeah. I am."

"Do you know what an avatar is?"

"That's the thing you create to represent yourself in a video game. Everyone makes themselves look like they're a lot hotter than they really are and goes off into some fantasy world to slay ogres and get virtual sex."

Charon laughed. Anya felt it rumbling under her fingers before the wind ripped it away. *"If it were only that easy. Let me back up a sec. Do you know what an archetype is?"*

"I'm not *entirely* stupid. I remember reading about Jung and his archetypes. They're constructs of ideal people that exist in the collective unconscious. Warriors, magicians, tricksters . . . that kind of thing. There was a guy on PBS a lot of years ago who talked about them." Anya was impressed with herself for retaining that much from Mythology 101.

"Joseph Campbell. Yeah, he's a trip. Great guy. And he's having a rocking good time in the Afterworld." Charon shook his head, and the air clawed through his Flock of Seagulls hair. *"Anyway . . . archetypes are these idealized*

mythological images. Remember what I said about thought giving life to form in this world?"

"Yeah."

"Pieces of those archetypes sometimes express themselves on the physical plane. They want to be timeless and eternal . . . so they don't want the physical world to forget about them. Otherwise, they stop existing here, too."

"Gah." The whole theory made her head hurt.

"The short version is, you've been touched by Ishtar. Or the timeless archetype of Ishtar, however you want to look at it. In ancient times, this would have made you a priestess or a god's favored champion."

"I'm her avatar in the physical world?" Anya struggled to keep up.

"You're one of her avatars, probably one of hundreds over time. Maybe thousands."

Anya's mouth thinned. "I got possessed a few months back by a demon who had been a priestess of Ishtar."

"You'll attract synchronicities that connect you to that archetype. It's totally unpredictable, but that's the way it works."

"And the salamanders?" she asked.

"The salamanders need a protector. You're a formidable threat, from their perspective. You're a Lantern, and you can see into their world. You've got the touch of Ishtar upon you. So, yeah, a perfectly rational fire elemental would want to latch on to you to mother its offspring."

"But Sparky just didn't pick me out of a crowd. My mother gave him to me."

"Remember what I said about pieces of archetypes

wandering into the physical plane? Somewhere, someone in your family picked up that salamander collar, and it found its way to you. You've been blessed by fire."

Anya's jaw hardened. She didn't like the idea that these bits of myth expressed themselves with conscious volition, regardless of the willingness of the recipient of their graces.

"This stuff is a lot like seeing ghosts," Charon explained. *"They're not part of everyone's daily consciousness. But when you can see beyond the mundane physical world, you realize the fingers of myth are all around you, touching and underneath everything. And here, on the astral plane, myths and ghosts are a lot more solid and powerful than they would ever be on your corporeal plane."*

"Look, Charon. I was raised to be a good Catholic girl. This is just a bit too New Agey for me to digest."

"Good Catholic girls don't devour ghosts, raise fire elementals, or go gallivanting off with motorcyclers on the astral plane." Charon snorted. *"I don't think Ishtar really cares about your upbringing. She liked you, and you became one of hers."*

Charon peeled off down one of the side streets, and Anya held on for dear life. He pulled the motorcycle off the street in front of Michigan Central Station and shut the engine off. The silence made Anya's ears ring.

On the astral plane, the train station looked much as it did in real life: a shattered black husk. But here, throngs of people moved past the windows and along the warped steel tracks. Anya could make out hats shading faces, the swish of skirts, hear the chatter of voices and the creak of luggage.

"They're ghosts." Anya's brow wrinkled, and she scrambled off the back of the bike.

"This place is what it's always been: a way station for spirits among planes. Spirits come here before they move to the Afterworld, whatever that destination may be for them."

Anya followed Charon up the steps. "So . . . this is the gate to heaven?"

"Or hell. And anywhere in between. From here, you can travel to any plane of reality. And the spirits don't have much choice where they go."

They passed through the doors into the crowded lobby. Hundreds of ghosts milled. They were images of people from many eras: women in bonnets, men in zoot suits, a child dressed in footie pajamas clutching a stuffed toy. No one seemed to notice the disparities in eras, and Anya wondered how long it had taken some of them to travel here. Some stared at a clock high on the wall, waiting with train cases and briefcases. Others flashed through the darkness like minnows in a pond, racing for the train platform. Long lines snaked to the ticket counter, which was made whole and full of glass. Anya watched as a shadow pushed a scrap of paper through the window to a ghost. The ghost at the head of the line, a teenage girl, took the ticket. She looked at the stub and burst into tears.

Charon wove through the crowd like a native New Yorker in a subway station. Anya struggled to keep up with him, trotting in his wake. From his high perch,

Sparky craned his head above the crowd. The bodies of ghosts pressed against her, cold as winter wind, chill fogging her copper armor. Sparky remained wound tight around Anya's neck like a spring. She shivered, and her armor rattled around her.

Charon paused at the edge of the train platform, peered into the darkness with his hands stuffed into his pockets. *"It's coming soon."*

"What's coming?" Anya's mouth was dry. She could see light beginning to prickle the edge of the tunnel, hear a terrible sound moving toward them.

"The train. It'll take you where you need to go."

The roar trembled the platform, whipping up wind and a scorching heat that shimmered in the air. A blackness thick as the dark at the bottom of any basement stairs rushed down the tunnel, blotting out the weak lights strung there like a cloud moving over stars.

"It's going to hell!" Anya shouted, feeling a visceral fear rise in her stomach. That sound could come from nowhere else.

"Not hell." Charon's voice was shredded by the black. *"But a road to it."*

Before she could turn and make a break for it, the shadow washed over the platform, sucking all the spirits like tissues in a vacuum cleaner. Anya crouched down and clutched Sparky, remembering tornado drills from elementary school. But the ghost train pulled her in as if she weighed nothing.

She felt an exquisite moment of weightlessness, of

falling. Her body lifted in its armor, and she could feel it loosen, spinning around her skin. Sparky's heaviness around her shoulders lifted, though her fingers still wound in his feet. Blackness surrounded her, punctuated only with sparks of light that she suspected came from her own retinas, perhaps a concussion. She could feel the eggs strung around her waist orbiting her like glowing planets. The vertebrae along her spine and the bones in her joints loosened, and she wondered for a split second if this was what the ghosts felt, ephemeral and fluid . . .

. . . and then she hit the ground. The blackness spat her out with a roar and a rush of wind on concrete. Her armor slammed around her as she took the impact on her left shoulder and hip, trying to shield Sparky and the eggs.

She groaned and rolled onto her back, Sparky squirming out of her grip with a huff. He stalked away, licking at his back as he shook his tail in irritation at the rough landing. Her fingers fluttered to the eggs strung around her waist, feeling nothing shattered. She blinked stupidly up at a streetlight, realizing that a soft skiff of snow had blown over the concrete. Snowflakes drifted in the streetlight like mosquitoes in summer. They melted when they touched her face and armor, tasting like iron and pollution.

"It helps if you hit the ground running." Charon stood over her, hands in his pockets.

Anya sat up, got her feet under her, and slowly stood. Where she'd fallen, she'd scraped an angel in the snow. "Shove it up your psychopompous ass, Charon."

Charon snorted. He fished in his pocket for a cigarette.

Snow didn't melt on the shoulders of his coat or in his hair, just collected there like dandruff. But Anya could smell something burning before he lit the lighter.

Her brows drew together. She was on a residential street, a familiar one. Though the aura around the streetlights was surreally soft and the numbers painted on the curb were fuzzy and indistinct, she recognized this place. She recognized the cracked macadam, the skeletons of crabapple trees planted too close to the street, the fire hydrant painted yellow. It was a place she hadn't been since childhood, a place she'd tried to forget.

Her voice was low, threatening. But a cold sweat had broken out under her armor, a sweat that had nothing to do with the snow. "Charon. Where the fuck are we?"

The flame of the lighter illuminated Charon's angular face, rendering it inhuman for an instant. *The train takes you where you need to go.*

"You also said the train went to hell."

Same difference. We've all got to go through hell to get where we're going.

Anya swallowed and turned to see her childhood home, burning to the ground.

CHAPTER SEVENTEEN

ANYA FROZE.

She froze as she had when she was a child, looking up and seeing the Christmas tree in flames. Then Sparky had dragged her out of the house. Her mother, upstairs, had been unable to escape. She'd died in the fire . . . the fire that had been twelve-year-old Anya's fault; her fault for sneaking out of her bedroom, for plugging the damn Christmas tree lights in, for falling asleep under its comforting glow with the salamander draped across her legs. The fire that had been ignited in the brittle Christmas tree—this was the first year they'd had a real one—by the multicolored lights that pulsed like stars.

She stood on the curb, fists clenched, unable to move. A hiccup congealed in her throat as she watched the flames lick through the broken front window of the little saltbox house. The husk of the Christmas tree shriveled through the smoke that began to peel and melt the vinyl siding. There were no sirens in the distance, no one coming. Only the crackle of flame and the trickle of the snow melting on the front lawn, draining away into the street gutters.

"This can't be real," she whispered to herself. Her vision blurred, turning orange in the glare.

Charon's voice seemed distant behind her. *"It is real. Real on this plane. Playing over and over, because you remember it."*

Sparky growled. He stood up on his hind legs and grabbed Anya's hand in his teeth, dragged her a step toward the house.

Her suspension broke, and her firefighter's instinct ignited. Anya raced to the front door, ripping open the screen door. The wooden door was locked fast. She front-kicked the door as hard as she could, aiming high for the lockset, the weakest point in the door. The sound was deafeningly loud in the silence, like a gunshot echoing in her helmet.

Crack.

Crack.

Crack.

Her armored foot finally rattled the lockset loose. One more hit broke it open, and she stumbled against the door sagging against the frame. Sparky lunged ahead of her, racing across the rust-colored shag carpet to the fire.

"Sparky!" she screamed.

The salamander dove into the flames, and Anya's heart lurched into her throat. She'd not run more than two steps after him when he emerged from the blaze surrounding the corpse of the Christmas tree, dragging a small body by the collar.

It was Anya. Anya as a child, curled into a ball with her fists over her face. She recognized the Wonder Woman pajamas. Sparky hauled speckled ass past the adult armored Anya, dragging the child out to the cold snow of the lawn.

It was exactly as she remembered, Sparky rescuing her. This parallel world was unfolding exactly as it had in the real world she knew.

Smoke billowed over her, and Anya's eyes watered and stung. Her gaze raced up the stairs. But it didn't have to unfold exactly like the past this time.

"Mom!" she yelled.

She stumbled up the stairs, feeling the heat of fire spreading under the stairs. On the living-room wall, she could see wallpaper blackening and curling. Lack of oxygen made her vision shimmer and buzz; smoke rolled up the steps, rendering the blackness deep and total.

Over the roar of the fire below her, she could hear voices:

"You can't have her!" It was her mother's voice, growling in the darkness.

Anya fumbled down the hallway on her hands and knees, trying to keep below the level of smoke. Her mother's bedroom was at the far end of the hall. Her armored fingertips clutched shag carpet that was beginning to melt, and she could taste the char in the back of her throat.

"She's mine." The voice that answered was one that she'd never heard, more a low hiss than human.

Anya pressed her hands against the closed bedroom door. As soon as she opened it, she knew that smoke would flood the room. She reached up for the brass doorknob, felt it sizzle against her hand through the armor. She turned it and tumbled into the room in a cloud of smoke, slammed the door behind her.

"Mom!" Anya cried.

Her mother stood barefoot in her nightgown, fists clenched. Her long dark hair floated around her in the updraft of the heat. She turned, and her face was a mask of fear and fury.

"Anya, get out!" she shouted.

Coughing, Anya looked past her, past her to the terrible creature standing before the closet door. It was the shape of a man, but there was no body. Its form was a shifting outline of flames, the heat shimmering before him and curling the plastic blinds of the window. A glass perfume bottle on her mother's dresser broke under the heat, as if it had been shot.

The shape extended a finger toward Anya. Its voice was the hiss and pop of flame warped into a human voice. *"I've come for her. She's one of mine."*

"No." Anya's mother was between them.

"You can't keep her from me."

"I've kept her from you for twelve years. I'll keep her from you for one more night."

Anya reached out and grabbed her mother's hand. She looked down and saw the hem of her mother's polyester nightgown begin to burn. "Mom, we've got to go, now!"

The flame-creature growled and hissed. *"That is not part of our bargain."*

Anya's mother turned to the fiery shape. *"What can I give you for a reprieve? For a pardon?"*

The creature shook its head. *"No pardon. But I will allow a reprieve."*

Tears streamed down her mother's face. *"What do you want?"*

"I'll take you."

Anya dragged at her mother's hand, but it seemed that the older woman had taken root, like a tree. Her mother turned, cupped her daughter's face in her hands. Tears sizzled in the impossible heat. On some abstract level, Anya knew that nothing human could survive in it.

"You have to let me go," her mother said, her face shimmering.

"No. I won't." Anya clutched her mother's wrists with armored hands. "Not again."

"It's not your fault. None of this is." Her mother's gaze flickered to the creature blackening the ceiling. *"It's mine."*

"We need to get the hell out of here!" Anya shouted.

She shook her head, wisps of dark hair flying. *"No. One of us must stay. One of us must stay with your father."*

Anya gawked at the monster. Her mind refused to comprehend, refused to process the scene further.

She grabbed her mother's arm, intending to throw her over her shoulder and carry her from this place. But the fiery shape of the man cast a wall of fire at her that knocked her over the bed into the far corner of the room. Drywall splintered behind her back, and Anya struggled to draw breath.

Through tearing eyes, she crawled over the bed. She couldn't make a sound above a squeak, couldn't say anything as her mother walked toward the creature with her head lowered. The creature took her mother in its fiery embrace. Anya smelled flesh singe and hair sizzle. For a moment, her mother was gloriously beautiful, her hair ignited in flames like an angel. Fire fell like a curtain over her mother, reaching up to the ceiling, dragging down half of a roof strut with a sound like thunder.

The floor buckled. Tangled in a burning bedspread, Anya slid to the hole in the floor. The burning fringe in her fingers broke away, and she slipped down the ruin of the ceiling, crashing into the inferno of the first floor.

Flames surrounded her, washed over her in rippling waves. It felt like lying in the ocean at low tide in the sunshine, the heat of the water rolling over her. It poured into her lungs in shimmering heat, and she could hear it pop and fizzle there.

Intellectually, she knew that she couldn't survive this. Nothing human could. But though she felt the heat roiling through her, she didn't burn.

And if she didn't burn, she *was* going to survive this. She wasn't going to be like her mother.

She brushed the crumbling drywall away, shoved a burning beam from her legs. She climbed to her feet, watching in fascination as the fire clung to her armor and raced down her gauntlets; it reminded her of spilling alcohol in her high-school chemistry class and tipping over a Bunsen burner to watch it burn on the near-indestructible stone surface. The brilliant light seethed like a living thing but didn't destroy her.

She breathed it in, feeling it flow down the back of her throat. It felt like when she devoured ghosts, that same burn and sting, like drinking absinthe.

Somewhere in the distance, she thought she heard the voice of the fire laugh.

The voice of the creature that was her father.

The fire roared around her, devouring the house. The skeleton of the steps crumbled, and the remaining roof beams groaned overhead. Anya stepped over the remains of the Christmas tree, past the blackened bricks of the fireplace and the flammable Christmas stockings gone up like marshmallows, melting onto the carpet of fire. She stepped over the broken glass of the front window frame, out into the cold night.

The fire had dissolved the snow on the front yard. Anya turned back to stare at it in all its terrible beauty, smoke obliterating the stars in the sky. The change in temperature fogged her armor, caused the gloss of sweat on her brow to flash-freeze to an instant chill.

In the driveway, Sparky and Charon waited. Sparky stood over the form of Anya's younger self. She was huddled into a small ball, her arms around the salamander's neck. Charon stood beside them, smoking a cigarette, watching the house burn.

Anya strode down the driveway to Charon. Steam rolled from her armor, and snow melted under her footsteps as she stalked up to him and struck him in the face with a closed fist. When her fist made contact, she could hear the sizzle of metal as it connected with his cheek. She'd half expected that her hand would slide right through him, like it would in her physical world. To her delight, it connected as thickly as real flesh. Charon had been right; myths and ghosts were more solid here. Satisfyingly so.

Charon fell back into the snow like a ton of bricks, dropping his cigarette.

She stood over him, glowering and steaming. "Why in the fuck did you bring me here?"

Charon put a hand to the red burn on his jaw.

"Why bring me here if I couldn't change anything?" Anya screamed at him. "Why bring me here if I couldn't save her?"

Charon sat up. *"You could never save her. But there were things you needed to know. . . . "*

"Fuck you, Charon. And the boat, train, whatever the fuck you rode in on." Anya turned to Sparky, knelt in the snow before the child and salamander wound up in a tight ball.

"Hey." She was afraid of touching the girl, afraid of burning her. But her younger self peered over Sparky's head with solemn eyes. "I'm sorry that . . . I'm sorry that I couldn't save her." A lump rose in Anya's throat, and she couldn't keep the tears from sizzling on her cheek.

The child disentangled herself from Sparky, stepped barefoot in the snow before Anya. Through blurred vision, Anya saw the little girl didn't leave any tracks in the snow.

"You weren't supposed to. You were supposed to save yourself." The girl opened her arms to embrace Anya . . . and disappeared, like ice melting in an oven.

Anya sniffled, her tears speckling the ground and burning through the snow. Sparky waddled up to her and licked her face. Like she did when she was a child, she threw her arms around his neck and sobbed.

Something plopped and sizzled as it fell to the ground.

Only then did she remember the eggs. In a panic, she reached around her waist for the girdle of eggs. She knew that they had to be kept warm, but Jesus Christ . . . had the fire she'd heedlessly run headlong into killed them? Had she hardboiled Sparky's eggs?

The egg that had fallen to the snow rolled, cracked open. A tiny, perfect replica of Sparky clambered out. In amazement, Anya lowered her hand to the ground, and the baby salamander crawled into her palm. It blinked and cocked its head at her. From its marble-like eyes, down to the speckles on its tummy, it was perfect.

The other eggs began to fall into the snow. One after another, the glass-like shells cracked, and orange newts waddled free, steaming on the snow. They rolled in the snow, scratched their heads with their rear feet. Sparky stood over them, licking them and fussing like a mother chicken with a brood of chicks.

Anya counted them. All fifty-one eggs were in various stages of hatching. Anya plucked pieces of eggshell from their dewy backs. She rapped a tough egg open on the curb to release its prisoner, just like Katie would rap a chicken egg on the edge of a mixing bowl to release the yolk.

Charon stood back, watching. Anya, noticing that the burn mark she'd put on his face was gone, glared at him. She'd hit him hard enough to break his jaw. He should be spitting teeth on the driveway, not watching her with that smug air of bored superiority.

He shrugged. *"I took a swim in the Styx. Like Achilles. Makes one pretty damn near invulnerable."*

Salamanders clambered up her armor, into her lap. As she watched, they seemed to flicker and grow. She guessed that they'd inherited Sparky's talent for changing shape.

Her relief at seeing that they had hatched safely was suddenly tainted with a stab of dread.

"What do I do with them now?" she groaned.

Charon dug another cigarette out of his pocket. *"Looks to me like you've got an army of salamanders. Which is exactly what you're gonna need to stop Hope."*

"They're . . . they're just *babies*," Anya growled at him, watching the hatchlings tumble in the snow and chase their tails in the bright light of the burning house. Like the child, they were innocents. And she wasn't going to take them into war. "They're not weapons."

"They're salamanders." Charon blew smoke into the sky. *"They're fearsome elemental creatures. Not children."*

A newt waddled up Anya's arm and wagged his tail. Fearsome, indeed. "They're not fearsome anything, Charon. They're too little to defend themselves."

"I wouldn't be so sure." Charon's eyes narrowed,

and he gestured at a shape shambling down the street. *"Watch."*

A ghost drifted along the street like a plastic bag pushed by the wind. It was the ghost of a man dressed in a long policeman's coat and sharply starched hat, the kind worn by cops in the 1940s. Anya supposed that the watchman was simply continuing his rounds in this plane, patrolling the streets in darkness. He twirled his baton as he walked, his feet making no tracks in the snow.

The salamanders lifted their heads, twisted toward the ghost, like sunflowers turning toward the sun. Tongues flickered out, and the salamanders skittered to the curb, watching. Chirps echoed through the crowd. Sparky stood behind them, staring at the watchman with black, marble-like eyes. The hair on the back of Anya's neck rose.

The ghostly watchman saw the fire billowing behind them, paused. He lifted his whistle to his mouth with white-gloved hands. A shrill note echoed over the snow and steam, to summon help. . . .

The salamanders swarmed him. They skittered down into the street and washed over him in a flailing mass of legs and tails. Their jaws opened and closed, tearing into the ghost with tiny teeth and claws sprouting from their feet.

Anya ran to the ghost. Charon blocked her, grasping her by her arms. She struggled with him, but he was surprisingly strong, holding her fast by her wrists. In horror, she watched as the salamanders shredded the defenseless ghost. It was like watching a nature documentary when army ants tore a ghostly beetle apart. The policeman blew his whistle for help, over and over again, until the wheezing sound became nasal, ragged, and stilled. The little salamanders ripped off shreds of ectoplasm and gorged themselves like dogs with fresh kill, while Sparky looked on proudly from the curb.

"What are they doing?" Anya shouted.

"Feeding."

"But salamanders don't eat—"

"Salamanders, like any other elemental, need energy to survive. Sparky gets what he needs from the electrical appliances in your physical world, from the occasional ghost you allow him to snap at, and from you."

Her brow wrinkled. "What do you mean, from me?"

"Lanterns put out a surprising amount of energy. Salamanders are attracted to that. He's probably licking at your aura as you sleep."

Anya tried to shake off the uncomfortable feeling of being a salamander snack, when a little newt disengaged itself from the seething mass. It waddled heavily across the yard, groaned, and lay on its back with its legs splayed open, displaying its full belly. It had grown a few inches since it had begun feeding upon the hapless night watchman, its belly distended as if it had swallowed a golf ball. Sparky gave it an approving lick.

Charon released Anya, but she remained rooted in place, staring at the salamanders wolfing down the shredded remains of the ghost. What was left looked like papier-mâché, a soft, ectoplasmic goo that was rapidly losing illumination, like crushed fireflies. Snorkling nasal sounds emanated from the scene as the salamanders licked ectoplasm from their snouts.

"Oh, my God," she breathed.

Charon smirked. *"I think your children are ready to go to war."*

A baby salamander ran gleefully away from the remains, scuttling over Anya's foot. His speckled tail kinked in joy, he trilled and scrambled away with glowing goo smeared on his face.

CHAPTER EIGHTEEN

"I'M NOT FOLLOWING YOU ANYWHERE." Anya crossed her arms over her chest. It was hard to take a serious stance with dozens of overstuffed salamanders crawling all over her, but she was going to try. She picked one up who was standing on her shoulder, licking her cheek, and set it on the ground to clamber on Sparky.

Charon frowned. *"Look, need I remind you what's at stake? Now that Hope has Pandora's Jar, she's got enough storage to suck up half the ghosts in the Midwestern U.S."*

"That's not the problem. The problem is that I can't trust you to take me where you say you will." Anya couldn't imagine a worse hell than the fire that had consumed her childhood home, but wasn't entirely sure that one didn't exist. Either way, she didn't want to find out.

"I don't have any control over where the ghost train takes us. You had to go here to resolve your . . . issues." Charon rolled his eyes. *"I don't like wasting time any more than you do."*

"Seems to me that you enjoy being psychopompous."

"Whatever." Charon turned his back. *"I'm walking back to the train to see if it will take me to Hope now. You can come, or not."* He ground out his cigarette with his heel and struck off down the street.

Anya glanced back at the house. Fire had chewed it down to a pile of blackened beams, stinking burned vinyl, and glittering glass. She didn't particularly want to sit around and watch it be reduced to embers. And she had no desire to pick through the wreckage for her mother's remains . . . or to see if that man-shaped creature of fire still lingered. Sighing, she clunked off after Charon. Sparky trotted along beside her, and the little salamanders tumbled along in their wake, nipping at her heels. Anya hoped they weren't still hungry. But maybe they could be convinced to gnaw on Charon.

The streets stretched out in ribbons of black and white, bits of snow spangling the darkness. Anya could feel the cold seeping into the seams of her armor as the warmth of the fire faded. Where the little salamanders hitched a ride, she felt scalding heat, as if they still retained some of the fire they'd hatched in. Sparky plodded along, his tail switching through the skiff of snow and obliterating Charon's footprints. Cold air whistled along the neck of Anya's armor like the sound of a child blowing across an empty bottle.

Charon paused at a railway crossing, then turned west on the tracks.

"It's shorter, this way," was all he said. He walked along the rail, boots sure-footed on the ice.

Anya's armored feet were too clumsy to walk like a bird on a wire. She lifted her feet and marched, stepping from one broad wooden railway tie to the next. Sparky hopped along beside her, with the little salamanders springing like grasshoppers behind them in the gravel and pieces of green slag.

After what seemed like hours, a now-familiar rumble echoed in the distance. Anya moved to get off the tracks, calling for Sparky and the salamanders. She could feel the vibration in the metal.

Charon stood on the tracks. *"We can catch the train from here."*

Anya blinked stupidly. "On the tracks?" She could see the train lights in the distance. "We'll get run over."

Charon shook his head. *"It's just like at the train station. Not pleasant, but you won't get killed."* He extended a hand.

Grudgingly, Anya took it, clambered up on the slippery second rail. Sparky huddled up against her leg, and she could hear the metallic clinks peppering her armor as the little salamanders clung to her.

Every instinct told her to run as the train plowed into view, a dark shape with a yellow headlight. Even though she knew it wasn't real, the whistle sounded real, the thundering on the tracks felt real, and her heart threatened to hammer out of her chest.

She glanced sidelong at Charon, balanced on the first rail. His expression was one of cool indifference, and his hand was cold in hers.

The lights washed over her, and Anya sucked in her

breath, bracing for the terrible impact that would flatten her like a soda can and fling salamanders all over the tracks for the next mile . . .

. . . but the ghost train roared through her, sucking her up in a whirl of darkness and snowflakes. Anya felt a sense of weightlessness, spiraling through black and tasting cold snow on her lip. As the roar diminished, she remembered to move her legs, to hit the ground running as Charon had warned . . .

. . . and her copper-covered feet slapped down on broken concrete. She pitched forward, dizzyingly, her stomach lurching into her throat and her feet rattling on the ground like a broken muffler dragged by a car. She managed to stay upright, despite Sparky's unbalanced weight clinging to her leg. She skidded to a halt.

It was raining salamanders. Little salamanders were spewed out of the darkness that washed over her. They rolled and scrambled on the pavement, aggrieved at the lack of gentility by the conductors of the ghost train, but seemed to be otherwise unhurt. Anya counted fifty. Had she lost one?

In a panic, she cast about, recounting, searching for the missing one. The ghost train receded in the sky like thunder, and Anya was already desperate to get back on board. . . .

"Lose something?" Charon pulled a salamander out of his pocket by its tail. Anya growled at him and snatched the writhing creature, clutching it to her chest.

"Poor baby," she cooed over it.

"It was eating my cigarettes, " he muttered.

The salamander belched, and it smelled like incense.

Anya turned on her heel. She scanned the empty lot they stood in. A traffic light strung over a nearby intersection cast red light on blacktop broken by weeds. A broken chain-link fence dissolved at the far end, beside a battered Dumpster. The topography looked familiar, but she couldn't place it. "Where are we now?"

"We're on Hope's doorstep, " Charon told her grimly.

Anya frowned. Yes . . . this was the place where Hope's headquarters stood in the physical world, but there was no building here. Nothing but trash blowing around the empty lot.

Charon crossed the broken pavement to the Dumpster. He put his shoulder to it and pushed it aside. Rats skittered out of the bottom, and it gave a rusty groan as it scraped across the ground. Anya blinked. That Dumpster had to weigh at least a ton. Either physical laws worked a lot differently here, or Charon was decidedly more inhuman than she'd thought. Maybe that was why the salamanders showed no interest in nibbling on him.

Charon paused to pluck away a yellow cheeseburger wrapper that had blown into his hair. *"Here."*

Anya stared down into a hole that had been covered by the Dumpster. It reminded her of storm cellars in old houses: a stone frame and steps leading down into blackness. It occurred to her that this was the same spot that the basement had occupied in the footprint of the original building. But somehow she doubted that she'd find an old store of office supplies and shelves full of dusty bottles in this place. Nothing was as it seemed on the astral plane, and she expected this would be no exception.

"How does this remain hidden?" Anya wondered if there was a truck that came by every week to pick up the astral Dumpster.

"It's an illusion. A bit of camouflage Hope's using to cover her tracks on this plane."

Charon descended the worn steps, and Anya followed. Sparky oozed down the stairs beside her, while the young salamanders leapt down the stone risers like Slinkies. There seemed to be no light in this place, but Sparky and the newts gave off a shifting amber glow that was sufficient to see by, casting writhing shadows on the earthen ceiling. Plant and tree roots reached down from above as they descended down the broken spiral staircase. The place smelled like winter, like cold earth: sterile and barren, with nothing living.

She heard water, wrinkled her nose. "What's that? The sewer?"

Ahead, Charon shook his head. He didn't seem to need the light of the salamanders to see by; he walked down the uneven steps as if he'd known them well enough to wear the dents in the tops of the steps. *"No. It's the Styx."*

Anya's breath caught in her throat. The staircase spilled out onto a silty causeway, into the broken edges of a canal hewn into the stone. It was man-made; the arches curved as far as the meager light reached over the shallow black water.

"Are you sure it's the Styx? Because it *looks* like a sewer."

Charon sighed. *"It's not the Styx. Just a weak tribu-tary. If you remember your mythology, it wrapped nine times around the perimeter of Hades."*

"I thought we were going after Hope." Anya clenched her fists, trying to resist the urge to strangle the psycho-pomp's laconic throat.

"This is where she's retreated, at least on this plane. We've got to bring the fight to her." Charon began to pace beside the bank, kicking at pieces of trash: moldering newspa-pers, plastic cups, soda cans. The salamanders seemed to recoil from the water. Perhaps fire elementals didn't care much for the Styx. Given its dubious origins, Anya didn't blame them.

"Does she know we're coming?" Anya clunked to the water's edge. There was no way she could swim across in her armor. She ran her fingers along the seams. She had no idea if her astral self was wearing clothes under her armor, but she figured that death's ferryman had seen it all. She took her helmet off and set it in a clean patch of gravel by her feet. She began stripping off her gauntlets.

"Probably not. Not yet." Charon was piling up empty milk jugs and was counting caps in one hand. In the other, he was dragging a dented green plastic kiddie pool in the shape of a turtle.

He stared at her trying to open her breastplate. *"What the hell are you doing?"*

"Getting ready to swim across," she said matter-of-factly, though her cheeks burned.

Charon looked at her as if she was stupid. *"Humans can't get into the water. This is the Styx."*

"First of all, jackass, this is a sewer. But I'll give you the benefit of the doubt, and say it is, at best, a tributary of the Styx. Second of all, the Styx made Achilles invulnerable. And lastly, you seem to have survived it. So kiss my ass."

Charon made a slicing gesture with the hand full of plastic caps. His expression was dark. *"You don't know the cost. All magick has a price, and the Styx is no exception. But, hey, if you want to walk around naked, don't let me stop you."* Charon turned away and began fitting caps on the plastic soda bottles and milk jugs, but Anya thought she saw a spark of wry amusement in his expression. Just for an instant.

"So . . . how the hell am I getting across? Is there a bridge somewhere?" Anya concentrated on wriggling her fingers back into her gauntlets.

Charon was tying the plastic bottles together with a piece of electrical cord, lashing them to the hard rim of the turtle pool. *"If you would stop talking and stripping and doing other distracting things, you'd see that I'm working on that."*

Anya gave him a sour look. At least he found the prospect of her nudity distracting. That was the only flicker of humanity she'd seen in him.

Charon turned his creation over. The kiddie pool resembled a warped artist's conception of a jellyfish, constructed of trash. Bottles of air were trapped under the rim, and Charon cast it in the water with a splash that made the salamanders scatter and hiss. The pool floated, tentacles of plastic and wire reaching out behind it.

"Here's your fucking boat."

Anya stared at the makeshift craft. "Um, thanks."

Charon pulled the raft close to shore, and Anya climbed on top of the contraption. The plastic wobbled and turned under her weight, crumpling even more when Sparky and the other salamanders leapt aboard. The newts squeaked and minced their way around the perimeter, afraid of getting their delicate toes in the water.

Anya shot Sparky a look. "You don't mind water in the physical world. Hell, you gave birth in a bathtub."

"The Styx is different." Charon released the edge of the boat, and it began to turn in a lazy circle.

Anya clutched the rim of the pool, under the turtle's chin. There wasn't room for Charon aboard the good ship Turtle. "What about you?" For a moment, she thought he wasn't coming along, and a pang of alarm struck her.

Charon walked into the water, his black coat flaring after him like the wing of a raven. He grabbed the electrical cord towline and dragged the turtle to deeper water.

"I took one bath in the Styx. Another won't fuck my karma up that much more."

Anya swallowed. Despite his cool demeanor, she was certain that this had to cost him something.

Charon waded into the water, up to his chin, and began to swim. Anya clutched the rim of the raft, while the salamanders cowered under and around her. She could hear their feet scraping against her armor as they clutched her tightly. Perhaps they were right to be afraid of the water.

The towing was slow going into the darkness, where water dripped in tunnels that wound around themselves. Though Anya couldn't detect much current, it seemed as if Charon occasionally struggled with an undertow that caused the electrical cord tether to groan and strain. More than once, she thought she saw something else moving under the water, and whispered to Charon in alarm. He merely grunted an acknowledgment and kept towing them into the black.

Anya shivered, and the newts rattled and reorganized themselves around her like locusts on a tree. Sparky blinked up at her, and she felt a stab of guilt. The way the newts had devoured the night watchman's innocent ghost bothered her. Anya never devoured a ghost without cause, but they were not encumbered by her sense of morality. Their atavistic hunger shocked her.

And yet . . . she was leading them into battle against Hope. Anya expected that Hope would level whatever spirits still remained under her control against her, including the contingent of missing museum ghosts. Many of them were ancient warriors and would know how to fight, whether they wanted to or not. And those ghosts, like the watchman, were blameless in all this. Could she destroy those innocent spirits, in order to keep others out of Hope's grasp?

She shook her head, dislodging a salamander perching

on her head. It dropped back to her lap, huffed, and began to crawl up her arm. Never before did she have such doubt about her work as a soul-devourer. She liked to think that she was different from the salamanders, that she didn't mindlessly eat ghosts out of primitive hunger. That she was human, capable of choosing right from wrong.

But her mother's revelation had cast doubt on that. Her memory shied away from the burning shape in her mother's bedroom. Her father. Anya's mother had never spoken of him before. Anya had always assumed that he was simply a man, perhaps a deadbeat guy with a drinking problem who had no interest in her. Anya had grown emotional calluses over the idea long ago, though some blister deep in her soul still wondered if he ever wanted her, ever wanted to know her.

And now . . . she knew that he *did* want her. And that he was a monster.

What did that make her?

A newt sat on her knee and chirped adoringly at her. Its tail twitched and it blinked, giving a tiny purr. How could she blame these creatures for doing what came naturally to them? It was like being horrified by watching lions take down a gazelle—there was no good or evil, just instinct. But it offended her human constructs of right and wrong.

Anya petted the salamander with the tip of her finger and wondered, Was she really any different? Would she be able to force herself to kill innocents to avert a larger disaster?

She knew in her heart she would kill to protect the

newts. Perhaps that was the only answer she needed for now. She'd sort out the humanity and the guilt later.

Charon had pulled the raft down a narrow tunnel and was tugging it to shore. It seemed as if the water weighed a great deal on him as it streamed down his coat. He dragged the raft up to the graveled shore and stumbled to the ground.

Anya leapt clumsily out of the turtle boat, the salamanders hopping out behind her like springs, squealing.

"Are you all right?"

Charon sat with his arms on his knees and head bowed, dripping. *"Yeah. Just gimme a minute to rest."* He lifted his head and stared up at the ceiling, breathing heavily.

His blond hair hung dripping over his burning blue eyes. Without the stiff punk spikes, he was actually an attractive man. Anya had the urge to brush Charon's sodden locks off his face.

Don't touch, her instincts warned her. *Poison.*

Whether her subconscious meant the water or Charon, Anya obeyed and knit her fingers behind her back. She supervised the remaining newts hopping to shore, taking a head count as they milled around on the bank.

The newts suddenly stopped, turned. A growling sound issued from the darkness beyond, so low and deep that it rattled pea gravel on the shoreline. Before Anya could react, Sparky lunged toward the sound, teeth bared.

"Don't," Charon gasped, but it was too late.

A massive black creature roared into view. Three dog-like heads snarled and salivated under lion-like manes.

Its body glistened like an oil slick, viscous and glossy. It charged Sparky, lashing a long black tail behind it like a monitor lizard's. Unlike the ghosts, this creature looked pretty damn solid.

Anya hurled herself in front of Sparky, skidding on her hands and knees in the gravel. The three-headed creature reared and Anya covered her head with her hands, waiting to feel teeth against her armor.

"Kerberos." Charon's voice sliced the air like the crack of a whip.

Anya opened one eye over her elbow. The creature sat on its haunches, all three heads turned toward the direction of Charon's voice. Anya took the opportunity to scramble to her feet and put up her fists.

"Sorry about that. This is Kerberos."

"Of course it is." Anya blinked at the pony-sized creature. With its jaws closed, the three heads looked much like Labrador retrievers. Anya noticed that the dog heads were wearing collars: a pink one with a dangling rhinestone tag that said *Princess*; a camouflage collar stenciled with the name *Grumpy*; a black leather collar that had the word *Bashful* lettered on it in silver charms. Princess cocked her head, hound dog ears lifted. Bashful was sniffing at Sparky, and Grumpy shoved his head under Charon's hand. Charon scrubbed Grumpy's ears and chin, baby-talking to him in something that sounded like Latin, but not quite. A twelve-foot length of broken chain rattled behind Grumpy's collar.

Anya retreated to Sparky and the newts, who were still

on high alert and milling near the shoreline like trapped lemmings. Sparky snaked around her knees, extended his spade-shaped head to sniff at Bashful's wet nose. He was rewarded with a lick.

"Is he . . . your familiar?" Anya managed, in a small, scraped voice.

"We're not joined at the hip, like you and Sparky are. Kerberos is stuck guarding the gate to the Underworld, most of the time. And Kerberos is more of a 'them' than a 'he.' " He paused to examine the broken end of the chain.

"Hence the collars?"

"Yeah. After a few thousand years, they sort of develop their own personalities." The three-headed dog put its paws on Charon's shoulders. Tail wagging, it slobbered on him with three tongues.

Sparky and the newts looked askance up at Anya. Anya didn't know what to do but shrug.

Charon rubbed the hellhound's sides, but his fingers came away red with blood. When Anya looked more closely, she could see a long gash extending along the dog's ribs. It was hard to see the red against the hellhound's smooth black skin, but she could see it shining a bit darker in places.

Charon's eyes darkened to the color of storms. *"Who did this to you?"*

Kerberos whimpered and laid down in the gravel, heads snaking and hound-dog ears flopping.

Charon turned on his heel and stalked down the riverbank. Kerberos trotted behind him. Anya, Sparky, and the newts followed warily in his wake. She wondered how many other pets Charon might have in this place.

The ferryman stopped a hundred yards distant, at a hole in the earthen wall flanking the sluggish river. The hole was covered by an iron gate speckled with rust and peeling green paint. Plain and unornamented, it was exactly the kind of gate Anya expected to find in a sewer. The gaps in the gate were wide enough to allow water and rats to flow through, but little else. The gate was closed with a chain and an ordinary padlock covered with a scum of duckweed.

Except for the large tear ripping through the hinges on the left side of the gate. The left panel had been ripped away from the wall, exposing a gap big enough for a person to crawl through.

Charon stood before the gate, glowering at the hole. Kerberos slunk behind him, its dragon tail tucked between its legs.

"It's not your fault," he muttered, rubbing the nearest pair of black ears. He unhooked the broken chain from Grumpy's collar and wound it around his wrist.

"What happened?" Anya asked.

"I'm guessing that this is Hope's work, roughing up Kerberos and breaking the gate to the Underworld."

Anya blinked. "That's the gate to the Underworld?" It was so . . . ordinary. She'd expected the gate to hell to look like one of the elaborately mosaiced Ishtar gates in the museum. Or that Rodin sculpture that was more than twenty feet tall and depicted scenes from Dante's *Inferno*. This was just . . . a pathetic little gate.

Charon rubbed the bridge of his nose. *"It's one of 'em, anyway. It's not fancy, but it works."* He kicked at a loosely swinging piece. *"Or it did."*

Charon pulled the piece of bent gate away and stepped through. Kerberos moved to follow him. *"Kerberos, stay."*

The hellhound sat back on its haunches before the gate.

Charon looked through the bars at Anya and the salamanders. His eyes burned very blue in the darkness beyond, like foxfire. *"You coming?"*

"To hell? Yeah, I guess so."

Anya shuddered and ducked through the broken gate.

CHAPTER NINETEEN

HELL WASN'T REALLY WHAT ANYA had thought it would be.

When she stepped over to the other side, she felt a palpable difference in atmosphere. At first, she tried to get her ears to pop, but couldn't quite get the sense of thick darkness out of her helmet. It felt . . . gooey, as if the air possessed an extra viscosity as it slithered down her throat and into her lungs. It felt like the mud sticking to her feet, as if the Styx reached far into the tunnel with watery fingers.

"Ugh," she muttered. Her mouth tasted like she was chewing on aluminum foil.

"You get used to it after a while," Charon said. She couldn't see him, but his voice sounded close. She didn't want to ask how long "a while" was for him.

The salamanders crawled through the bars behind her, crowding behind her legs. Sparky leaned against her, his gill-fronds twitching. They cast a warm amber light that picked out the rough-hewn edges of a tunnel with a low ceiling, so low that it nearly scraped the top of Anya's helmet when she stood. Charon had his back to her, dark coat melting into the shadows. He gestured with his chin to the tunnel ahead.

"If I were Hope, I'd be looking for a place to hide Pandora's Jar."

"Hell is a good place."

Charon turned and gave her a wry smile. Anya forced herself not to take a step back. His eyes gleamed foxfire blue, an inhuman color in the half-dark. *"She's got to find a way to hide it in your physical world. But that thing acts like a beacon on the spiritual planes. She's got to put it someplace where she can easily defend it, where few people—or spirits— would be willing to come after it."*

"Um . . . " Anya raised her hand. "Question . . . I can see why Hope wants to hide Pandora's Jar here . . . but if this is the classical Underworld . . . isn't there a Hades who will mind her encroaching on his territory?"

Charon pressed his mouth into a grim slash. *"The Underworld is a big place. And the gods of the Underworld have a lot of shit to deal with—you'd be amazed at the recordkeeping alone. The actuarial department takes up an area the size of Manhattan. Shit slips by them, every once in a while. And Hope is one of those things."*

"You're telling me hell is a slow-moving bureaucracy?"

"Pretty much. You humans are up to about a hundred and fifty thousand deaths a day. That's a lot of administrative overhead that doesn't leave much time for chasing down megalomaniacs hauling around spirit jars."

"Do you get overtime?"

"No." His mouth curled in a half-smile. *"But the higher-ups are not happy that Hope is trying to move in on their turf. They weren't happy with her doing it in the physical world, and if they knew that she'd moved into the Underworld—even this backwater province of it—they'd be furious."*

Anya crossed her arms. "So . . . why can't we let somebody farther up the food chain deal with her?"

"By the time that happens, she may be strong enough to take over."

"What?"

"You heard me. Pandora's Jar is not a toy. It can hold thousands of spirits. She can stake out some substantial real estate in the spirit world, more than most avatars." Charon smiled mirthlessly. *"There's a lot more at stake here than just you, me, the salamanders, and the museum ghosts."*

"I don't—" Anya began, but her attention was arrested by movement at the end of the tunnel. Something flickered in the dark.

Sparky lowered himself to the ground and hissed, tail lashing. From the corner of her eye, she could see Charon unwinding the chain around his knuckles. He held it loosely in one hand, and its tail rattled to the ground.

Anya stood her ground, chin lifted. The newts, who had been bouncing like popcorn around her, were frozen, watching.

Her resolve faltered when she saw the ghost.

Leslie drifted into view in her bathrobe, her feet barely

gliding along the floor of the tunnel. She wore a dazed expression, her hands stuffed into her pockets, bumping into walls as she drifted.

Anya's throat constricted. Leslie's ghost must have been one of the ones still trapped in the bottle Hope wore around her neck.

A newt jogged forward for a bite.

"No," she snarled at it, and it retreated behind her, chastened.

Anya moved forward. Charon grabbed her arm, but she shrugged it off. *"You can't trust a ghost down here . . . and they can hurt you."*

"Leslie . . . " she said.

Leslie blinked at Anya, drifting closer. She tipped her head in confusion.

"Leslie, it's Anya. Do you remember me?"

The ghost sidled up to her, squinted at her face.

Sparky growled a warning.

Anya licked her lips. "Leslie, do you know where you are?"

Suddenly, Leslie's ghosts hands ripped out of her robe pockets. Anya glimpsed the sharp edges of metal in Leslie's fists before the metal flashed and skipped against her copper armor.

Anya stumbled back, still startled by the knowledge that ghosts could actually hurt her on this plane. This was their world, their rules. Leslie was armed with knives. Though her expression was still clouded, her hands flashed with purpose.

Hope's purpose. The bitch knew they were here.

The salamanders surged up behind Anya like an orange tide. She screamed at them to stop, but they swarmed over her like locusts.

"You all right?" Charon asked, picking Anya up off the floor.

"Yeah." She fingered the scars in her armor. "She—"

"She's under Hope's control. There's nothing to be done for it."

The ghost flailed with the sparks of metal in her hand. Sparky plowed into her, knocking her off her ghostly feet. The newts had begun to tear into her, snarling. She slashed at them in broad arcs, making little contact.

Anya looked away. "There has to be another way!" she insisted. Tears stung Anya's eyes. Leslie had been an innocent.

"The only way to break the spell is to break the vessel."

Beyond the feeding frenzy, she could hear sighs and scrapes emanating from farther down the tunnel. Her hair stood on end. One look at Charon's face told her that Leslie wasn't alone, that the other ghosts under Hope's spell were coming for them.

The salamanders, caught in gustatorial delirium, looked up, gill-fronds twitching. They could smell them, smell the ghosts coming and the thrill of the fight. Even Sparky turned to the darkness, tail switching in anticipation.

Anya muffled a sob, stood beside Sparky. Charon was right: There was no other choice. Once committed to this path, she had to give herself fully to it.

She opened her hands as the first wave of ghosts rumbled down the bend of the tunnel, feeling the dark void in her chest open and blossom. It growled hungrily, just as fevered as the salamanders gnawing on ectoplasm behind her.

"Come on," she challenged them.

The tunnel was narrow enough to require the oncoming ghosts to march shoulder to shoulder, three abreast. The first row was familiar: She recognized the samurai ghost from the museum and one of his compatriots. And Bernie. The ghost of the bespectacled artifacts dealer in his slippers was incongruous beside the helmeted warriors, but for the sword he held in his grip. Anya recognized it as the missing sword that had hung over his mantel. Amber light from the salamanders glittered on their blades and armor as the ghostly warriors bore down on their targets.

The salamanders struck first. The newts ran just below the reach of their swords, hissing and clambering up their ankles and the backs of their legs. The samurai struggled to reach their backs, snarling, as the salamanders burrowed underneath their armor laces. Sparky tried to keep their attention distracted to the front, snapping at their distracted parries and thrusts.

A newt was hurled back by the edge of a sword, landing at Anya's feet. It mewed piteously, grievously wounded. Anya reached to scoop the creature up as its amber aura flickered. Seeking comfort, it dragged itself up her arm and curled up in the lip of her armor around her neck. She could feel its thready breathing and warm ecto-plasm leaking down her collarbone.

Rage boiled in her throat, and she lashed out at the ghosts. She cast her hand out, palm open, and tried to de-vour the nearest ghost.

On the physical plane, this power was often subtle. Most onlookers, as well as Anya herself, rarely saw more than a flicker of pale energy dying out as she swallowed it. But here she could see the full, terrible ramifications of what had seemed, before, like a simple act.

The samurai's ghost half turned toward her, katana lifted. As if he were constructed of little more than ciga-rette smoke, he began to fray at the edges, pulling apart like a dandelion blown by a child. When she inhaled, she felt the cold smoke sliding down her throat and pooling in the bottom of her lungs. He tasted like dust. The ghost howled as he was shredded and devoured.

Beside her, Charon swung Kerberos's leash over his head. It made contact with a samurai's throat with a sickening rattle. Charon drew the samurai close, ripped a newt out of the samurai's fist, while Sparky clung to the samurai's sword arm. The ferryman viciously kicked the samurai, striking his armor with a clang that sent him stumbling backward and released the tension from the chain. Charon slugged him, hard enough to knock the hel-met from his head and send it ringing to the floor. Sparky lunged up to tear the ghost's throat out. As the samurai fell, he began to fade, like an overexposed photograph, dissipating into the darkness.

Bernie confronted Anya, sword clutched awkwardly in a two-fisted grip. He swung at Anya, and she deflected the blow with the elbow of her armor.

"I'm sorry, Bernie," Anya muttered. She grasped his wrist, and her breath rattled in her throat. She felt the ectoplasm that made up Bernie's ghostly form begin to soften in her grip, like candle wax melting in the summertime.

Bernie howled. The sword rattled to the ground. Anya held on. Held on as her fingers and breath chewed through his skin. He tasted like carbon and burned things as he dissolved in her throat.

A second line of the ghost army was already pushing behind the first. Anya glimpsed the embroidered skirts of the Bohemian girls from the museum, fingers clawing the air near her face.

Anya reached for them, reached out for them with her hands and the black emptiness in her chest. She felt them dissipate, soft as moths fluttering down her throat. They screamed, hundreds of years of history silenced in one breath.

One breath.

And another.

She reached for the ghosts, the newts flowing like orange fire before her. She could hear the lash of Charon's chain on the left, Sparky's growl on her right. She reached out for the ghosts beyond.

Some, she knew. Some, she didn't. She recognized Katie's magnificent Egyptian; he tasted like myrrh when she breathed him in, shattering like sand when she touched him. Sparky was mauling a man in a letter carrier's uniform. Pieces of mail shook free of his mailbag like white birds from a magician's hat before dissolving into black. The crazy old man from the museum clambered to Anya, swinging his staff. Anya balled her fists, ducked. Though his eyes were clouded, she sensed some spark of independent volition in him. Or craziness.

"Ishtar," he hissed. *"Beware Erishkigal's poison."*

Anya's brow wrinkled. The old man was still living in his myths. He struck at her again with his staff. Anya batted it aside. When she swallowed him, she tasted something bitter, like fresh earth and onion roots.

She kept pressing forward, devouring ghosts. But she couldn't help but feel the air thickening, that she breathed more shallowly. Her lungs ached as she moved through the spirits, pulling them apart like taffy. In the physical world, she'd devour maybe two ghosts in a month—these were more ghosts than she'd taken in a lifetime. And she could feel her body beginning to resist, to ache under the strain.

"Anya!"

Charon's voice snapped like a whip over her, and she turned. But she was an instant too late. Something struck her armor, slamming her to the floor like a tin can. She tasted blood in her mouth.

"What the fuck—" she groaned, clutching her shoulder. She rolled over to see Charon's boot beside her head.

His body jerked as he stood above her, and she could hear him muttering, ". . . *two, three* . . . "

She looked beyond to see the museum security guards. They were armed with guns, as they had been in life. Charon was counting the shots as they advanced, shots that were tearing into his coat. The bullets were shockingly real on this plane, chewing into Charon.

Anya gasped, clawing the air before her to dissolve the ghosts.

". . . *four, five* . . . " Charon stumbled.

They had at least six shots in each revolver. No matter how much swimming Charon had done in the Styx, he wouldn't be able to keep standing.

She pulled the first one into her throat, nearly choked. Her chest was filling, and she struggled to devour the second, coughing. More ghosts were filling the corridor, filling the void left by the guards. Newts swarmed into the darkness, but the ghostly columns seemed to stretch too far into the distance. And Anya couldn't help but notice that there were fewer newts than when the battle had begun. A lump rose in her throat.

Charon fell to his knees, hands wrapped around his chest. Anya thrust his limp hair away from his face: "Are you all right?" It was a damned stupid question to ask a man who'd been shot.

"*Yeah.*" Charon took a shuddering breath. He reached up to finger the dent in Anya's armor. "*You?*"

"Okay." The armor had deflected the bullet, but it would leave a hell of a bruise. She could feel hot stickiness inside the armor, trickling down to her palm.

She hauled Charon to his feet. Sparky appeared at his side to take part of his weight.

"We've gotta break their formation," he growled. *"Get past the bottleneck."*

Anya nodded, turned her head to cough into her elbow.

Charon snatched her arm, and Anya saw that her gleaming armor was speckled with blood.

"How many ghosts have you devoured?" he demanded. He pressed his hand to her forehead, as if she were a child with a fever.

"I don't know. I —"

Charon ripped open the latches of her armor, pulling open her breastplate.

"What the fuck do you think you're doing?" Anya moved to cover herself, though she had an overriding urge to slug him. She felt cold air on her skin.

"Shit." Charon's blue eyes burned as he stared at her chest.

Anya looked down and nearly threw up.

When Anya took a spirit, it left a burn mark on her in the physical world. They eventually healed, usually over a period of weeks, and rarely scarred. But the battle, the dozens of ghosts, had reduced her flesh to burned bloody blackness. She looked as if someone had taken a blowtorch to her. Her skin felt numb under her fingers. Beyond it . . . she could almost touch that blackness that devoured ghosts.

"You're burning out." Charon's eyes seared into hers.

"Lanterns can only take so many spirits before they burn out."

"Why didn't you tell me this shit?" she demanded.

"I assumed that you knew your limits." His eyes were frosty, accusing.

"It's not like I eat these motherfuckers for breakfast." But now she understood what the old man's warning meant—the ghosts were poison to her. Too many, and . . .

Charon looked over her head at the newts. They were holding the line, but just barely. *"We've got to figure out a way to retreat."*

Anya shook her head, fumbling with the closures on her breastplate. Sparky wound worriedly around her legs. "No. We keep going."

Charon glared at her. *"Here's the plan. The newts and I drive a line up the middle. You get behind us. When we get to the end of the line, you break out ahead for Hope. Sparky will cover you."*

Sparky slapped his tail on the ground. Anya hoped he was taking notes.

A howl and a whinny sounded from the tunnel.

"Shit," Anya muttered. That could only be Pluto.

"Let's go." Charon pulled the chain tight between his hands. Sparky fell into line beside him, and they began to push against the bottleneck. Anya plucked up Bernie's sword from beside the body of a newt that was fading away like a wisp of smoke. Charon's chain lashed into the battle, and Sparky launched himself into the fray. Anya

stayed behind them, hacking at ghostly limbs that snaked through the spaces between.

Ahead, she could see Pluto rearing. Gallus clung to the saddle. The ghost-horse rolled an eye, foaming at the mouth. The end of Charon's chain wrapped around the horse's neck, and the ferryman pulled with all his might.

The horse struggled and wobbled in the crowd of ghosts, crashed down with an inhuman scream.

Gallus hacked himself out of the trap of ghost-limbs and tack, howling, *"You killed my horse!"* Tears glistened in his eyes under his helmet, and he raised his sword to behead Charon, whose fists were still tangled in the chain.

Anya thrust Bernie's sword between them, clumsily blocking the blow.

Newts clung to Gallus's back, chewed at his shoulders, but he cried, *"That was my horse! Pluto has been my horse for two thousand years. . . . "*

A well of pity rose in Anya, and she tenderly reached out to touch his wet cheek.

She breathed him in, in the same breath as the broken and twisted horse. She tried to be gentle. She felt them mingling in her lungs, smoky and musky, bound together for all time. . . .

She smiled sadly. The cold breath of the spirits seized her throat, paralyzing her breath. She couldn't inhale. Couldn't exhale. She felt as if she was drowning, could hear nothing but the echo of blood thumping in her helmet. She felt the sting of the ghost-burn crawl up her chest through her throat, seizing her voice.

Charon was holding her by her arms, shouting at her. He shook her so hard that the helmet rattled off her head.

But the thunder of her blood blotted him out. She could feel the poison of the burn spreading up her face, numbing it and crawling blackly over her vision.

The last thing she remembered was falling over Charon's shoulder with Sparky tangled in her legs.

CHAPTER TWENTY

IT FELT AS IF THE ghost train had taken hold of her again, that queasy sense of weightlessness washing over her.

Anya opened her eyes in the familiar setting of the Devil's Bathtub, and she sighed in relief. The old tin ceilings, the scarred wood floors, the jewel-toned bottles perched behind the bar, even the layer of dust on the stained-glass lamps over the bar—all of it familiar. She was home.

But then she realized that the perspective was all wrong.

She was floating at the ceiling, the stamped tin tiles close enough to touch. Below her, she could see her physical self sprawled in the bathtub fixture on the floor, the center of a flurry of activity.

Her body had sunk into the change-filled bathtub. Brian was straddling her, pumping her chest with interlaced hands. Each thrust rattled change from the bathtub onto the floor. A fire extinguisher rolled on the floor, bits of chemical foam smeared on the floor and in the coins. She smelled something burning, and wondered what it was.

"You came back." Renee floated beside Anya.

Anya chewed on her lip. "I don't understand. Why am I not down there, with them?"

Renee tenderly touched Anya's cheek. *"Honey, you're slipping away."*

Jules was shouting into the telephone at a 911 operator, and Katie was running out the door to flag down paramedics. Max stood behind Ciro's wheelchair, the old man's hands clutching his chest. Tears were streaming down the old man's cheeks.

". . . five, six, seven, eight . . . " Brian counted out the chest compressions.

". . . five minutes," Jules was saying. "She hasn't breathed in five minutes . . . how the fuck should I know?"

Anya looked down. The silver cord connecting her astral double to her physical self was severed. She fingered the frayed edges of it in her hand, blinked.

Brian lifted her limp body's head to straighten her airway. "You. Don't go," he whispered as he pressed his mouth over hers and forced a breath into her throat.

It wasn't the cold breath of a spirit. Anya could taste it. It felt warm. Alive.

Anya coughed, sputtering up against arms that held her.

"Brian," she whispered, fingers wound in his shirt.

"Wrong place," a voice told her. *"Drink."*

Lukewarm water slid past her lips down her throat. It tasted like slime, and she hacked it out.

She blinked, her vision fuzzy. She wasn't in Brian's arms, but in Charon's. She lay across his knees in the crook of one elbow. He held a filthy bottle of water in his free hand. His coat smelled like gunpowder, and she realized her fingers were twined in the bullet holes. Sparky licked Anya's face.

"What is—" she was overtaken by another fit of coughing.

Charon's eyes crinkled in relief. He capped the bottle and stuck it in his pocket. *"Water from the Styx."*

Her eyes widened. "You said it was poison."

"Just a sip." Charon's eyes darkened. *"Don't worry. You're not invincible . . . and you'll pay for that later."*

"The newts . . . " She struggled to sit up.

Charon gestured with his chin. *"They're tough little bastards."*

The newts scuttled through the tunnels, feasting on shreds of fading ghost-flesh. Their amber light flashed from one corner of the tunnel to the other, like fireflies.

She reached around her neck for the newt that had tucked himself into her armor. The body felt cold and stiff. With a lump in her throat, she laid it on the ground. Sparky nosed over it, whined, as it began to fade.

"How many survived?" Anya asked, self-consciously disengaging her fingers from Charon's coat.

"More than half," Charon said. *"Even in the physical world, that's a pretty good survival rate for salamanders in the wild."*

Her vision blurred, and she wiped her nose. "I guess."

Charon hauled her to her feet as easily as if she were a doll. *"C'mon. Let's go kick Hope's ass."*

Anya nodded. With her arm wrapped around the ferryman's waist and Sparky at her heels, she followed him into the dark tunnel.

The newts had made vicious work of the ghosts. Smears of glowing iridescence smeared the walls. Anya could make out handprints and spatters of what would have been blood in the physical world covering the walls in what looked like glow-in-the-dark paint. The marks gleamed eerily in the dark. In a corner, three newts fought over the remains of Marie Antoinette's head, the curls of her wig strewn on the floor of the tunnel like seaweed.

The tunnel turned back on itself several times and opened up into a large, echoing chamber. The chamber reminded Anya of when she'd gone to Shenandoah Caverns as a child: a rocky room with a vaulted ceiling, studded with stalactites and stalagmites. Deep in crevasses, water and quartz gleamed. Water dripped from somewhere distant.

"Hope," Charon called. *"It's over."*

Something moved in the pitch. "You can't hold me."

Sparky's amber light cast shifting shadows, before finally illuminating a figure perched on a four-foot jar. Pandora's Jar appeared much the same as it did in the physical world, except the paint was fresher. At the foot of the jar, Bernie's artifacts were strewn. Anya recognized some of the bottles and bits of jewelry glinting in the light.

But Hope was not the same on this level. The creature

perched on top of the jar reminded Anya of the gargoyles she'd seen on gothic churches: warped head, leathery wings, and hands curled into claws. It was Hope, in this world. Anya thought it a more realistic depiction.

"Ah. Death and the Lantern have come to take my treasures," the creature using Hope's voice hissed. Her mouth was filled with needle-like teeth; Anya figured that they were hell to floss.

"Your army's been chewed to pieces, Hope." Anya narrowed her eyes. "Give us the jar."

Hope slithered from the top of the jar. "Be my guests. Forever."

She shoved it over, and the mouth of the jar rolled to face Anya, Sparky, and Charon. The interior of the jar shimmered with crystalline blue light, a glow that bent and warped the air. It sucked at them, and Anya dug her armored heels into the dirt. But the vortex at the lip of the jar widened. Charon stumbled. Sparky wrapped his tail around a stalagmite, his claws churning in the air for Anya. Through the howl of air, Anya felt herself slipping toward the mouth of the jar. Her arm popped out of its socket, and she watched as her fingers warped and stretched, like light before a black hole.

This must be what it feels like to be a ghost when I devour them, she thought. Her hair lashed past her face, stretched out beyond her hip by the jar's terrible gravity.

"Nothing can escape that," Hope cackled from the shadows behind it. "Nothing. Not an elemental. Not a Lantern. Not even Death himself."

Charon growled at her. *"You know better than that."*

"The Underworld will be mine. Without you to protect it, I'll begin my collection of spirits over again."

The soft, sandstone stalagmite Sparky clung to splintered. He clawed in the dirt, tail stretched into an infinite spiral, pulled toward the jar. Pebbles rattled past him, sucked into its gaping mouth.

Anya snarled. There was no way she'd let that bitch take Sparky. She turned her full attention to the shadow behind the jar, and let go.

She skidded past Charon and Sparky, twisting and turning in the maelstrom vacuum of dirt and light. She let herself be sucked into the rim of the jar. She clutched the rim with all her strength in twisted fingers. She looked over the rim at Hope's dark shape and glowing eyes . . .

. . . and breathed in.

Hope shrieked. Anya felt the metallic taste of Hope in her throat, curling into her lungs like smoke. If she was going to spend the rest of eternity stuck in a jar with Charon and Sparky, she was damn well going to take Hope with her.

Charon's chain flashed past, slamming into the edge of the jar. The jar fractured, splintering quartz fragments in Anya's face.

The vortex spun out and collapsed like a dust devil, leaving Anya with two feet in the cracked jar and a chain around her wrist. Hope was nowhere to be seen, but Anya could feel the disgusting taste of expensive perfume in the back of her throat.

"Ow," she muttered, spitting sand out of her mouth.

Sparky scuttled up and licked her face, wrinkled his nose. Apparently, he could smell it, too.

Charon gave Anya a hand up, nudged the edge of the jar with his foot. The fracture extended from the lip of the jar halfway through the picture painted on the side. Pandora's peplos was cleaved neatly in half. He righted the jar, fingering the scar.

"The magick's gone from it," he said. *"Any ghosts put in it would leak right out."*

Anya sighed. "Charon?"

"Yeah?"

"At the risk of sounding like a petulant Dorothy, I want to go home."

He smiled, and this time the light seemed to touch his eyes. *"I'll take you to your train."*

Sunlight streamed through the high windows of the train station, passing through the ghosts milling in the crowd. Charon and Anya walked slowly though the crowd, trailed by Sparky and the newts. The newts darted around feet, clambered up briefcases, and harassed the ghosts at the ticket counter.

"What am I going to do with them?" Anya asked. She'd counted thirty-two newt survivors. She was relieved that they'd made it, but dreaded the chaos they'd bring to her daily life.

Charon shrugged, hands in his pockets. *"They're big and strong enough to make their own way in the world."*

"Charon, they're just babies. . . ."

"Look." He gently turned her around and pointed. The newts were hopping away through the crowd to the train platform. They leaped off one by one, whisked away by the ghost train.

Anya's eyes filled with tears. She felt like she'd been punched in the gut. "Where are they going?"

"To new homes. I imagine many of them will attach themselves to artifacts, like the ones in Bernie's collection. There are probably a few idiot witches out there trying to summon salamanders. Some of them will probably hang out around ironworks and firehouses—that's just what they do."

Anya rubbed her eyes. "Bye, guys."

The last newt paused on the platform. It turned to Anya and chirped before it flung itself into darkness.

Charon awkwardly patted her shoulder. *"I'll look in on them once in a while. I swear."*

Anya nodded, unable to speak. She looked away, into the crowd of ghosts.

Something snagged her attention. While most of the ghosts were bent on their destinations, oblivious to their surroundings, one ghost watched her. He stood in a closed phone booth beside the ticket counter, his hands folded over his hat.

She recognized him from his morgue photograph.

He was Calvin Dresser, the computer scientist who was the model for Brian's neural network, ALANN.

Anya walked briskly to the phone booth, reached for the handle. It was locked. Calvin looked at her sadly, trapped behind the door.

"He's in limbo," Charon said. "I've never seen anything like it. He can't move backward or forward, though he's fully aware. Very curious case."

"How do I get him out of here?" Anya's breath fogged the glass.

Charon tipped his head, hands clasped behind his back. "You could break him out."

Anya doubled her armored fist and broke the glass near the handle. The glass spidered and shattered, trickling down the door frame. The man inside didn't flinch. He stepped hesitantly outside of his glass prison.

"Hello, Anya," he said.

"Hello, Calvin."

He tipped his hat. "Thank you for freeing me. I knew you would somehow."

Calvin smiled and walked away into the crowd toward the platform, whistling. Her heart swelled to see him free and on his way.

"You did well." Charon watched him walk away. "You could have my job someday."

Anya's skin prickled. "Hope called you 'Death.'" She couldn't help but feel as if Charon wasn't telling her the full truth . . . about himself, or about the Styx.

Charon waved his hand dismissively. "Hope's full of shit. She doesn't know Hades from Hestia."

"Mmmm . . ." Anya was dubious. "I have questions."

"Save 'em for later. Sleep on it." His blue eyes darkened. "Don't ask any questions you don't really want answers to."

"You'll be at the morgue?" she asked.

"I'm always around. You can use the coin I gave you to come back." He leaned forward and kissed her cheek. His lips were cold, and he smelled like gunpowder and winter.

Anya smiled at him. She would have questions. She clucked for Sparky, walked to the edge of the train platform. Ghosts stood on the edge, hopped off into the roar of wind like grasshoppers for a lawn mower.

Anya steeled herself for the journey, taking Sparky into her arms. She waited her turn, got ready to step off . . .

. . . when she glimpsed a familiar face a few yards down, and her heart plummeted to her stomach.

Ciro.

He wasn't in his wheelchair, and she nearly missed him. Instead, he was walking, dressed in a sharply creased suit, with a starched shirt and red bow tie. A beautiful young woman dressed as a flapper was on his arm: Renee. Renee stood on her tiptoes to kiss Ciro, and her face shone like the moon.

Together, Renee and Ciro stepped off into space. The ghost train sucked them up an instant before it took Anya.

Anya woke, not to the rushing darkness of the train but to a blinding white light.

"Ow," she muttered, tried to turn over. But she was tethered by a stinging sensation in her arm. Her fingers closed around plastic IV tubes, and her vision cleared to reveal harsh fluorescent light. She smelled disinfectant and heard the beeping of machines.

A hand lay heavy across her brow. She blinked up to see Brian leaning over her.

"Hey, you," he said.

"Hey," Anya whispered. Her throat was dry, raw as if she'd swallowed bleach. She wondered if that was from swallowing the spirits, but guessed that it could have been from the scrape of a breathing tube. She looked down, saw that Sparky was lying beside her in the hospital bed, between her hip and the rail. He stared at her with his head between his front feet, his tail twitching slightly. She scrubbed his gill-fronds, and his tongue snaked out from his mouth.

"What happened?" she asked.

"Renee told us that you'd gone to the astral plane, so we watched, waited. For hours. And then . . . you stopped breathing. We got you started again, but you were gone for a good five minutes."

Anya scraped her hand over her hospital gown. Her chest ached, and she could feel the scrape of bandages taped to her skin. "What's all this?"

Brian frowned, and she could see the circles under his eyes. "We smelled something burning after you went away. Max searched the bar, but we discovered . . . it was you. Your skin was blistering, burning." He took his glasses off, rubbed the bridge of his nose. "We poured water on you. Jules hit you with the fire extinguisher, but you kept . . . smoldering. Then . . . then you stopped breathing." His voice crackled a bit.

Anya reached for his hand. "It's okay. I'm back."

He opened his mouth to say something more, but the pastel curtain surrounding Anya's bed got pulled aside. Marsh, wearing a slightly rumpled dress shirt and loosened tie, nodded at her. Anya wondered how long he'd been waiting. That was positively disheveled for Marsh.

"Kalinczyk. The duty nurse said you were awake." His voice was as crisp and businesslike as ever.

"Thanks for coming, Captain," she croaked.

"Thought you'd want the news. We found Hope."

Anya's fingers clutched the rail. "Where?"

"Found the truck outside her headquarters, found her in the basement. Found her dead, crammed into Pandora's Jar." Marsh's mouth turned. "We've got no idea how she got down there, or how she got the jar down there."

Anya swallowed. The jar had been a funerary jar. The irony of Hope being trapped in the bottom of the jar was not lost on her. "How did she die?"

"Gina at the ME's office thinks it was a stroke. But we can't figure out how she got crammed in there."

Anya's nails bit into her palm. "Did the jar get back to DIA?"

"Yeah, but they're not happy. It's been damaged—got a crack in it like the side of the Liberty Bell. I imagine that they'll be suing Miracles for the Masses for repair costs." Marsh leaned forward and awkwardly patted her shoulder. "Get some rest. I'll give you the reports when you get back."

He ducked behind the curtain and vanished.

Brian watched him go, his expression pinched. Anya

tugged his sleeve, wanting to wipe that expression from his face. "It's okay, Brian. Everything's going to be fine."

He shook his head, blew out his breath. "No. No, it's not." He clutched her hand. "Ciro . . . Ciro had a heart attack."

Anya's heart plummeted, and she suddenly remembered seeing the old man's face at the train station. "Is he—" She knew the answer already, but couldn't force herself to say: *Is he dead?*

Brian shook his head. "He didn't make it, Anya. I'm sorry."

Anya pressed the back of her hand to her mouth. The sob that snagged in the back of her throat sounded for all the world like a devoured spirit trying to escape.

"Ciro said he never wanted to leave this place."

Jules stood before the bar at the Devil's Bathtub, head bowed. The mirror behind the bar captured his reflection: the creases in his forehead, the sport coat that he couldn't button around his middle, the Bible in his hands. The mirror reflected Anya, Brian, Katie, and Max. It reflected the blue funerary urn perched in the center of the liquor bottles, the urn containing Ciro's ashes.

"Anya . . . do you sense him anywhere near here?" Katie asked. She was dressed in a floor-length black thrift-store dress for Ciro's memorial service. The attempt at somberness made her seem even more the witch.

Anya bit her lip, buried her face in Brian's shoulder. His suit jacket smelled like mothballs. She wiped her nose on the back of one white glove from her firefighter's dress blues, her cap tucked under an arm. "No. And I don't see Renee, either." The lack of music made the place eerily silent.

Sparky leaned against her side, chirping softly. She knew he felt the loss of Ciro, as well as the loss of the newts. She'd woken in the middle of the night to see him moving his feet as he dreamed, calling for the newts like a mother cat who'd misplaced her kittens.

Jules sighed in relief, closed his Bible. "He's in a better world now. So's she."

The remains of DAGR stood in awkward silence. Anya looked up at Brian. His left hand dipped in his pocket to graze the surface of his iPhone. She knew that he'd lost ALANN—he said that the neural network supporting the intelligence had "spontaneously dissolved." Anya hadn't been able to bring herself to tell him yet what had really happened . . . that she'd set him free.

Somehow she doubted that she ever would. He didn't—wouldn't—understand. And she had no idea how far the chasm of his lack of ethics dug into his character. She hoped it was simply a superficial blemish . . . but she wasn't able to get past those doubts. Not yet. Perhaps not ever.

"What's gonna happen to the Devil's Bathtub?" Max asked, digging at the tie around his neck. It was one of Jules's ties, and was too long for him.

Katie laced her hands behind her back. "Ciro had a will. From what his lawyer said, the Devil's Bathtub goes to Anya."

Anya jerked her head up. "What?"

"He said that Anya was family. That we all are."

Anya blinked back tears. That crazy old man was more a father to her than her own . . . whatever it was. She'd been trying not to think of it, but her thoughts kept returning to the flaming man in her mother's bedroom . . . and what that meant.

Jules pressed his thick hand to the top of the bar, watched the steam form around it on the high-gloss finish. "He shouldn't have died," he growled.

"He was an old man, Jules," Katie said.

"He shouldn't have died." Jules glared at Anya. "He was too fragile for this shit. For all of this shit. He should've been upstairs listening to his old record albums."

Brian spoke over the top of Anya's head. "The old man did what he wanted to do, Jules."

"I'm sorry he's gone." Anya's voice tremored, and her eyes glossed with tears.

A thick silence descended over the room. Katie moved behind the bar and began pulling glasses and pouring drinks. Anya stared at the ice crackling in the tumblers, wishing there was something she could do to bring Ciro back. But where he had gone, she didn't think he'd want to come back. She remembered the sublime look on his face when he and Renee were waiting for the train. This world could offer him nothing like that.

"And what about us?" Jules asked, climbing onto a bar stool. "What about DAGR?"

Anya shook her head. "I don't know, Jules. I can't see the future. For any of us." She looked up at Brian, squeezed his hand. "All we can do is keep fighting."

Anya slowly drove the Dart back to what remained of her house. She parked on the curb while staring at the street, refusing to look over into the yard, at the scene of the fire. Brian had insisted on coming with her, but she wanted to do this alone.

She took three deep breaths. Christ, she could smell the char from here, with the windows rolled up. In the passenger seat, Sparky whined. DFD had ruled the fire at her house to be an unfortunate electrical fire, brought on by a wiring defect in the new HDTV. Anya knew better but kept her mouth shut.

She popped open the door, tucked a box of garbage bags under her arm. She walked up the sidewalk, staring down at her feet, heart hammering. Finally, she forced herself to look up.

The house was a complete ruin. The scene was cordoned off by yellow fire line tape and a movable chain-link fence to secure the scene. She had Marsh to thank for that. The hulk behind it was a charred, soggy black mess of broken brick, burned timbers, and curled shingles. Puddles of ash and gluey muck extended into the yard, blackening the white feet of her protective Tyvek suit. Blades of new green crabgrass poked above the sludge.

Anya unlocked the padlock holding the chain around the fence, pulled the creaking fence aside. Sparky wiggled in before her. He planted himself on the front step and whined.

Anya sighed. The little guy deserved to say good-bye to this place, too. She shoved open the charred ruins of the front door. Sparky bounded inside, mewled piteously when he saw the jagged roof timbers collapsed onto the living-room floor. The refrigerator still stood, though blackened, and the copper pipes could be seen reaching through the walls.

Anya kicked through some glass to the kitchen. She opened the fridge door, wrinkled her nose. Nothing worth salvaging there. She pawed through the cabinets, finding a couple of pots that might still be usable, if cleaned. Cast iron survived anything, she told herself, and dropped them into the garbage bag.

She opened the hall closet, where the washer and dryer stood. She rooted through them for clothes. They smelled like smoke but could probably be cleaned. She stuffed them in another garbage bag, headed to the bathroom, where Sparky's nest had been.

The tiles had blackened, Sparky's mobile was charred to its wire armature, and the linoleum was scorched. But she could see the mass of crystal inside the tub. Except for a carbon film over the quartz, it was largely intact. She fingered a fracture in the geode formation, pulled a piece of it free. The size of her fist, it still managed to glitter in the gray light from the sky above. She threw it in a bag. Anya made a mental note to call an excavator to get the rest out of here. Sparky's nest didn't seem like the kind of thing that should go to the dump.

Her rubber ducky collection sat on its shelf, watching. The ducks had warped and blackened in the heat, but she couldn't leave them behind. Anya stuffed them into the bag.

Sparky howled from the bedroom, and Anya came running. He paced in the corner of the room, where his salamander bed had stood. The bed was a soggy ruin, but he was still digging at it, like a dog trying to dig a hole under a fence.

"Sparky . . . "

Something glinted in the ruin of his bed, a yellow gleam that blinked off and on in response to Sparky's pawing. Anya pulled apart the bed to find his Gloworm, a little stained but still intact. Its cherubic face lit up when she squeezed it, and Sparky chortled with glee.

Anya carefully wrapped it in a clean garbage bag, smiling. These things were relics of a former life. But like the salamander collar that had survived the fire at Anya's childhood home, they were worth saving for the future.

Desire is stronger after dark...
Bestselling Urban Fantasy from Pocket Books!

Bad to the Bone
JERI SMITH-READY
Rock 'n' Roll will never die. Just like vampires.

Master of None
SONYA BATEMAN
Nobody ever dreamed of a genie like this...

Spider's Bite
An Elemental Assassin Book
JENNIFER ESTEP.
Her love life is killer.

Necking
CHRIS SALVATORE
Dating a Vampire is going to be the death of her.

KICK SOME BUTT

with bestselling Urban Fantasy from Pocket Books and Juno Books!

SHADOW BLADE
SERESSIA GLASS

Sometimes you choose a path in life.
Sometimes it chooses you.

DEMON POSSESSED
STACIA KANE

Detroit is burning...but it's just the beginning.

EMBERS
LAURA BICKLE

Is she going on a dream date...Or a date to hell?

AMAZON QUEEN
LORI DEVOTI

Being an Amazon ruler can be a royal pain.
